THE LAND BEYOND THE CLOUDS

VALERIE BISHOP

LIGHT
PUBLISHING

Cover design and book layout by
Drai Bearwomyn McKi

Printed in the United States

ISBN 978-0-9801937-7-0 hardcover

ISBN 978-0-9801937-6-3 paperback

Published by LIGHT PUBLISHING

1482 East Valley Road Suite 369

Montecito, CA 93108

www.landbeyondtheclouds.com

www.valeriebishop.com

This book is dedicated to my Mom
who gave me the love of reading and a life
that allowed me to find my own path home

And to my Dad
for his courage and sacrifice
which allowed me to follow my path

ACKNOWLEDGMENT

For my husband's unwavering love & support
Tom's hours of tireless editing & friendship
Jan's open & supportive heart
And the 'girlfriends'

Without all of you, Anna would have
never found her way home

THE LAND BEYOND THE CLOUDS

VALERIE BISHOP

CHAPTERS

ONE – THE FARM

TWO – THE LAND BEYOND THE CLOUDS

THREE – LOYAL FORCES OF THE OPPOSITION

FOUR – FOUR MR. DOBBS

FIVE – SCHOOL OF IMES

SIX – AMRAK STATION

SEVEN – CANDY LAND

EIGHT – AUNT B

NINE – THE SURPRISE

TEN — THE ESCAPE

ELEVEN – LEVIE

TWELVE – THE FORTRESS

THIRTEEN – PUZZLING

FOURTEEN – WAFER TOWN

FIFTEEN – CARDBOARD CITY

SIXTEEN – THE SEARCH

SEVENTEEN – ZEEBEE

EIGHTEEN – YALI STREAM

NINETEEN – QUILRUM VALLEY

TWENTY – SOOPOIL RIDGE

TWENTY-ONE – THE CRYSTAL PALACE

CHAPTER ONE

THE FARM

"It's going to be a long, hot, boring summer," Anna thought as she sat cross-legged in the barnyard, idly watching an anthill.

It wasn't that Anna didn't like summer. After all, it was so much better than going to school. It's just that there wasn't much for an 11 year-old to do on an old farm. I mean, you can only spend so much time watching anthills.

It was different when her grandpa was alive. The farm was a working farm then, and Anna and her grandpa did everything together.

He called her Sweetpea and taught Anna all the important stuff in life, like how to milk a cow, which wild berries you could eat and how to whittle the perfect stick for roasting marshmallows. Grandpa had great faith in Anna. He put her in charge of feeding the chickens and even let her drive the tractor while sitting on his lap.

Grandpa was a man of many talents. He could make a quarter come out of Anna's ear and skip a stone clear across a pond. Grandma called Anna 'Grandpa's Little Shadow', because you could always find her wherever he was.

He died in the cold of winter. The following spring, Grandma sold off all the animals; all except for a few chickens and Millie, the old grey goat.

The only things that remained of the farm were a weather-beaten clapboard farmhouse, an old red barn full of cobwebs, stale hay and a jalopy that Grandpa had loved, and some sixty acres of overgrown pasture where the cows used to graze.

Anna sighed. "I sure do miss my grandpa," she said to the ants. But the ants were too busy to pay much attention. Anna wondered if they even knew she was there, watching their every move.

Anna had been coming to her grandparents' farm for summer vacation for as long as she could remember. The farm had become her second home, and she genuinely enjoyed being there, but it wasn't the same without Grandpa.

At the beginning of each June, Anna's mom would say, "The city is no place for a child to spend the summer, especially cooped up in an apartment all day. You should be out in the fresh air and sunshine."

And so, as soon as the school year ended, an old hand-me-down suitcase with Anna's summer clothes and a few toys was packed and loaded in the car. They would then make, what seemed like a long drive to an 11 year-old, the trip from Toronto to her grandparents' farm on the outskirts of Grimsby, an area known for its rich red soil and acres of fruit orchids.

Anna loved her grandma. After all, she did make the world's best peanut butter cookies, but Grandma didn't play with Anna. At least not the way her grandpa used to. Besides, on the drive up to the farm, Anna's mom kept reminding Anna to 'mind her manners and not bother her grandma.' Anna's mom was concerned that Anna would be too much for Grandma, now that Grandpa was gone. Anna promised her mom she wouldn't be any trouble. So, other than helping Grandma with the occasional batch of cookies, Anna was pretty much left to fend for herself.

It had only been a week since her mom had dropped her off and she had already done everything there was to do on the farm. She was restless and dreaded the idea of spending the entire summer with nothing to do except watch anthills, which was only slightly more exciting than watching grass grow. If only Grandpa were here. He had a way of making even the most ordinary day exciting. Anna never knew what to expect when she was with him. There was always something to see or learn or explore. How was Anna ever going to make it through this summer without him?

Anna looked up from the anthill to see Jed coming around the corner of the house. At least she had Old Jed, Grandma's dog. He was one of those hound dogs with all the extra skin. He looked like his body was three sizes too small for his skin. He reminded Anna of those people on the diet pill TV commercials. You know, the ones that stand in the middle of a huge pair of pants that used to fit them before they lost all their weight.

Grandpa used to say that Jed was as old as the hills. Anna didn't know how old that was; she just knew Jed was older than her, which is really old for a dog. Jed was now the only company Anna had. Sometimes, when Jed wasn't napping in the shade of the cherry tree, he would join Anna for a walk through the nearby woods. He liked to sniff the forest floor and every so often would even chase a squirrel or groundhog.

Anna liked to hunt for trilliums in the forest and collect strips of birch bark. Once she wrote a secret message on a strip of bark and put in it an old green bottle. She sent it down the creek that ran the length of the farm. Anna was hoping the creek would take it to the Great Lakes, where someone would find it washed up on a distant shore in the USA. But instead, Anna watched as the bottle hit a rock, cracked and sank.

Jed lazily wandered towards Anna, yawned and plopped down, creating a cloud of dust from the dry earth. Anna coughed and looked down at her clothes. She was covered with the barnyard. Grandma was not going to be pleased, especially since they were planning on going into town that afternoon.

Her brand new white Keds sneakers, which Anna liked to wear without socks, were now more gray than white. Anna had always been thin, but the growth spurt she'd had in the spring left her "all arms and legs," at least according to her mom.

Her blue jeans, which Anna wore rolled up, had a hard time staying up, as Anna had yet to develop curves. Her mom told her not to worry, but Anna was tired of waiting for 'Mother Nature to take its course.' Anna's pale yellow t-shirt might as well have been on a boy. Her shoulder-length brown hair was also flat. She sometimes wore it in a ponytail, but not today. Anna's fair skin was a nice backdrop for the few freckles that appeared on her nose during the summer.

Anna wasn't plain, but she wasn't beautiful either. At least not like her mom. Everywhere they went people turned to look at her. Anna was sure her mom could have been a model or a movie star, but instead she was an assistant manager at a shoe store, which is where she had met Anna's father. At least that is what she was told. Anna had

4

never met her father. She didn't know why, but her mom didn't like to talk about him. One snowy afternoon, while rummaging in the closet looking for an extra shoelace for her ice skate, Anna found a faded picture of her dad and mom on their wedding day. That was as close as she had ever gotten to him.

The one thing that Anna did have in common with her mom was her beautiful eyes. They were as big as a full moon and such a dark brown they were almost black. Her mom loved to tell the story about how after Anna was born, all the doctors and nurses kept commenting on the color of her eyes. "Have you ever seen eyes on a new-born like that before? Why, they are as dark as midnight," Anna's mom overheard one of the nurses say to another.

Grandpa had once told Anna that the eyes were the window to the soul, but she was pretty sure she had never seen anyone's soul by looking in their eyes. Or if she had, she didn't know it.

Anna stuck her hand in her pocket and rubbed her lucky stone. She found it last year during one of her many expeditions with Grandpa. Anna was hopping from one river rock to another along the farm's creek. She had stopped to wait for her grandpa, who was walking along the banks, when something in the water caught her eye. She almost fell in reaching for it.

"What have you got there, Sweetpea?" Grandpa asked as he caught up with her. Anna handed him the stone.

Grandpa carefully examined it as if it were a diamond. "Ah, a lucky stone," he said as he handed it back to her.

Anna looked at the stone with new found respect. It looked like an ordinary stone to her. "A lucky stone? What makes it lucky?"

"Well, of all the stones you could have picked up, you chose that one. I'd say that was very lucky, at least for the stone," Grandpa said with a wink.

Anna smiled at hearing this. The stone was almost completely translucent and as smooth as tumbled glass. It felt good to Anna's touch and now had a permanent home in the front-pocket of her jeans.

In Anna's back pocket was a blue and white bandana. It was identical to the one her grandpa had always carried with him. He used his to wipe his brow, dab blood from Anna's scraped knees and even to carry a few eggs from the henhouse to the kitchen. A bandana was a mighty handy thing to have.

Anna's bandana had been a Christmas present from her grandpa. The tag read: "To Sweetpea. One never knows when you might need a bandana. Love, Grandpa." It was the last present she received from him. Anna now took it with her everywhere, even though it hadn't proved to be particularly useful, at least not yet.

Anna turned her attention back to the anthill. One of the tiniest ants had found one of the stale pieces of bread that Grandma had thrown into the barnyard for the blue jays and robins. Not that the birds wanted the old bread, but it's what Grandma always did with leftover bread. This one ant had decided it was *finders keepers* and had staked claim to a particularly large piece. Anna watched in amazement as the little, teeny-weenie ant carried the huge piece of bread that was at least a squillon times bigger than he was. The ant wasn't exactly carrying the bread. It was more like a series of pulls and pushes, yanks and jerks, shoves and tugs. Nevertheless, it was working and the bread was slowly making its way towards its destination, the anthill.

"Jed, look at that ant. How is he ever going to get that piece of bread into the tiny hole on top of the anthill?" Anna asked, admiring the ant's strength and perseverance.

Jed looked up and tilted his head as if to say, "I have no idea."

Anna continued to watch the struggling ant; so much energy and determination for a stale piece of bread. She considered helping the ant, but decided not to, remembering how much she liked to do things on her own.

The ant was almost at the bottom of the anthill when Anna felt a raindrop, then another and another.

She looked up, "Ah, nuts!" she exclaimed, seeing that the clouds were about to burst. She ran for the open door of the barn. Jed was close behind; he really could move when he wanted to. They made it, right before the heavens opened up. Anna was so absorbed with the ant that she hadn't even noticed the dark clouds that had formed in front of the sun. She watched as the rain came down in buckets, upset that she had to leave the little ant before he'd reached his destination. The dry earth greedily drank in the rain.

Anna could tell from the look of the clouds that it was only a sun shower and would soon be over. Her grandpa had taught her how to read the weather. "You can't be a farmer, if you can't read the sky," Grandpa used to say.

Sure enough, within a couple of minutes the rain stopped as suddenly as it had started. The pastures were glistening with raindrops. The air had that sweet smell that only happens after it rains. Anna walked back into the barnyard to check on the little ant.

"Wow!" she exclaimed, abruptly stopped in mid-step and stared straight ahead.

There in the distance, through an opening in the clouds, was a brilliant beam of sunlight streaming down to earth. It created a radiant ladder of light. The bottom of the ladder landed somewhere in the little forest beyond the pasture.

"Look Jed, Jacob's Ladder!" Anna exclaimed pointing. "Isn't it beautiful?"

Anna remembered the first time she'd seen Jacob's Ladder. She was six or seven years old and was with Grandpa on the farm. The ladder had also appeared right after a sun shower. Grandpa pointed to it and told her it was a weather phenomenon known as Jacob's Ladder. The ladder of light had disappeared almost as quickly as it had appeared. When she asked her grandpa where it had gone, he said, "The Ladder Keeper that lives in the clouds has pulled it up."

"The Ladder Keeper?" Anna questioned.

"Yes, he is the one responsible for putting down and pulling up the ladder," Grandpa explained.

"When will he put it down again?" Anna asked.

"That's up to the Ladder Keeper. The trick is to get to the bottom of the ladder before he pulls it up."

Anna wanted to know what was at the top of the ladder.

"Nobody knows, because nobody has even made it to the top the ladder. Or, if they have, they never lived to tell about it," her grandpa had said with a wink and a smile.

Anna had seen many Jacob's Ladders since then, but none had ever been this close.

"Come on Jed. Let's go find the bottom of Jacob's Ladder." Jed just looked at her, but didn't budge.

"Never mind, I'll go myself." Without thinking twice, Anna turned and hightailed it towards the little forest; where the bottom of the ladder was sure to be. Running as fast as her spindly legs could carry her, she galloped through the pasture.

The long, damp grass tickled her legs. Anna never once took her eyes off the golden ladder of light. She was out of breath by the time she reached the edge of the forest, but Anna knew there was no time to spare and rushed into the forest.

"Oh, please, Mr. Ladder Keeper, don't pull up the ladder, not yet," Anna begged.

She then heard Grandma calling her in for lunch. Anna paused, but only for a moment. She was determined to find the ladder before it got pulled up.

Now, well into the forest, Anna could no longer see the ladder when she looked up, only trees. She left the well-worn forest path and headed deeper into the woods. The underbrush made it difficult to run, but this didn't deter her. Anna darted to and fro, first one way then another. She just had to find the ladder; it had to be here somewhere. She kept looking until she couldn't look any longer. Exhausted she stopped to catch her breath.

"Nuts!" she cried out in frustration. Anna wasn't one who gave up easily but by now the Ladder Keeper had surely pulled up the ladder.

As she turned back to find the path, Anna froze. There, in a small clearing in the middle of the forest, stood the radiant ladder of light. Anna stared at it in wide-eyed wonder. It was even more beautiful than she had imagined!

Translucent rays of light were woven together to form the rungs of the ladder. It looked as delicate as a spider's web. The light shining from the ladder was so bright it almost hurt Anna's eyes. She could barely believe she had actually found it. If only her grandpa could be here.

Now what do I do? she wondered. Fear momentarily held Anna, but she realized that there was no time to waste. If she was going to climb the ladder, she had to act now. Any moment the Ladder Keeper could pull the ladder up. Anna seized the opportunity and ran to the ladder. Trembling, she reached out and touched one of the rungs. Her fingers tingled and glowed. It was a pleasant feeling, like being tickled from the inside.

Mustering up a bit more confidence, Anna placed her other hand on the ladder's rail. The tingling spread through her like a wave. The ladder looked very fragile but was surprisingly sturdy to the touch. Anna cautiously placed her right foot on the first rung and was instantly engulfed by radiant light. Her whole body shone.

She hesitated only a moment before she began to climb. The shimmering ladder, although soft as a rose petal, was extremely strong

9

and easily supported her.

She would have been far more frightened except that the light somehow gave her a sense of confidence and inner strength. Slowly, one by one, she scaled the radiant rungs. Is this real? she wondered. Am I really climbing a ladder made of light?

Anna rose steadily, confidently, rung by rung until she was above the tree tops. She stopped to look out over the land.

"Wow! I'm so high," Anna thought as she watched Jed wandering around the barnyard, looking somewhat lost. Anna couldn't see her grandma; she must have gone back into the house. From up here, everything on the ground looked the size of ants.

Anna looked up. High above her the ladder disappeared into a ceiling of thick, white clouds. It was still a long ways up and Anna began to doubt her decision to climb the ladder. What had she been thinking? But she couldn't give up, not now. She just had to find out what was at the top of the ladder. She took a deep breath and was about to start climbing again when the ladder began to quiver then shake.

"Oh no," Anna cried. She knew exactly what was happening. The Ladder Keeper was getting ready to pull up the ladder. Anna momentarily thought about climbing down but she knew it was too late. She grabbed the shimmery rungs with both arms and braced herself.

With a violent jerk and the speed of lightning, Anna and the ladder were pulled skyward towards a small opening in the cloud. Anna screamed as she held on for dear life.

Within seconds, Anna was whisked through the clouds. The ladder instantly disappeared, but not Anna. She still hurtled skyward. Higher and higher she flew.

Finally, Anna began to slow down, then stop—traveling neither higher nor falling—perfectly suspended in air. It seemed like an eternity before she started to fall, but fall she did, slowly at first, then picking up speed with each passing moment.

"Ohhhhhhhhh noooooo!" Anna screamed.

CHAPTER TWO

THE LAND BEYOND THE CLOUDS

I t is a well known fact that your life is supposed to flash before your eyes right before you die, but for some strange reason, the only thing Anna could think about was one of her least favorite classmates, Sharon Wintertown. Sharon was the class drama queen and the self appointed star of any situation. Anna could hear her now, "Poor, poor Anna. My dearest, closest friend. Oh, how I'll miss her." Everyone who heard it would roll their eyes, knowing it wasn't true. Sharon barely noticed Anna, and they were anything but friends.

Why am I thinking about her now? Anna wondered as the air whisked past her on her descent. It doesn't matter, none of it matters.

It'll all be over soon. Why did I ever climb that ladder?

A thick blanket of white clouds was now the only thing separating Anna from the cold, hard ground. Anna wondered what it would feel like to go through the clouds—she didn't have to wonder for long. As she entered the clouds, they instantly engulfed her. They were thick, billowy and strangely inviting.

"It won't be long now, until I'm splattered like a bug on a windshield," Anna thought as she waited to break through the other side of the clouds. But instead of going straight through the clouds, Anna began to slow down.

Was she imaging this? Were the clouds really slowing down her descent? The clouds continued to thicken and were now so dense they reminded Anna of falling onto the fluffy, goose down duvet on her bed at Grandma's house.

The clouds really were breaking her fall, she wasn't imagining it. Anna continued to slow down until, much to her amazement, she came to a complete stop—in the middle of a cloud.

"This can't be happening," Anna thought as she lay perfectly still, completely surrounded by billowy clouds. "I must be dreaming. Either that, or I am already dead."

After a few moments, Anna mustered up enough courage to sit up. She tentatively reached out and touched the cloud that encircled her. Her hand went right through it. How could that be? How can her hand go through the cloud and the cloud still be solid enough to support her? This certainly was a strange place.

Cautiously, Anna stood up. Much to her relief she found the clouds reassuringly solid. She took one step, then another. She had a hard time keeping her balance. It was like walking on a giant marshmallow. Anna could barely believe it, but she really *was* walking on a cloud. She wondered if this was Cloud Nine, or if clouds even had numbers.

Anna could only see about a foot in front of her. Being in the middle of a cloud was like being in the middle of a heavy, white fog.

"Hello, is anyone there?" Anna called out, hoping the Ladder Keeper was still around. Anna listened for a reply, but there was none.

A gentle breeze began to blow. The clouds swirled around her, gently caressing her. The wind picked up. Spinning and whirling, the clouds seemed to dance, with Anna as their partner.

Slowly the clouds began to clear until Anna could see the sky. It was an amazing blue that reminded her of blue Jell-O. Stretched out before Anna was a carpet of clouds. There was nothing but brilliant, white, fluffy clouds for as far as the eye could see. Anna was dazed. How can this be?

"What do I do now?" Anna thought. Not knowing what else to do, she started to walk, tentatively at first, then with more confidence as she gained her balance. It didn't seem to matter in what direction she went because it all looked the same—a vast landscape of clouds. Even so, Anna was reluctant to venture too far for fear of falling off the end. She wondered if this was how Christopher Columbus felt, afraid that he might fall off the edge of the world if it turned out the world really was flat.

Something shiny and bright in the distance caught her eye. It was too far away to tell what it was. Anna started to walk towards it, figuring it was as good a direction as any. As she got closer, the glistening object began to take shape. It wasn't long until Anna stood in front of two very ornate wrought iron-like gates. They shimmered and sparkled, and appeared to be made of the same radiant light as Jacob's Ladder. The gates were attached to two golden pillars, like giants standing guard.

Anna could see through the elaborate scrollwork of the gates to the other side and stepped closer to have a peek. It looked the same on the other side as it did on her side. Just clouds and blue sky, for as far as she could see. She noticed that there were no walls on either side of the gates.

How strange. Why have a gate if you can easily walk around it to get to the other side? Anna wondered.

She took a deep breath and gingerly reached out and touched one of the gates. It swung open with ease and grace. Hesitatingly, she stepped through the gate. Anna was not prepared for what lay before her. What had a moment ago been clouds and blue sky was now a scene straight out of a story book on steroids.

Everything was in hyper-color, like being in a Technicolor movie. There were tall, unusually-shaped trees, like you would see in a Dr. Seuss book. A few feet from her was a rushing brook of thick red liquid. Beyond the brook was a meadow covered with polka-dotted flowers. And in the distance, pink cliffs shot straight into the air.

Anna walked to the little brook and put her fingers into the red liquid. It was thick, like syrup, but felt cool and wet, just like the water in the creek on the farm.

Hearing a rustling noise behind her, Anna quickly turned around, and then froze. In front of her stood a most peculiar-looking man. He was tall and slender with long, flowing white hair and a matching beard. His piercing blue-green eyes were the color of a tropical ocean on a postcard. The lines on his face were deeply cut, but the twinkle in his eye defied his age. He wore a striking purple robe trimmed with gold embroidery. In his left hand, he carried a long walking stick made from a deep mahogany colored wood. The splendid stick was topped with a large clear stone that reflected the light that hit it. The man seemed to shine.

"Hello Anna," he said. "There is no reason to be alarmed. My name is Odin."

Anna's tongue was a little thick, but she finally managed to sputter, "You know who I am? How do you know my name?"

Odin smiled. "Ah, yes—questions. I imagine you have quite a few questions."

Come to think of it, Anna did have a lot of questions. So many that she didn't know where to begin.

As if reading her mind Odin said, "Well, you have come to the right place. For here you can find all of the answers to all of the questions, for all of time."

"You can?"

Anna wasn't sure she wanted to hear the answer to her next question, but she asked it anyway. "But where am I? Am I...am I dead?"

Odin threw back his head and laughed. "Dead? Heavens no, far from it. You are in *The Land Beyond the Clouds*."

"*The Land Beyond the Clouds*? But where exactly is that?"

"*The Land Beyond the Clouds* is everywhere and nowhere. It is where you are and where you are not. It is where you came from, and where you are going."

Anna began to twirl her straight brown hair, something she often did when she was unsure of herself. "I don't understand."

"I know my child, but you will. For now, why don't you come with me? There is someone waiting for you."

"There is? Who?"

"You'll see." Odin turned and started down a well-worn path that led towards a forest of giant yellow sunflowers.

Anna wondered who could possibly be waiting for her in this strange land. She quickly caught up with Odin. Anna wanted to ask a thousand more questions, but for now she decided it was best just to follow, even though Anna wasn't much of a follower.

They entered the sunflower forest. The fragrance was intoxicating. Sunflower seeds littered the ground. Pink and orange birds with crooked beaks and big feet flew from flower to flower dining on the seeds. Deep within the forest of flowers they came upon a quaint little stone cottage. It had a thatched roof and a large wooden door with a peephole. Beneath the windows on either side of the door were window boxes full of purple tulips that were singing a cappella. Anna couldn't quite make out the words, something about 'walking on the soles of your feet.'

Odin opened the door and gestured for Anna to enter. Inside, it looked like an ordinary cottage. Which was a great relief compared to the Technicolor world Anna had just left. There was a great stone fireplace along one wall. Nestled around it were a rocking chair and a big green easy chair that had seen better days. Adjoining the sitting room was a small kitchen with a simple wood table and chairs. Opposite the fireplace, on the other side of the cottage, were a couple of doors that led to two small, modestly furnished bedrooms. The cottage was humble but warm and inviting. Anna began to relax, at least a little bit.

Odin pointed the crystal on the end of his walking stick towards the fireplace. A spark jumped onto the stacked wood, and a fire began to blaze.

"Come, sit by the fire," Odin invited.

A little dumbstruck, Anna sat down in the easy chair. Although she wasn't cold, the warmth of the fire felt good. Before she could settle in, one of the bedroom doors opened, and a teddy bear came bouncing out. As soon as he saw Anna, he ran across the room and flung himself at her, wrapping his furry little arms around her neck.

"Anna, Anna! Oh how I've missed you! I've been waiting for such a long time, I thought you'd never get here," the little teddy bear squealed in delight.

Sitting back in her chair, Anna stared at the furry bear in disbelief. No. It couldn't be, but it looked exactly like the teddy bear she got on her sixth birthday. "Tedith, is that you?" Anna finally managed to ask.

"Of course it's me," Tedith giggled, hugging Anna even tighter.

Tedith was a fuzzy, orange teddy bear with a sad looking green satin ribbon around his neck. He had been Anna's constant companion until last summer, when he had mysteriously disappeared from the farm. Anna was heartbroken at having lost her friend.

For days Grandpa helped Anna search high and low for Tedith, but he was nowhere to be found. After they had finally abandoned their search, Anna's grandparents took her into town and told her she could have anything she wanted from the toy store, which was a rare treat. But Anna didn't want anything. She wanted Tedith. Grandpa finally bought her a stuffed bunny rabbit, but Anna never did take to it, and left it at the farm when she returned home at the end of the summer.

"What are you doing here? What happened to you last summer?" Anna asked, trying her best to make sense out of everything that was happening. "I thought you…" Anna abruptly stopped talking as it dawned on her that she was having a conversation with a stuffed toy. At least he used to be a stuffed toy.

She was about to ask Tedith why he could talk, when, what looked like a cuckoo clock on the wall above the fireplace started to chime.

A little door on the clock opened and out flew four tiny fairies, each a different color. The fairies began dancing to the music coming from the clock. Their dance reminded Anna of the ballroom dancing competitions her mom liked to watch on TV. She wasn't sure, but she thought it might be a waltz. The fairies danced so gracefully, all except for the little blue fairy who was noticeably out of step. During a spin, it bumped rather hard into the yellow fairy, sending her flying half-way across the room. Anna couldn't help but giggle.

When the music stopped the fairies flew around the room

sprinkling fairy dust then returned to the clock.

"Ah, four o'clock. Tea time," Odin proclaimed happily as he headed off to the kitchen to put on the kettle, leaving Anna and Tedith to catch up.

Anna sat for a moment trying to get her bearings. "I don't understand," Anna finally said, looking deep into Tedith's eyes. "How come you can speak? Why are you alive?"

Tedith shrugged. "I'm not really sure, but it's been this way ever since I got here. Last summer was terrible. One minute I was on your bed enjoying a little nap, dreaming of honey, and the next thing I knew, Old Jed had me in his mouth and was carrying me outside towards the cornfield. He kept tossing me up in air and catching me. I knew he was only playing, but I didn't like it one bit. Besides, my fur was getting all wet with his slobber. Yuck. Then your grandmother called him in for dinner. He dropped me like a hot potato and ran towards the house. I was shaken up but not hurt. Back then, I couldn't move or talk or anything, so I simply laid there waiting, hoping you would find me. Night fell and the stars came out. It was very peaceful but oh how I wished I were snuggling in bed with you."

Tedith took a deep breath and continued, "The next morning I could hear you and Grandpa looking for me. If only I could have called out to you. At one point you were only a few steps away from me, but the corn was too high. You couldn't see me. When night came again I started to lose hope. I fell asleep and when I woke up I was here, in *The Land Beyond the Clouds* and I was alive, which I must say took a little getting used to. I wasn't sure what to do. Luckily, Odin found me and I have been living with him ever since. I really love it here. Odin has been really great, but I missed you so much. Now that you are here, everything is perfect."

Odin returned to the sitting room. A silver tray, floating four feet off the ground, followed him. "Over there," Odin directed, as he pointed to a small table in front of the fireplace.

The tray gently floated towards the table and landed delicately; careful not to spill its contents. The tray held a well-used, brown-betty teapot—the same type Anna's grandma had—three cups with saucers, milk, sugar and a plate of assorted finger sandwiches and fruit tarts.

"Milk and sugar, Anna?" Odin asked as he settled into the rocking chair.

"Ah, yes...yes please," Anna replied, her eyes as big as the teacup saucers.

"Tedith?"

"Do you have any honey?" Tedith asked hopefully. "Could I have mine with milk and honey?"

Odin smiled. "But of course, I should have known you would want yours with honey." He tapped his walking stick on the ground twice. A little honey pot floated in from the kitchen and landed on the tray.

"And I'll have mine with just milk," Odin said.

The contents of the tray came to life. The milk pitcher began pouring milk into each of the cups. The teapot poured tea over the milk. A silver spoon dipped into the sugar bowl and placed a teaspoon of sugar in Anna's cup. The honey pot drizzled sticky honey into Tedith's teacup. Three spoons stirred the cups of tea in unison. Then the perfectly prepared cups of tea floated towards each of them. Anna, a little unsteady, reached out and took hold of the cup hovering in front of her.

"Ahhh," Odin sighed, as he took a sip of tea, "nothing quite like a wee spot of tea. You haven't had lunch yet, have you Anna?"

How did he know that? Anna wondered. She shook her head as she looked at the overflowing plate of sandwiches.

Odin, noticing Anna's uncertainty, reached out and took a cucumber sandwich.

"You have to go get them, my dear. They don't come to you," Odin explained with a wink.

Anna chose an egg salad sandwich. Tedith helped himself to a peanut butter and honey sandwich, but only because there weren't any plain honey sandwiches to be had.

Even though everything was so strange and new, Anna was starting to feel better, and was happy to be sitting by the fire enjoying afternoon tea. It certainly had been quite the adventure. Who knew that climbing the ladder would have landed her in such a strange place? Anna thought of her grandpa as she reached for another sandwich. He would have been so proud of her. She wished he was there with her now. He loved a good adventure. Anna's thoughts then turned to home.

"Odin?" Anna said, placing her now empty tea cup on the tray.

"Yes, Anna." The rocking chair creaked as Odin moved it back and forth.

"Um, it's been very nice to meet you and I am so glad to have found Tedith," Anna said, giving Tedith a little squeeze, "but I really should be getting back home before my grandma starts to worry. She was calling for me right before I got here."

"Ah yes, home. Such a lovely place, home," Odin said, staring longingly into the fire.

"I was wondering if you could you please tell me how to get home?" Anna asked.

"I'm afraid I can't help you there, my dear."

Anna shivered, even though she was sitting right next to the fire. "What do you mean you can't help me? Does that mean I am stuck here?"

"Oh no, I didn't say that. You just need to figure out how to get home yourself. We all do."

Anna didn't like what she was hearing. "I don't understand."

"You see, my dear, there is no one way home that works for everyone. Why, there are as many paths home as there are people and you, Anna, must follow yours. It's really very simple. Put one foot in front of the other, and don't stop until you get home."

"So, I can walk home?"

"In a manner of speaking, yes, you can. But the mode of transportation isn't relevant. The important thing is to start, keep your eye on where you want to go, and simply keep going. Keep going even when you don't think you can go any further. Keep going even when the way isn't clear. Keep going even if there are those who don't want you to go home."

Anna started to get scared. "What do you mean? Why would someone *not* want me to go home?"

Before Odin could answer, the clock struck once, indicating that it was half past the hour. The little door on the clock opened and out flew the blue fairy. It did a quick, awkward dance, sprinkled a little fairy dust around the room then returned to the clock.

"My, how time flies. Well, my dear, I must be going," Odin said as he stood.

Anna was stunned; she was just starting to feel safe. "You mean you're leaving me here? By myself?"

"Oh, no, not at all."

Anna was relieved to hear this.

"Tedith will stay with you," Odin said, patting Tedith on the head.

"But, but you can't leave. I don't know how to get home," Anna protested.

"Trust yourself Anna, and you will be fine. Every heart knows the way home."

Before Anna could say another word Odin turned towards the door and walked right through it—as if it wasn't there.

Anna gasped, jumped up from her chair and ran after him. She flung open the door. "Odin!" she called out, but he was nowhere to be seen.

Anna stood looking into the sunflower forest, bewildered and frightened. Tears welled up in her eyes. The tulips in the flower box were singing a sad cowboy love song.

"Oh Tedith, what am I to do?"

Tedith put his arms around Anna's leg. "It's all right Anna, we have one another and we will find our way home."

"Really? You really think so? Everything is so strange here. I don't even know where to start."

"Odin said it was really simple, didn't he? He said we just need to keep our eyes on where we want to go and not stop until we get there. Right?" Tedith asked, looking up at Anna reassuringly.

"That is what he said, didn't he? But where do we begin?"

Tedith paused. Anna did have a point. The one thing he knew about *The Land Beyond the Clouds* was that it was vast. He'd been exploring it since he had arrived and had barely scratched the surface.

"How did you get up here?"

Anna wiped a tear from her cheek. "I climbed up a ladder made of light; Jacob's Ladder. I almost made it to the top before the Ladder Keeper pulled it up."

"Well then, if you climbed up the ladder, we can climb down the ladder," Tedith said optimistically.

"But how are we going to find the ladder? It was gone when I landed on the clouds."

"Who is this Ladder Keeper guy?"

"I don't know. I just know he's in charge of Jacob's Ladder. He's the one that puts it up and down."

"That's our answer. We need to find the Ladder Keeper and ask him to put the ladder down."

"But I don't know even know what he looks like. I never saw him. He was gone by the time I landed on the clouds."

"Maybe we should go back to where the ladder was. Maybe he'll be there again."

Anna sighed. "I guess we could give it a try. I can't think of anything better to do," Anna said, suddenly feeling very tired. "But before we go, can we rest for a bit? It's been quite the day."

Without another word, Tedith took Anna by the hand and lead her back to the fire. He then went to the bedroom and returned with a patchwork quilt. He wrapped it around Anna as she curled up in the big easy chair. He jumped into the chair and crawled under the quilt next to Anna. It was one of the things he missed most about being with Anna, cuddling with her.

As Anna eyes became heavy with sleep, she heard an animal howling in the distance. She shuddered and pulled Tedith closer to her. Despite their uncertain future, it wasn't long before they were both fast asleep.

CHAPTER THREE

THE LOYAL FORCES
OF THE OPPOSITION

It was a moonless, black-as-coal night. The fire in the little cottage had gone out long ago. The little door on the clock above the fireplace opened. Twelve fairies flew out, but instead of doing their usual fairy dance, they hovered directly over Anna and Tedith who were still sound asleep.

"Hurry, we don't have much time," said the little purple fairy.

The pink fairy flew down and brushed Anna's cheek with her wing. Anna stirred and swatted at the fairy as if she were a fly but did not wake.

The yellow fairy flew to Anna's ear. "Anna, Anna, wake up, wake up!" she urged in her loudest voice.

Sleepily, Anna opened her eyes. Seeing the fairies hovering around her, she jolted awake and accidentally knocked Tedith on the floor.

"Hey," Tedith called out as he landed with a thump.

"My name is Latanya," said the purple fairy. "You must listen to me very carefully. We don't have much time. *The Loyal Forces of the Opposition* will be descending on the cottage any moment now—looking for you."

"*The Loyal Forces of the Opposition?* Why are they looking for me?"

"They don't want you to go home."

Anna gulped. "What do you mean? Why don't they want me to go home?"

"They want to rob you of your…"

A bone-chilling shrill rang out deep from within the sunflower forest. It was a sickening sound and sent shivers down Anna's spine. It reminded her of a wounded animal dying a slow, painful death. Anna was sure she had heard the dreadful sound before, but where?

"It's too late. They're here…hide...hide!" Latanya urged. The fairies quickly returned to the safety of the clock. Grabbing Anna's hand, Tedith lead her into one of the bedrooms.

Tedith opened the closet door and pushed Anna inside. As soon as he closed the door, another ear-shattering shrill rang out. They heard the tulips in the flowerbox under the windows scream as the front door was kicked in with a force that shook the cottage. The fairies, although safe in their clock, trembled in fear.

The closet smelled like old gym socks. It was crammed with strange clothes and an odd assortment of sports equipment, including a bowling pin, a field hockey stick, a croquet mallet and a water polo ball.

Tedith put his paw up to his mouth, indicating for Anna to be very quiet.

In the front room stood three identical intruders. They had chalky white skin, hair as white as snow, and piercing red eyes. Their stark white uniforms, complete with white knee high boots and long-flowing white capes, gave them a ghostly appearance.

They were identical in every way, except one. A large medallion hung from a heavy chain around the neck of one of the intruders. The medallion was very ornate to the point of being gaudy. In the center of the medallion was a big colorless stone, not unlike the stone on the end of Odin's walking stick.

"We're too late, Donovan," said one of the intruders to the one wearing the medallion.

"Nonsense, they've got to be here someplace," sneered Donovan. "Tear the place apart."

Anna shuddered with fear. The two companions listened as furniture was overturned, curtains were ripped down, and the contents of kitchen cupboards thrown onto the floor.

"Check the bedroom," Donovan commanded.

"It won't be long 'til they find us," Anna thought.

Tedith was squirming all over the place. Anna wished he would be still. Tedith maneuvered himself behind her and pushed on the back of the closet. A little door swung open. Tedith climbed through and gestured for Anna to do the same. They heard footsteps approaching. Anna struggled to fit though the small opening. Tedith grabbed her hand and pulled with all his might. Anna's belt loop was stuck on something. She unhooked it, squeezed through the opening and quickly shut the trapdoor.

The closet door swung open. Anna and Tedith held their breath. The intruders rummaged through the contents of the closet. They were only inches from their hiding place.

"Ouch," cried one of the intruders as a billiard ball rolled off the top shelf and landed on his head.

"They're not here, Donovan. They've escaped. Someone must have tipped them off," the intruder said, rubbing the goose-egg sized lump on his head.

"They couldn't have gotten far. Let's go. I'm not through with them yet," Donovan snarled as he led the way out of the bedroom, past the ruins of the cottage and through the opening where the front door once stood.

Anna waited until she was sure they were gone before she spoke. "Wow! That was close! Who are they and why don't they want me to go home?"

"I don't know, but the sooner we find the Ladder Keeper the better. I think it's safe to go back inside," Tedith said as he pulled on the handle of the trapdoor. The door didn't budge.

"Anna, help me with this."

They both took hold of the door handle and pulled and pulled and pulled, but the trapdoor remained shut.

"This is useless," Anna said, letting go of the handle.

"Maybe there is something to pry it open," Tedith suggested. They began to explore the dark space with their hands for something, anything that might help.

"Ouch!" Anna yelled, as she banged her head on the ceiling. The space was only high enough for her when she remained on her hands and knees. Anna stretched out both her arms and found that she could reach either side of their hiding space. Using her hands she explored the space furthest away from the trap door. She kept expecting to bang into a wall, but didn't.

"Tedith, I don't think we are in a room. I think we are in a tunnel."

"Really?"

"Yeah, it leads this way," Anna said. "I think it leads to the back of the cottage. It must be an escape route. Follow me, but stay close."

They made their way down the tunnel. It was slow going since Anna had to crawl and it wasn't long before her knees were red and sore.

The tunnel was musty and damp and much longer than the length of the cottage. If it didn't lead to the back of the cottage, where did it lead?

"Look... light! We are almost at the end," Anna said, just as her knees were about to give out.

"Yea!" Tedith exclaimed as he squeezed by Anna and ran towards the light.

He jumped out of the tunnel and was almost hit by a speeding horse and buggy. Tedith tumbled back into the tunnel. "Whoa, that was close."

Anna crawled past Tedith and peeked out of the tunnel. In front of them stood a quaint little town that seemed to belong in the 1800's.

"Where's the cottage?" Tedith asked, looking at their strange surroundings.

"I don't know," Anna said, rubbing her knees. "Let's go find out where we are."

They carefully emerged from the tunnel onto a cobblestone street. An assortment of shops lined the street which was bustling with people going about their business. The women carried parasols and wore long dresses, gloves and pretty bonnets. The men wore top hats, which they tipped as they passed by other townsfolk. A sign hanging above the street read: "Welcome to Merryvale. Come Join the Merriment."

"This isn't anywhere near where I found the ladder," Anna said, taking in the commotion of the little town.

"Maybe someone in town knows how to find the Ladder Keeper," Tedith offered.

Anna certainly hoped so but had her doubts.

They wandered into the town.

"Let's go in here." A little bell hanging from the door rang as they entered the shop.

"Wow!" Anna exclaimed.

Dozens and dozens of hats in every shape, color and size lined every inch of the tiny shop. Some were decorated with brightly colored ribbon, while others were fashioned with silk flowers and lace. They were the most beautiful hats Anna had ever seen. But among all the exquisite hats, one stood out above the rest. It was displayed on its own table in the center of the shop, as if taking center stage. It was made entirely of peacock feathers. Anna walked around the table admiring it. At one angle it looked green, at another blue, and at yet another turquoise. It was truly remarkable.

Anna had a thing for hats. She had a decent collection of baseball caps at home. Anna's mom used to tell her that she had one of those faces that looked good in any hat. And it was true. It didn't matter if she was wearing a cowboy hat, toque, or ball cap; they all looked good on her.

An older gentleman, not much taller than Anna, emerged from the back of the shop wearing a grey pinstripe suit, a stiff-collared white shirt and spats. The buttons on his vest strained to contain his waist. His spicy aftershave greeted them first. It smelt like the aftershave her grandpa put on when he cleaned up before going into town.

The gentleman twisted his large handlebar mustache as he greeted Anna and Tedith formally with a deep bow. "Mr. D.B. McGillicutty, proprietor, at your service."

He didn't seem to be at all alarmed by Anna and Tedith's

appearance, even though Anna felt very much out of place.

"Hello," Anna said hesitantly while twirling her hair. "I'm not sure you will be able to help us but we are looking for the Ladder Keeper."

"The Ladder Keeper?" Mr. McGillicutty said, looking puzzled. Anna knew this wasn't going to work.

"Yes, sir, the Ladder Keeper. The one in charge of Jacob's Ladder."

"Oh, you must mean Mr. Dobbs. We don't see much of him in town. He's a bit of a loner."

"You know him?" Anna was pleasantly surprised. "Could you tell us where we might find him?"

"He travels quite a bit for his work, but if he's not away, you should be able to find him at home. He has a little house a few miles from town. When you leave the shop, turn left and follow the road out of town. When you arrive at a four-way crossing, follow the sign to Summerland. Down the road a bit is a small forest; a path will lead you through it. On the other side you will see a bridge. Pay the Toll-Master the toll. On the other side of the bridge is Mr. Dobbs's house. You can't miss it as it is the only house for miles around."

"Did I hear you say that you have to pay a toll to go cross over the bridge?"

That's right, young lady. One gold coin."

"A gold coin!" Anna gulped. "But we don't have any money, let alone a gold coin."

"Well, I am sorry, but that's the standard toll for bridge crossing in these parts. Now, may I interest you in a hat?"

"A hat? No. Thank you but no," Anna said a little disheartened, still thinking about needing a gold coin.

Mr. McGillicutty, sensing Anna's distress said, "Wait right here." He headed into the backroom and returned with an old used hat, which was actually more like a beanie than a hat. It was faded lime green and was covered in red and brown polka dots. Anna thought it was the ugliest hat she had ever seen.

"Here, this is for you. Try it on" Mr. McGillicutty said, beaming as he handed the hat to Anna. Reluctantly, Anna took it and put it on.

"Why, it looks lovely on you! Just lovely," Mr. McGillicutty exclaimed, clapping his hands together as he stepped back to admire Anna. "Please, take a look in the mirror."

Mr. McGillicutty held up a hand mirror. Anna didn't want to look, but she did. She tried her best not to cringe when she saw her reflection. Anna didn't think it was possible but she had finally found a hat she didn't look good in. The image in the mirror was nothing short of hideous.

With all the beautiful hats in the shop, why did Mr. McGillicutty have to give her this one?

"Thank you, but I can't accept this. Really" Anna said, wanting to be rid of the hat as quickly as possible. She didn't want to hurt his feelings but she didn't want the hat either.

"Of course you can, my dear. You would make an old man very happy."

"Alright," Anna mumbled reluctantly, "...but only because you insist. Thanks again for your help with Mr. Dobbs, and um-ah, for the hat."

"Good luck. I hope you have a light-filled journey," Mr. McGillicutty said as he bowed and held open the door for them.

"What a strange thing to say," Anna thought... 'have a light-filled journey.'

Anna and Tedith stepped out into the bright sunlight and headed down the street.

"I didn't want to be rude. Mr. McGillicutty seemed like such a nice man, but what am I going to do with this hideous hat?"

"It's not really that bad," Tedith said with a little giggle.

"Yeah, right. Well, I'm not going to be seen in it," Anna said as she removed the beanie from her head, folded it in half, and stuck it in her back pocket.

With a heavy heart, Anna walked on. "How are we going to get across the bridge if we can't pay the toll?"

"I don't know," Tedith replied. "But I am sure we'll think of something."

A loud commotion was coming from the far end of the town. They watched as townspeople ran into shops and ducked behind bushes. Then, an ear-shattering shrill rang out. Anna's stomach turned over. She knew exactly who that sickening sound belonged to. She picked up Tedith and darted into a nearby alley. They huddled together as they watched three pure white horses gallop through town, carrying Donovan and his men.

Then Anna remembered where she had heard that horrific shrill before. It had been in a dream, a nightmare actually. She was being chased by a ghostly white figure; all the while it was making that horrible sound. In her dream Anna ran as fast as she could, but it was no use, the figure caught up to her. He was about to grab Anna by the neck when she woke up in a cold sweat, gasping for air. She was so relieved it was only a dream, but even after her mom had given her a glass of juice, she couldn't fall back to sleep. She couldn't get that terrible sound out of her head. She laid awake the rest of the night tossing and turning.

Anna wished she was dreaming now and that she'd wake up, home, in her own bed. How can something from a nightmare be real?

When the sound of the horse's hooves had faded into the distance, Tedith peeked out. "The coast is clear. Let's go."

"Do you think they are still looking for us?" Anna asked, stepping out from the alley.

"I don't know, but I don't want to wait around to find out. The sooner we find the Ladder Keeper, and get home, the happier I will be."

"Yeah, but how are we ever going to get a gold coin?" Anna asked as they continued to walk down the street.

"I don't know exactly, but I am sure we will find a way," Tedith said, trying to sound reassuring.

The townspeople had begun to resume their activities as if nothing had happened. A cute boy about Anna's age was passing out flyers on the street corner. His hand brushed hers as he handed her a flyer. Anna cheeks turned scarlet. "Thank you," she said, averting eye contact with him as she read the flyer.

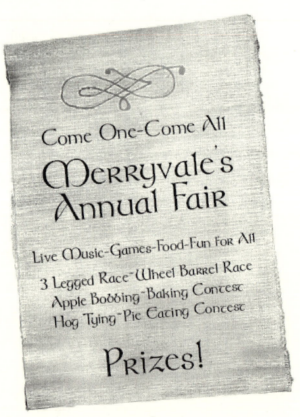

Come One-Come All

Merryvale's Annual Fair

Live Music-Games-Food-Fun For All
3 Legged Race-Wheel Barrel Race
Apple Bobbing-Baking Contest
Hog Tying-Pie Eating Contest

Prizes!

"Excuse me. When is the fair?" Anna asked with a little, shy smile.

"Why it's today. They are setting it up right now in the town square. I'm going to enter the three-legged race with my brother. This year they are giving out a gold coin to the winner of each contest," the boy enthusiastically explained.

Tedith lit up. "Really? A gold coin! Can anyone enter?"

"Yep, it's open to everyone," the boy answered as a band began to play strange music from the town square.

"That means the fair is beginning. I gotta go and get ready for my race. Maybe I'll see you there." Anna blushed again as she watched the boy packed up his remaining flyers and run towards the music.

"Thank you, and good luck," Tedith called after him. "That's it, Anna. We'll win one of the contests!"

"What? What are you talking about?"

"You heard him. They are giving out a gold coin to each winner. It'll be a cinch. We'll win a contest, get the gold coin, find the Ladder Keeper and go home. The only question is what contest should we enter?" Tedith said, studying the flyer.

"I don't know, Tedith. Do you really think we can win?" Anna asked apprehensively.

"Of course. We have to. It's our only chance. Now let's see what contest." Tedith said as he continued to read the flyer. "Hmmm, my legs are too short for the three-legged race."

Anna started to feel a glimmer of hope. Maybe Tedith was right, maybe they could win a contest. Anna looked at the flyer.

"Bet I could win the baking contest with the peanut butter cookies my grandma taught me to bake, except we don't have an oven, so that's out."

"We don't have a wheel barrel, so we can't enter that contest."

"What about the pie-eating contest? I bet you could win the pie-eating contest." Tedith said.

"Well, maybe," Anna said, over the rumbling of her tummy. "I haven't eaten since yesterday."

"Then it's settled. The pie-eating contest it is. Come on, let's go get you signed up," Tedith bounced down the street as they followed the strange music towards the fair.

The town square was a large grassy park, with a large white gazebo in the middle. Little paths meandered through the square under large oak trees and past fragrant flowerbeds. Today the square was a beehive of activity.

Anna and Tedith entered the excitement and made their way through the crowds, looking for the pie-eating contest. The music from the band was getting louder and stranger. Anna giggled as she spotted the band. It was an all-women tuba band. No wonder the music sounded so weird. One of the musicians was so thin Anna wondered how she managed to hold up the huge tuba.

As they continued through the crowd they passed a clown juggling balls and merchants selling balloons, hot dogs and funny hats. Anna definitely didn't need another one of those.

"Hey, watch where you are going," Tedith yelled as a man walking on stilts almost stepped on Tedith as they passed by.

"Over here," Tedith yelled, tugging on Anna.

They walked up to a colorful booth, over which was a banner: *"Pie Eating Contest—Register Here."*

"We would like to sign up for the contest," Tedith said to the lady in the booth who looked like she had enjoyed more than her fair share of pies.

"You're in the nick of time, we are about to start. Print your name here," the woman said, pointing to the entry list with her chubby finger, "then go take a seat in front of one of the pies."

"What type of pies are they?" Anna asked, as she printed her name as neatly as she could.

"They're banana cream pies. Now hurry, go to your place. And good luck."

Anna loved banana cream pies. She sat in front of a large, luscious pie. Anna looked down the row. There was a least a dozen constants she would have to beat. Sitting beside her, a man three times her size was cracking his knuckles, as if that was going to help him eat the pie quicker.

A man in a straw bowler hat and red-and-white-striped vest turned to the assembled crowd. "Ladies and Gentlemen, welcome. I will be your Master of Ceremonies for Merryvale's annual pie-eating contest. The rules are simple. The first one to eat the entire pie wins one gold coin." The MC held up the gold coin for all to see. Anna knew she had to win. It was her only chance to get home.

"Okay, contestants, keep your hands behind your back, and when I say 'GO,' dig in."

Anna's clasped her sweaty palms behind her back.

"Are you ready?" the MC asked. The contestants nodded in unison. "On your mark, get set, GO!"

The contestants dove into their creamy pies.

Anna ate the sweet delicious pie with abandonment.

"I simply have to win," she thought.

Over the screaming crowd, Anna could hear Tedith, cheering her on, "Go Anna, go."

Anna took great big bites of the pie, chewing as little as possible before swallowing. She could barely see through the bananas and cream that now covered her face. "I sure could use some milk," she thought.

"You are almost there contestants, keep going," the MC encouraged.

Anna was on her last mouthful and was about to swallow when the MC called out. "We have a winner! Freddy Parson, for the third year in a row." The applause for the winner was deafening.

The MC held up the arm of a frightenly thin boy at the end of the table, whose face was so covered with pie, the only thing you could see was his pointy nose sticking out of the cream.

Anna swallowed her last bite, it didn't go down well. She couldn't believe it. How could she not have won the contest? Anna wiped the sticky pie off her face with a towel the fat lady handed her. She then joined Tedith in the crowd and watched as the MC handed the skinny boy the shiny gold coin, the gold coin that should have been Anna's, the gold coin that was her ticket home.

"We're never going to get home now, Tedith." Anna said, watching her hope vanish into the boy's pocket.

"It's not the end of the world, Anna. We'll think of something else. We'll find another way to get a gold coin." Tedith tried his best to console her, but he wasn't at all sure that they would find another way.

Disheartened, they wandered through the crowds. They passed the apple-bobbing contest and the fire eater. They saw a man throw daggers at a lady spinning on a wooden board. They stopped to watch the three-legged race. The cute boy who handed Anna the flyer came in third. Anna wasn't the only one who had her hopes squashed today.

After they had wandered through most of the fair, they sat down on one of the park benches away from the crowds. Anna took the little hat out of her back pocket and laid it on the bench next to her; it sure was ugly. She decided to throw it into the next trash bin they passed. They sat in silence, contemplating their fate when a man walked by them and tipped his hat. Anna nodded back. The man took one more step, stopped, turned around and approached them.

"Excuse me, but I couldn't help but notice that little hat sitting there. Is it yours?"

"This?" Anna said, picking up the crumpled hat. "Yes, it's mine."

"Would you mind if I had a closer look?" asked the man.

Anna shrugged. "I guess not." And handed him the hat. She looked at Tedith as if to say, "I wonder what this is all about?"

"Exquisite, simply exquisite," said the man as he carefully examined the hat as if it was a fine piece of jewelry.

"You have quite the treasure there, young lady. The Bitterman beanie is very rare, especially one that is in as fine a condition as this one."

"The Bitterman beanie? That's something special?" Anna asked, surprised.

"Oh my yes, to a hat collector like myself it is very special indeed…and valuable."

"Did you say valuable?" Tedith lit up.

"Yes, quite valuable. Why, under the right conditions at a hat auction, this beanie could be expected to fetch as much as forty gold coins," the man explained.

Anna's mouth dropped open. The man handed the beanie back to Anna. She held it with newfound respect.

"Thank you for letting me have a look at it," the man said as he tipped his hat he turned to walk away.

"Excuse me sir, would you be interested in buying the…what did you say it was called…Bitterman beanie?" Tedith called after him.

The man turned around. "It's a wonderful specimen. Truly it is, but I'm sorry I can't afford such a rare treasure."

"How about one gold coin? Could you give us a gold coin for it?" Tedith offered.

The man looked stunned. "One gold coin. Oh, no, that would be completely unfair," the man responded.

"Please sir, you would be doing us the greatest service," Tedith said.

"Are you serious? It doesn't seem right," said the man.

"Yes, we are very serious. You really would be helping us," Anna said, getting the drift of where Tedith was headed.

"Well, I feel a little strange about this," the man said, pulling out a small change purse from his pocket.

"Here… here are four gold coins. It's all I have with me, but I insist you take them," the man said, handing Anna the coins.

"Thank you, sir. Thank you very much," Anna said, handing the beanie to the man.

"No, thank you! The boys down at the hat club will never believe it," the man said, beaming as he walked away with his new found treasure.

"Can you believe it? Who would have thought that that old hat…I mean beanie…was worth so much? And to think I was going to throw it away," Anna said as she took out the bandana from her back pocket, wrapped the coins in it, then put it back. "It just goes to show you that you shouldn't judge a book—or a beanie—by its cover. Thank you, Mr. McGillicutty. Thank you. Now, let's go find the Ladder Keeper."

CHAPTER FOUR

MR. DOBBS

With a light step and a pocket full of gold Anna and Tedith followed Mr. McGillicutty's directions and headed out of town. The streets of Merryvale were deserted; everyone was at the fair. They walked past a general store and an old-time barbershop, the kind with a red and white-striped pole on one side of the door and a life-sized wooden Indian on the other. Anna stared at the wooden Indian as they passed it. She was amazed at how life-like it looked.

"Hey, did you see that?" Anna asked in astonishment.

"See what?" Tedith asked, not having a clue what she was talking about.

"That wooden Indian winked at me."

Tedith gave her one of those looks you give someone when you think they are one bulb short of a full string.

"What? You don't believe me?"

"Come on, let's go," Tedith said, not at all convinced.

"I swear. He winked at me." Anna turned around to stare at the Indian but it was frozen in place.

It wasn't long until the cobblestone street of Merryvale turned into a dirt road with deep grooves where the wheels of the buggies had dug in. The road wound through sweet meadows dotted with ancient trees. It reminded Anna of the countryside by her grandparents' house, which turned Anna thoughts to her grandma. The last time she saw her, Anna was perched on Jacob's Ladder high above the trees. Anna never missed lunch, especially when it was grilled cheese sandwiches, which was what her grandma was making when Anna had disappeared.

"Grandma must be in quite a state wondering where I am," Anna thought as she stepped up the pace.

"The sooner we find the Ladder Keeper the better," Anna mumbled under her breath.

It wasn't long until they came upon the four-way crossing Mr. McGillicutty had told them about. They followed a rickety old signpost towards Summerland. The road was dusty and unexciting; they made good time. Anna sure hoped Mr. Dobbs would be home when they got there.

"Look, Anna," Tedith said, pointing.

A small forest stood in the distance, just like Mr. McGillicutty had described. But something didn't seem quite right. The sky was a deep blue, the sun shone brightly and there wasn't a cloud in the sky, except for one large foreboding cloud looming directly above the forest.

The closer they got to the forest, the more unsettled Anna

became. They stopped at the edge of the forest and cautiously peered in. It was dark and thick with underbrush. The whole thing gave Anna the creeps.

"I don't know, Tedith. I don't like the looks of this place," Anna said, fidgeting with the lucky stone in her pocket.

An owl called out from deep within the forest.

"That's strange," Anna said, "Owls only come out at night. I've never heard one in the daytime before."

"It'll be fine, Anna," Tedith said in his bravest voice. "Besides, it's the only way to the Ladder Keeper."

"Okay, but let's get through it quickly."

They warily entered the forest. With every step they took, it got darker and more creepy. Several times they heard what sounded like scurrying feet behind them but when they turned around they saw nothing.

"I think someone or something is following us," whispered Anna.

Suddenly, a large screeching owl swooped at them. The big bird knocked Anna off balance; she went down hard, hitting her head on a tree root right before everything went black.

"Anna, Anna. Wake up," Tedith whispered, gently shaking his unconscious friend. Anna moaned as she slowly opened her eyes; her head throbbed. It was pitch black. She couldn't see a thing.

"Tedith?" Anna asked, somewhat bewildered.

"Shhhh… quiet," Tedith urged.

"Where are we?" Anna whispered, rubbing a huge lump on the side of her head.

"Oh Anna, it was terrible. After the owl knocked you down, dozens of disgusting, smelly, weasel-like animals with yellow eyes and pointy teeth pounced on us. I tried to fight them off, but there were too many of them. They dragged us through the forest and threw us into this pit."

Anna slowly stood up. She moaned. She was bruised, scraped and ached all over.

"How long have we been here?" Anna asked, still holding the side of her head.

"Several hours. I am so glad you are awake. I was really worried about you. I kept trying to wake you, but you were out cold."

The full moon broke through the tree tops, giving Anna just enough light to get her bearings. The pit was about six feet in diameter and about nine or ten feet deep.

"Where are the weasels now?"

"I'm not sure, but I think they are somewhere in the forest. I haven't seen or heard them since they threw us in here."

"Let's see if we can get their attention. I want to see what we are dealing with." Anna started to yell. "Let us out of here! Let us go! Let us go!"

Anna kept yelling until she heard the scurrying of feet. Anna gasped as she looked up. Dozens of glowing yellow eyes looked down at them.

"Let us out of here," Anna insisted.

"Quiet!" commanded one of the weasels. "You are in no position to demand anything. You should be grateful there is a bounty on your head or we would have eaten you and your furry little friend long ago." The weasels all snickered.

"We have sent word to *The Loyal Forces of the Opposition* that we have you. They will be here in the morning for both of you."

Anna trembled at hearing this.

"Let's go," said another pair of beady yellow eyes. "We'll be back in the morning to collect you and our handsome reward. Sweet Dreams!" the vermin mocked.

The yellow eyes vanished into the black of night as the weasels scurrying back into the forest.

"Did you hear that? Donovan has put a bounty on our heads. What does he want with us? Why doesn't he want us to go home?" Anna asked, pacing back and forth.

What had Anna gotten herself into? She wished she could trade all of this in for a long, hot, boring summer on the farm watching anthills. It was funny that when she was on the farm all Anna wanted was something exciting to do. Now that she was here, all she wanted was to be back on the farm. Why does the grass always look greener on the other side of the fence? Then, when you get there you realize it's full of snakes, or in this case, weasels!

"We've got to get out of here," Tedith said as he began running his paws along the sides of the wall. "Maybe we can climb out."

They both searched the walls of the pit for anything that might help them escape.

"Over here, Tedith. There is a rock protruding out of the wall, just above my head." Anna put her hand on the rock. It was smooth and well-worn, as if she wasn't the first one to touch it. This gave her the willies. How many other people had tried to climb out of the pit? Anna found another rock for her foot. She carefully hoisted herself up. Her free hand searched in the darkness for something else to grab onto. She found a root and used it to lift herself further up.

"Good going, Anna," Tedith encouraged quietly, careful not to arouse the attention of the weasels.

Anna slowly made her way towards the top of the pit. She was about two feet from the top when her foot slipped and she tumbled down.

"Ouch!" she cried as she landed with a hard thump. "Darn. I was so close." Anna brushed herself off and tried again. This time she only made it half-way up before she slipped.

"This isn't working, Tedith. I am not going to be able to climb out." Anna said, rubbing her elbow, which she had whacked when she fell.

"But we have to get out of here. We can't let them turn us over to Donovan. I don't know what he wants with us but it can't be good."

Tired and sore, Anna sat down on the cold ground. There was nothing more she could do. Maybe there would be some way to escape when the weasels took them out of the pit in the morning, before giving them to Donovan.

Suddenly Tedith jumped to his feet. "I've got it!

"Got what?"

"I know how we can get out of here. You can throw me to the top."

"What?"

"You got a good throwing arm. I've seen you play catch with Grandpa. You can throw me to the top."

"I don't know, Tedith. It's awfully high and if I miss, you could really get hurt."

"I'm willing to take that chance. It'll be fine, really. Besides what other option do we have?"

"Alright, but I hope you know what you are asking me to do." Anna picked Tedith up. "Okay, you ready?" Tedith nodded.

"On the count of three. One...two...three." With all her might, Anna threw Tedith skyward. He landed on the edge of the pit and started to slide down. Anna prepared herself to catch him. But instead of falling, Tedith caught hold of a clump of grass. He struggled to hold on. He kicked his leg over the edge and hauled himself up.

"Good going, Tedith!" Anna cheered quietly. Tedith looked around cautiously. Deep within the woods he saw the glow of the weasel's campfire.

"Now how do *I* get out? Maybe you should run back to town and get someone to help us."

"We don't have time," Tedith said, "You were knocked out for a long time. It's going to get light in a little while. Besides I have another idea. Hold tight. I'll be right back."

Before Anna could protest, Tedith disappeared.

"I hope he knows what he is doing," Anna thought as she shivered.

It seemed like forever before Tedith finally poked his head over the edge of the pit. "Here, take this." He threw something in the pit. Anna grappled for it in the dark. "It's a vine. I've tied it to a tree. You can use it to climb out. Hurry!"

"Do you really think it will hold me?" Anna asked, grabbing the vine.

"It has to."

Anna gave the vine a good tug. It seemed to be strong enough. She took a deep breath and began to climb up the side of the pit. The vine cut into her hands, but she kept going. She was almost to the top when she lost her footing; she slipped but managed to hang on. With one final heave, she pulled herself over the edge.

"Way to go Anna," Tedith squealed as he jumped on her.

"Let's get out of here before they discover we're gone." Anna looked into the darkness. "I'm all turned around. Do you know which way to go?"

"This way," Tedith said, leading Anna deeper into the forest. "The path is over here, I saw it when I was looking for the vine."

They found the path and quietly followed it. It led them to the weasel's camp. They could hear the weasels snoring as they approached. They carefully tiptoed past the pack of sleeping, snoring, smelly weasels. Once they were a safe distance, Anna and Tedith ran as if their lives depended upon it, which they did. They finally emerged from the forest as the predawn light turned everything a soft gray.

"Look," Tedith said, pointing into the distance.

Anna was so relieved to see the bridge. It was now the only thing standing between them and going home. With new found hope they ran toward their salvation.

"That's strange. Anna said as they approached the bridge. "It doesn't appear anyone is here. Maybe Mr. McGillicutty was wrong. Maybe we don't have to pay a toll after all."

"Wait, what's that?" Anna froze. "Do you hear that?"

"I don't hear…" Then Tedith heard it. "What is that? It's disgusting."

The sound reminded Anna of the retching sound she made just before she threw up after she ate too much junk food at the Country Fair.

"I don't know but it seems to be coming from over here. They followed the sound down the riverbank. There, under the bridge, a giant of a man was snoring loudly.

"Boy, I'm glad you don't snore like that," Tedith said, covering his ears.

"That must be the Toll-Master," Anna said, tiptoeing under the bridge.

The Toll-Master turned over in his sleep and was now facing Anna. He was as large as Big Foot and smelled twice as bad. He swatted at a fly buzzing around his head with his massive hand.

"Wake him up, Tedith," whispered Anna.

"No way. I'm not going to wake him. You wake him," Tedith replied, staring at the snoring giant.

"Oh all right, I'll wake him."

Anna took a deep breath and stepped within arm's length of the huge man.

"Mr. Toll-Master," Anna called out gingerly. The giant swatted at her as if she were one of the flies. Anna jumped out of the way, barely avoiding being hit.

"Try again," Tedith, urged.

Anna leaned over and shook his shoulder. "Helloooooo…Mr. Toll-Master."

The giant abruptly sat up, whacking his head on the underside of the bridge, which he didn't seem to notice. Or, if he did notice, he didn't seem to care. "Huh… Who's there?"

"Sorry to disturb you, but we would like to cross the bridge."

The giant, still groggy, crawled out from under the bridge. Now standing, he towered over them like a mountain. He wore a faded red plaid shirt and overalls that were worn, frayed, and three sizes too small for his colossal body. His brown eyes bulged out and were topped with a bushy uni-brow that ran from one side of his forehead to the other. His basketball sized head was shiny and bare except for a long, thin tuft of hair that he combed across his head in the hopes of concealing his baldness.

"Now, what do we hav' here?" the giant said in a sweet voice, with a thick Scottish accent. "My, it's a wee girl and a little teddy bear. Dinna see the likes o' ye in these parts much. Ye say ye wanna cross me bridge?" The giant then let out a huge yawn. The smell coming from his vast mouth was repulsive. Anna almost covered her nose but didn't want to be rude.

"That's right and we have the toll," Anna said, reaching in her pocket, unwrapping the gold coins and holding one out for the giant.

"Well, that's grand," said the Toll-Master, taking the coin. "It's a wee early. What brings ye to these parts anyway?"

"We are looking for the Ladder Keeper."

"Aye, Mr. Dobbs. You're in luck. He returned home yesterday from one o' his business trips. He dona get many visitors. His house is over the river and doon the path a wee bitty. You canna miss it."

"Thank you sir, we best be going."

"Nice seein' ya; hav' a nice day," the giant said while stretching and scratching his big belly.

As Anna and Tedith walked across the bridge, they could see a little house in the distance.

"Oh, Tedith, imagine it, we are almost home!"

Anna couldn't believe she would soon be face to face with the Ladder Keeper. Ever since Grandpa had told her about Jacob's Ladder and the Ladder Keeper, she had an image of some noble old soul, lovingly attending the ladder. What a princely calling. Jacob's Ladder was so beautiful, fleeting and ethereal; it must be tended by a very special person.

As they approached Mr. Dobbs' house, they noticed that it was little more than a shack. The house leaned slightly to one side and its tin roof had numerous patches. The front door hung by one hinge and held an elaborate brass door knocker, which seemed out of place on such a humble dwelling. The blue paint on the shutters was cracked and peeling. One of the shutters flapped in the wind, making a loud slapping sound as it struck the side of the house. There was a flowerbox under one of the crooked windows filled with dead daisies. It was not at all how Anna imagined someone so noble would live.

It was still very early, the sun barely on this side of the horizon. Anna hoped she wouldn't be waking up Mr. Dobbs.

She approached the door cautiously, looking at Tedith for reassurance. He nodded his encouragement. Anna took a deep breath, reached for the fancy brass door knocker, and tapped it against the door. Nothing happened. She tried again, this time a little louder. The door abruptly swung open. Squeaking on its one hinge as it did.

Anna could see through the open door into a ramshackle front room, which was in an even worse state than the outside of the house.

"Yah!" barked a bent-over, shaggy old man whose face was at least four days away from its last shave. He wore a pair of mismatched pajamas; blue striped on the top and paisley print on the bottom. It definitely looked like Anna had awakened him.

"Ah, Mr. Dobbs?"

"Yah, who wants to know?" the old man yawned.

Anna was so taken aback by his appearance; she could barely get her words out. "Umm, my name is Anna and well, ah..."

"Spit it out, girl." The grumpy old man snapped. "What do you want?"

"I want to go home," Anna blurted out.

"Home! Then what are you doing here? Go home," he said and slammed the door in their faces. The whole house shook.

Tedith, seeing Anna's shock and disappointment, stepped up and pounded his paw on the door. The door flung open again.

"What? You're still here?"

Anna, finding her courage replied, "Yes, we are still here. I need you to put down Jacob's Ladder so I can go home."

"What are you talking about?" The old man's leathery skin seemed to crack as he talked.

"That's how I got here. I climbed up Jacob's Ladder."

Mr. Dobbs studied Anna's face for a moment.

"Oh yah, I remember you. I was getting ready to pull the ladder up when I looked down and saw you climbing. Huh, I thought you had fallen back down to earth and were long dead."

"No sir, I hung on to the ladder for dear life and landed on the clouds."

"Hmmm, that's never happened before and I have been tending to the ladder for over five hundred years. Everyone always falls back down to earth, and is flattened dead."

"Well, for some reason I didn't fall. So, you see sir, I need you to put the ladder back down so I can go home."

The old man snorted. "What? You think I can put Jacob's Ladder down any old time I want? All of the conditions have to be right. My job is very scientific. Cloud coverage, atmospheric pressure and precipitation levels all have to be exact. You're sadly mistaken if you think I can put the ladder down just because you want me to. I mean really…you have quite the nerve asking me such a thing."

"But…then how am I to get home?"

"How would I know? I *do* know you can't stay here. And don't bother me again." He slammed the door on them for a second time.

Anna looked at Tedith with tears in her eyes. "Did you hear that? We can't climb down the ladder which means we are stuck here. I'm never going to see home again."

"It doesn't mean that at all Anna. Just because we can't go down the ladder doesn't mean we can't get home."

"It doesn't?" Anna sniffled.

"Of course not. So what if we can't get back the way that you got here. Didn't Odin say, 'the way to get home was to keep your eye on where you want to go and keep on going'?"

"He did say that, didn't he?"

"Yes he did."

"But if we don't go down the ladder, how do we get home?"

Tedith had to think about that one for a moment. "Well, Odin also said to 'follow your heart,' it would lead you home. Do you remember?"

"Yeah, I remember him saying that."

"So what does your heart tell you to do?"

"My heart? I don't know. I don't know how to listen to my heart."

Tedith didn't know how to listen to a heart either; after all it had only been a short while since he had one.

"Close your eyes," Tedith instructed.

Anna took a deep breath and closed her eyes.

"Now, try to listen to your heart."

With all her might Anna strained to hear her heart. After a couple of minutes, she opened her eyes.

"Well, what did you hear?" Tedith asked hopefully.

"The only thing I heard was the sound of my heart beating."

"Oh," Tedith said, clearly disappointed.

The door to the shack swung open. "Quit making all that racket. I'm trying to sleep. Now get out of here!" Mr. Dobbs yelled and slammed the door for the third time.

"Come on Anna, let's go. Maybe the Toll-Master knows a way for us to get home."

Anna shrugged and followed Tedith towards the bridge. On the other side of the river, the Toll-Master was standing over a little fire, stirring something in a large black caldron.

They stepped onto the bridge.

"Hold on there a minute, Lassie. You canna' cross the bridge wi'out paying the toll," the giant called out.

"But we paid you, not ten minutes ago," Anna protested.

"Them's the rules. Ye wouldna want me to get into trouble now would ye'?" The Toll-Master asked.

Anna sighed, unwrapped another gold coin and held it up to show the Toll-Master.

The Toll-Master smiled. "Alrighty then, come on o'er lass."

"I'm glad that man insisted on giving us more than one coin for the beanie," Tedith said.

"Yeah, me too."

"I thought ye were going home," the Toll-Master said as they walked towards him.

"We were… I mean we are… just not the way we thought," Anna said as she handed the giant the shiny coin.

"Well it's a lovely day for a journey. Ye hungry? I was makin' me-self some breakfast."

Tedith's stomach started to rumble at the mention of food. "Really? You sure you wouldn't mind?"

"Mind, no. I'd enjoy the company. Don't see too many folks in these parts and I got plenty to share." The Toll-Master walked over to the fire. He plopped a big spoonful of grey glop from the simmering pot onto a tin plate and handed it to Tedith. Based on the looks of it, Anna wasn't so sure she was hungry after all.

"So, ye say you're going home? Where exactly is home?" the Toll-Master asked as he handed a plate of mush to Anna.

Tedith took a tentative bite and was delighted at how good it tasted.

"Toronto is home, but I am staying at my grandma's farm for the summer, which is just outside of Grimsby," Anna said through a mouthful of food.

"Hmmm, I canna say I hav' heard o' it."

"Toronto is in Ontario…Canada."

"Canada, eh? Is that anywhere near Merryvale?" the giant asked, picking his teeth with a stick he had found on the ground.

"Merryvale? No, Canada is a country, just north of the United

States." The giant still looked puzzled.

"You don't know where the United States of America is? I thought everyone did. What about Earth? Surely you have heard of planet Earth?"

"Earth? No canna say that I hav'."

Anna was astonished that he had never heard of Earth. It was then that she knew she was much farther away from home than she ever imagined.

"I was kind of hoping you could tell us how we might get home."

"Afraid I canna help ye, lass. I've n'er been further then me wee bridge here, but I hear Merryvale is a nice town. Maybe someone in town can help ye."

Anna knew they couldn't go back to Merryvale. But what were they going to do? Anna wondered, staring into the fire.

As the Toll-Master poured himself another cup of tree-bark coffee, an all too familiar bone-chilling shill rang out across the land. Tedith dropped his plate and shuddered. Food splattered everywhere. The terrible sound was coming from the forest.

"Oh no! It's *The Loyal Forces of the Opposition.* They must have discovered that we escaped. I was so focused on getting to the Ladder Keeper, I forgot they were coming for us this morning," Anna said in a panic.

"Please sir, you have to help us. They are looking for us!" Anna begged.

"Donovan is after you?"

"Yes, you know him?"

"Aye, everyone knows about him. But why are they—"

"Please, there is no time to explain. Will you help us?" Anna pleaded.

The Toll-Master, not a man of deep thought, thought for a

moment, then ran under the bridge, dragged out an old wooden raft and pushed it onto the river.

"Here, ye two get on."

Tedith and Anna jumped on. The Toll-Master gave them a good shove.

"Luck be w'i ye! Hope ye have a light-filled journey," the Toll-Master called after them as the river carried them downstream.

Anna again wondered. Why did everyone keep telling her to 'have a light-filled journey'? What does it mean?

The raft was made from rotting logs held together with frayed rope. It wasn't very sturdy but anything was better than nothing at a time like this.

Tedith grabbed a long pole that was lying on the raft and used it to guide them down the river. They moved along at the speed of the moving water, which was a decent clip, but wasn't nearly fast enough for Anna's liking. The more distance they put between them and Donovan, the better.

Anna kept looking back, expecting at any moment to see *The Loyal Forces of the Opposition*. But so far, they were nowhere in sight.

The river had begun to pick up speed. The raft began to bob and weave as the river's current became more forceful.

Anna had always wanted to go white-water rafting, but not on a rickety old raft, and especially not when her life depended upon it.

The water was now fierce. Tedith was doing his best to steer the raft with the pole, but the river had a mind of its own and soon snatched the pole right out of his hands.

"Hang on Anna," Tedith yelled over the sound of rushing water. The raft rose and fell violently to the rhythm of the now furious rapids. Huge waves swallowed the raft.

"Oh no!" Anna cried. "Hold on Tedith, hold on." The raft was headed straight for a waterfall.

Anna thought about the people that used to go over Niagara Falls in a barrel. She wished she had a barrel now.

The raft plummeted over the waterfall. The force of the water tore the raft apart.

"Ahhhhh," Anna yelled as she fell head first into the cold, deep water at the bottom of the waterfall. Deeper and deeper she went. Cold, dark water surrounded her. She was sure her lungs were going to burst; she couldn't hold her breath much longer.

Anna then felt a pair of arms around her. She looked around and saw a beautiful woman with long, flowing blond hair. She was lifting Anna to the surface. Anna broke through the water, gasping for air. The woman gently swam over to the bank of the river and laid Anna down next to Tedith, who was also struggling to catch his breath. Anna couldn't believe her eyes. Before her were two of the most exquisite women she had ever seen. Only they weren't women, they were mermaids.

CHAPTER FIVE

SCHOOL OF IMES

The mermaid looked at Anna with great concern. "Are you alright?"

Anna was too stunned to say anything. She just stared at her beautiful rescuer. The mermaid had intense turquoise eyes that matched the color of the water, long flowing hair that was so blond it was white, skin as fine as porcelain and iridescent purple scales on her tail.

"My dear, are you alright?" asked the mermaid again.

"Yes, I think so. Thank you. Thank you so much."

"That was quite the fall you and your little friend took. My name is Leah and this is my sister Neah."

Anna looked at Neah, who was tending to Tedith, then she looked at Leah, then back at Neah.

"Yes," Neah giggled. "We are identical twins, which is very rare for mermaids."

"And how are you, little fellow?" Neah asked Tedith, while stroking him under his chin. "You gave me quite the scare." Tedith couldn't take his eyes off of the mermaid; he was mesmerized by her unworldly beauty.

"Tedith?" Anna said, trying to break his trance.

"Uh, fine, fine. Really I am fine. Thank you for rescuing me," Tedith said, as he gazed at the mermaid who was still stroking his chin.

The lagoon they had fallen into was surrounded by a lush tropical jungle. The waterfall that was fearsome and raging just a moment ago now filled the air with the calming sound of falling water.

"Where are we?" Anna asked.

Before the mermaids could reply, there was a rustling in the jungle behind them. They turned around to see a raven-haired maiden, dressed in a long pink robe, step out from the thick foliage. She bowed deeply towards them. Without saying a word, she wrapped Anna and Tedith in the thick white towels she was carrying. Anna was shivering and was grateful for the warmth of the towel.

The woman began to walk back into the jungle. She turned around, indicating for them to follow her. Anna wasn't quite sure what to do.

"It's alright, you can go with her. You are in good hands. She won't talk to you but she can help you," Leah said with a smile.

"Where is she taking us?"

"You'll see," Neah said. "There is nothing to be frightened of."

"How do we ever thank you? You saved our lives."

"No thanks are necessary. You will find many people are more than willing to help you on your journey home," Leah said.

Anna wanted to ask how she knew they were going home, but before she could, both mermaids disappeared into the clear turquoise water with a flip of their tails.

Anna wrapped the towel tightly around her and walked towards the maiden. Tedith, still under the spell of the mermaid's beauty, was frozen in place. Anna, smiling, went over to her little friend.

"Come on dreamy eyes. Let's go." Anna said, as she gently guided Tedith towards the maiden. They followed her into the tropical paradise. Magnificent trees, bearing ripe fruit, lined the path. Multi-colored birds called out and monkeys swung from branch to branch. Giant white flowers growing from long vines permeated the air with the sweetest aroma.

It wasn't long until the path led to a small clearing. They approached a thatched roof hut, no taller than a playhouse. It was the first of six identical huts standing in a semi-circle. The maiden opened the door. Anna and Tedith had to duck to fit through the threshold.

They could not believe their eyes. What was a humble hut on the outside was a stately mansion on the inside. It reminded Anna of the class trip she had taken to the Parliament buildings in Ottawa, only here, beautiful women were everywhere. They were all dressed in identical robes in four different colors; pink, blue, green and purple. Most of the women had long hair. Some wore it down and flowing while others wore theirs up, decorated with flowers.

All of the women carried a single leather bound book. Each woman they passed nodded at them. But what was most remarkable was the silence. Even though many of the women walked together, no one spoke.

The maiden led them through a grand foyer, up a monumental marble staircase, down a long hall and into a well-appointed bedroom. It was just like the kind you would find in a fancy hotel. On the bed was a set of clothes that were identical to the outfit Anna was wearing, except they were dry and clean. There was even a new fresh green ribbon for Tedith. A bowl of fruit stood on a table along with a pitcher of water.

"Can't you at least tell us, where are we?" Anna asked, hoping the maiden would talk to them. But the maiden just smiled and walked out of the room, closing the door behind her.

Anna, still wet and shivering, decided to change into the fresh clothes. They fit perfectly. She transferred the gold coins wrapped in the bandana and her lucky stone into her new jeans. Tedith toweled himself off. When his orange fur was dry and fluffy Anna helped him tie his new ribbon around his neck.

"I wonder where we are," Anna asked.

"I don't know, but I'm hungry. Tedith walked over to the bowl and picked out a ripe plum. "After all, I barely got to finish my breakfast this morning."

Tedith bit into the sweet fruit. He moaned in delight as the juice ran down his chin. Anna smiled at Tedith's utter pleasure in eating. She walked over to the large window. It overlooked a formal courtyard and garden. Crushed rock pathways crisscrossed through an exquisite rose garden. Four marble dolphins spurted water from their mouths into a large fountain. Birds perched on its edge, drank and splashed.

Anna sighed. It was nice to be warm and safe, but where were they? And how was this going to help them get home? Anna had decided to go find someone she could ask when there was a knock at the door.

"Umm, yes, come in," Anna called out.

The door opened and a maiden wearing a purple robe walked in and bowed. "My name is Sofia. Would you be so kind as to follow me?"

"Where are we?" Anna asked, relieved that someone was talking to them.

"You are in the School of Imes. We are very pleased that you are here. Please come with me."

Anna sighed. "But *where* are you taking us?" Anna was frustrated, she wasn't one who was easily lead and wanted to know what was going on.

Sofia turned and without a word looked deeply into Anna's eyes. There was something about the way Sofia gazed at Anna that immediately calmed and reassured her. Anna knew that words weren't the only way to communicate and decided, at least for the time being, to follow.

Sofia led them back down the grand stairway and through a large glass door that lead into the gardens that Anna had admired from their room. They followed the path past the fragrant roses, the dolphin fountain, and into a tall bamboo forest. Anna stuck her hand in her pocket and rubbed her lucky stone. Anna hoped that wherever Sofia was taking them it would help them get home. The bamboo forest gave way to a vast open field.

Anna gasped. In the middle of the field was a magnificent stone pyramid, just like the ones in Egypt. Sofia stopped at the base of the pyramid, and a door slid open. She indicated for Anna and Tedith to enter, then bowed and returned to the school.

As soon as they entered, the door slid shut behind them.

"Wow," Tedith said as he gazed upward. From the outside, the pyramid looked like it was made of solid stone but the inside of the pyramid was made of glass. They looked right through the pyramid into the clear blue sky. It was like being in a huge greenhouse.

In the center of the pyramid was a circle of twelve women dressed in white robes. This was the first time Anna had seen any one dressed in a white robe. Anna and Tedith stood by the door a little dumbstruck.

"Welcome, Anna. Welcome, Tedith. Please join us in the middle of circle," one of the women said.

As they walked towards the women two of them moved aside so they could enter the circle.

"Please have a seat."

Anna and Tedith sat on two glass chairs which appeared to have been placed there expressly for them.

"Welcome to our school. We have been waiting for you. My name is Sidea and I am the headmistress." Sidea seemed to radiate light. She had lavender colored eyes, long, flowing black hair and skin that reminded Anna of silky black satin. She held a long ebony staff that had a crystal on the end of it, like the one on Odin's walking stick and Donovan's medallion.

"Excuse me, but you said you were waiting for us. How did you know we were coming?"

"Odin paid us a visit last night and told us to expect you."

"Odin! Is he still here?"

"No, my child. He left almost as soon as he arrived."

"But…how did he know I was coming here?"

"Odin knows many things, my dear. He told us to take good care of you and Tedith, and to assist you on your journey home if we could."

Anna was disappointed. She would've liked to have seen Odin. She had a lot of questions for him. But at least he had asked them to help her.

"What kind of school is this? It's not like any school I've ever seen before."

"The School of Imes is one of the oldest schools in *The Land Beyond the Clouds*. Women come here from all over to learn about truth. The color of the robe you see each of them wearing indicates the level that the student has obtained."

"This school teaches truth? I didn't know truth was something you could study. We don't have anything like that at the school I attend."

Sidea laughed and said, "No, I don't imagine you do. The schools on earth are more dedicated to mental knowledge. Our school is dedicated to assisting each student in discovering the truth that is in each of us. Now, how might we assist you on your journey home?"

"Well, could you tell us how to get home?" Anna asked, pretty sure she knew what the answer would be.

Sidea, appreciating Anna's attempt, smiled. "I'm sorry, my dear, no one can tell you how to get home. As Odin explained, everyone must find their own way and there are as many paths home as there are people. However, if you like, we could assist you in learning more about your path home."

"Really? That would be great! How do we do that?" Anna asked, with newfound hope.

"Close your eyes," Sidea instructed.

"You aren't going to ask me to listen to my heart are you? I already tried that and nothing happened."

Sidea just looked at Anna with her piercing lavender eyes.

"Okay, okay. I'll give it another try." Anna closed her eyes, even though she was sure this was going to be a waste of time.

Sidea spoke in a soft rhythmic tone. "I want you to think about going home. Connect with the deep longing for home that lives deep within you. Think about all of the reasons why you want to go home; your family, your friends, where you live, the things you like to do." Anna wasn't prepared for the tears that welled up in her eyes as she thought about everything she loved in her life and how much she missed all of it.

"Now, let your thoughts go. Let go of your past and any

thought of the future. Let go of everything and be in the ever present *now*. Within the present lies the truth, the truth that will lead you home. Your path lives inside you Anna, you have only to be open to it." Sidea paused. "Take your time. When you are ready, tell us what you see."

Anna strained to see something. "I don't see anything. There is nothing there."

"Beyond the nothingness lies your path. Let the image come to you like a gentle breeze. It's there. Trust yourself," Sidea directed.

Anna took a deep breath and gazed into the vast nothingness within her. Then she saw a golden light. It was very faint at first, but then it grew brighter. Anna couldn't believe that the light was coming from inside her but it was. Within the light an image was beginning to emerge. It was a little fuzzy at first but then it became clearer.

"You see something, don't you?" Sidea asked.

Anna nodded, afraid that if she spoke, the image would disappear.

"It's okay. Tell us what you see."

"I'm not quite sure. It's some type of building, only I can see right through it. I think it's made of glass, like the inside of the pyramid. No wait, it's not glass, it's crystal," Anna said, amazed at how clear her inner vision was becoming. It was like watching a movie being projected onto a screen. "I think it's a palace, a crystal palace. It's perched on a mountain top, in the middle of a vast mountain range. It's seems to glow from some inner light," Anna stared in awe at the vision inside of her.

"Very good, Anna. When you are ready you can open your eyes," Sidea said quietly.

Anna was reluctant to open her eyes. Something about the palace gave her a deep sense of peace and contentment.

"Anna?" Sidea encouraged.

Anna slowly opened her eyes. Everyone was very still, very

quiet. Too quiet.

"What? What is it? Did I say something wrong? Will finding the Crystal Palace get me home?" Anna asked, wondering what was going on.

Sidea broke the silence. "Yes, I dare say it will."

Anna felt relieved. At least she now had an idea of what she was looking for but there was still an uneasiness in the room. "What is it? What aren't you telling me?"

Sidea tried to find the right words. "Of all the ways someone can get home, going through the Crystal Palace is one of the most difficult and dangerous."

Anna shivered. "It is? Well, then I'll just go another route, one not so dangerous. After all you did there are a lot of paths home."

"I wish it were that simple my dear. As Odin explained, everyone has their own unique path home. If that is the path that has revealed itself to you, then that is the path that is perfect for you. I am afraid there is no other path home for you."

Anna shuddered at hearing this.

Sidea walked into the center of the circle. She used the crystal on the end of her staff like a writing instrument and started to draw in the air. She drew an upward spiral and it magically appeared, as if she was drawing on a blackboard.

"This spiral represents *The Land Beyond the Clouds*. Even though it looks like a single spiral, it's actually a multi-dimensional spiral. All the paths home are contained within this one spiral. Although they all lead to the same place, home, no two paths are alike. Each path contains exactly the experiences *you need* to make it home. Along the way, you will encounter many different lands, civilizations, and realms. Which ones you encounter depend on your unique path up the spiral. Many of these societies are friendly and helpful, such as ours and Merryvale. However, many are dark and foreboding, full of all manner of negativity." Sidea paused as she carefully chose what she was going to say next. "To get to the Crystal Palace you will have to go through some of the darkest and most dangerous places. *The Loyal Forces of the Opposition* has a very strong foothold in these lands."

Anna went pale. "Did you say *Loyal Forces of the Opposition?*"

Sidea nodded.

"I don't understand. Who are they and why are they trying to prevent me from going home? What could they possibly want with a girl and a teddy bear?"

"It's simple my dear. It's their job. Everything in the universe has an opposite. Up has down. In has out. Positive is balanced by negative. Even light has dark. *The Loyal Forces of the Opposition* is the opposite of your heart's desire, which is to go home. It is their responsibility to keep you, and everyone, from their heart's desire. And I must say, they are very good at what they do. They will use every method they can to stop you. You must want to reach home above all else and be ever vigilant and single-minded. Never take your focus off your destination. The closer you get to home, the stronger their pursuit will become. It will take all your wit and willpower to overcome them. Only the bravest and truest will make it home. But if you persist, you will get home."

Anna couldn't believe what she was hearing. It sounded hopeless. She looked over at Tedith who seemed to be in a state of shock. His orange fur even looked pale.

"What if I decide not to go?"

Sidea smiled and said, "The heart wants what the heart wants. You could delay your journey, but sooner or later you will follow your heart home. We all do."

Anna signed. "And you are sure that the Crystal Palace is the only way for me to get home?"

Sidea laughed, "It wasn't I who picked your path my dear; it was you. Trust what was revealed to you. Although it might not seem like it now, your path is perfect for you. You have everything you need to complete your journey, but you must trust yourself and keep going, no matter what you encounter."

Anna still wasn't ready to accept her fate. "There has got to be another way. If there are so many paths, I don't understand why I can't take a different one."

"I know, my child. The mind's job is to try to understand but there are some things that can't be understood until they are experienced. Trust yourself Anna and all will be well."

Anna sighed deeply, full of doubt and worry.

"Now it is time for you to continue. I will escort you to the edge of our civilization. There, we will say our goodbyes."

Reluctantly, Anna and Tedith followed Sidea out of the pyramid, through the gardens and back into the main building. They passed several students as they made their way to the front door. Anna wished she was one of them. She didn't want to leave the comfort and safety of the school.

"This is where we must part," Sidea said, opening the same door they had entered. "I wish you a light-filled journey."

Anna wanted to ask Sidea why everyone kept saying that to her, but somehow knew that was something she would have to figure out for herself.

"Thank you for your assistance. I really do appreciate it," Anna said. "Can't you at least point us in the right direction?"

Sidea smiled at Anna, bowed silently, and closed the door.

CHAPTER SIX

AMRAK STATION

Anna was surprised once again to see that the outside of the magnificent building was nothing more than a grass hut. *The Land Beyond the Clouds* sure was a strange place. At home she knew what was what. But not here, everything was so different.

Why did getting home have to be so difficult? At least she now knew what she was looking for; the Crystal Palace, but she had no idea where to start. It was all so confusing.

"Which way do you think we go?" Anna said looking at their surroundings.

"Maybe the mermaid can tell us where to find the Crystal

Palace," Tedith suggested hopefully.

Anna smiled at her little friend's attempt to see the beautiful mermaids once more. "I don't think so, Tedith. It's becoming pretty clear that we have to figure this out for ourselves."

"Well, what about the other huts? Maybe the Palace is in one of them," Tedith offered as he studied the five other huts.

"I don't know if that is such a good idea, Tedith. There is no telling what is behind those doors."

"All right, what do you think we should do?"

Tedith had a point, they didn't have many options. They could either go back into the jungle or try another hut. "Okay, let's check them out but be careful."

Tedith approached the hut next to the school. "Do you think I should knock?"

Anna shrugged. "I guess so."

Tedith rapped lightly on the door. Nothing happened. Tedith put his ear to the door. "I don't hear anything."

"Try knocking a little harder," Anna encouraged.

Tedith rapped loudly; still nothing.

"Let's try another hut," Anna suggested.

Tedith knocked on the door of the next hut, but again, no one answered.

He knocked on the door of each hut but still nothing.

"Maybe we should try opening the door without knocking," Tedith said as he stood in front of the last hut.

Before Anna could answer, a blood curdling shrill rang out from the tropical forest. Donovan!

Without thinking twice, Tedith grabbed the door handle and pulled. Thankfully, the door swung open. They both jumped into what they hoped would be the safety of the hut.

"I can't believe Donovan is so close," Anna said, holding on to

Tedith. The inside of the hut was black as midnight and smelled of the ocean.

"My, my. What do we have here?" A booming voice asked high above them.

Anna and Tedith had been so relieved to be in the hut they hadn't realized they were not alone.

As a light switch was hit, the inside of the hut was flooded with light. Two beady eyes looked down at them through a pair of round, metal-rimmed spectacles that were held together with scotch tape. The glasses were perched on the nose of a giant green turtle, standing on his hind legs. He wore white sneakers and gym socks. A faded conductor's hat was perched on his massive green head. He held an oversized clipboard and, stuck behind his right ear, was a badly chewed pencil.

Anna was shaking. "Ah, I'm Anna and this is Tedith."

"I see and what are you doing here?" the reptile asked, looking down at them over the tops of his glasses.

"We…we…we are looking for the Crystal Palace," Anna stuttered.

"The Crystal Palace you say?"

"Yes, so…so…so we can go home."

"Well, come on in. My name is Marlin, I am the Transport Director. I will be assisting you today. Right this way."

Marlin saw Anna give Tedith a look that clearly asked, "Do you think we should follow him?"

"Of course, you can go back where you came from," Marlin said with a sly smile.

"No, no, we are coming," Anna said eagerly. Wherever he was taking them had to be better than going back to where Donovan was looking for them.

They followed Marlin down a short corridor. A set of double

glass doors slid open as they approached.

Anna was flabbergasted. One moment they were in an old town, then a jungle, then a mysterious school, and now this....

The space was massive. It had to be three or four times larger than a football field. Along one wall were dozens of glass elevators with numbers above them. They were taking off and landing at lightning speed. The place was a hub of activity. All sorts of...what would one call them...'critters?' were running around. Some of them were familiar to Anna, such as penguins and giraffes. Most, however, Anna had never seen before. One of them reminded her of a poodle, except that it was bright pink and had two heads and six legs. There was also a blue, beetle-like thing with a very long nose, and a critter with green and white-striped fur that hung down to the ground, but stood only as tall as Anna's knees.

"Excuse me but where are we?" Anna asked Marlin, who was obviously used to all the commotion.

"Where are you? Why, you are in the Amrak Transport Station, of course."

"The Amrak Transport Station?"

"Yes, we provide realm-to-realm transport, for all the beings of the known and unknown universes. Those glass pods transport you from one realm to the next," the large turtle explained as he pointed to the wall of glass elevators.

"Those aren't elevators?"

"No, they are pods. Transportation pods. Now, where did you say you were headed?"

"Ah, the Crystal Palace," Anna said, overwhelmed by everything she was seeing.

"Well, as I am sure you know, we can only take you up one realm at a time. The Crystal Palace may or may not be on the next realm you visit."

Marlin flipped though several pages on his clipboard. "Let's see…Anna and Tedith… Anna and Tedith… ah, yes. Here you are. It says here that the next realm you are to visit is the Pink Realm. Hmmm, also, says that this is your first visit with us."

"Our names are on your clipboard?" Anna asked, confused.

"Oh, course. If you were not ready for your next realm, you would not have been able to enter the Amrak Station. Only those who have completed the level they are on can go onto the next one. Of course, you can always visit the levels below the one you are on, just not the ones above it. Many of the folks you see here today are going on vacation, visiting some of their favorite places. Others, like the two of you, are ready for their next realm. The realm you are going to, the Pink Realm, is very intriguing. Yes indeed, most intriguing. You can have anything you can imagine on the Pink Realm. A new bike, the latest clothes, endless honey pots," Marlin said, winking at Tedith. "You have only to imagine it. The Pink Realm is a very seductive realm. Your wildest dreams can come true on that realm. People have been known to get lost in the Pink Realm for eons. The only problem is that none of it is real. It's all an illusion, a 'figment of one's imagination,' so to speak."

"What do we do when we get to…what did you say it was called, the Pink Realm?" Anna asked, not at all sure she liked the sound of all this.

"Why, you continue your journey home, of course."

Anna looked confused, so Marlin continued, "Just deal with whatever you encounter. Do the best you can but always remember that what you see on the Pink Realm is an illusion."

A booming voice over a loud speaker, like the kind you hear at sporting events, announced: "Passengers destined for the Pink Realm please report to Platform Three. Departure is in five minutes."

"Well you two, that means you. Come with me." Marlin walked

them through the massive station. Anna tried her best not to gawk at the weird beings they passed. They stopped in front of the glass pod with the "3" above it. The doors were open. Tedith immediately got in. Anna wasn't so eager.

"You sure this is how I am going to find the Crystal Palace?" Anna asked, not wanting to get into the pod.

"You'll be fine," Marlin said, "just remember that no matter how good it all seems, what you really want is to go home."

Anna reluctantly joined Tedith in the pod. It was old and rickety and had a musty smell. It was empty except for the operator, who reminded Anna of a purple aardvark. He wore a grey flannel uniform and little cap, which was a least three sizes too small. He sat on a little stool in the corner, in front of a panel of buttons that looked like they had been pushed a million times. The whole thing reminded Anna of the old fashioned elevator in a department store. You know, the type of elevator that has an operator calling out each floor. Anna giggled as she thought of the purple aardvark calling out, '5th floor ladies lingerie.'

Anna and Tedith moved to one side to let a family of orange beings, that resembled a cross between a duck and a camel, enter the pod.

"Come on Doodles, don't dawdle," said the mother to one of her several offspring.

"Watch your step," said the pod operator to the youngsters as they entered.

"We're going on vacation," said Doodles to Anna. "My mom says I can eat as much yellow slime as I want...yum! I can't wait."

Anna was not quite sure how to respond. She couldn't imagine anyone looking forward to eating slime, yellow or any other color.

Doodles then pinched Tedith on his arm.

"Ouch," Tedith called out, rubbing his arm.

Doodles snickered, "Sorry, I didn't think you were real."

Tedith backed away and stood behind Anna.

"Okay, that's everyone," the purple aardvark said, pushing a button that closed the glass door. "Welcome aboard. Our destination today is the Pink Realm, where your wildest dreams can come true. Before we continue, there are a few guidelines. First, I will count down from five. During this time, imagine where you would like to go. Keep a clear picture in your head. When I say 'Now' you can open your eyes and you will be in the place you imagined. Second, be sure to hold hands with the people you are with so that you all end up in the same location, which will be where the oldest one in the group imagines." Turning to the children, he said smiling, "So you little ones, no sense imagining a toy store, 'cause you aren't going to get there."

"Ah nuts," said Doodles.

The purple aardvark turned and looked at Anna and Tedith. "And finally, a friendly reminder. Where you are going is an illusion. So for those of you who are trying to get home, your imagination, no matter how good, isn't going to get you there."

Anna sighed, "Oh well, so much for that idea."

"Okay it's time. Please hold hands with the folks you are with."

Anna's sweaty palm took hold of Tedith's tiny fur paw.

"Now, close your eyes and imagine where you would like to go."

Anna closed her eyes and squeezed Tedith's paw.

"Five...four..."

The pod rumbled as it started to move upward. Anna's mind went blank. Other than home, there was no place she wanted to go.

"three...two..."

The pod accelerated.

Anna franticly searched her mind for someplace to go. Someplace nice, someplace safe, someplace far away from Donovan.

Then it popped into her head.

"one...now...."

CHAPTER SEVEN

CANDY LAND

A loud clap echoed throughout the pod. Then silence. Anna stood perfectly still. She was afraid to open her eyes.

"Wow!" Tedith exclaimed. "Anna, open your eyes. You gotta see this."

Anna squinted enough to let in a little light. The only thing she saw were big blocks of color; pink, mint green and white.

Tedith shook Anna. "Come on Anna, open your eyes. It's all right. It's more than all right! You aren't going to believe where we are."

As Anna's eyes slowly opened, her mouth dropped. She blinked a few times to make sure what she was seeing was real.

"Look at all this candy," Tedith exclaimed.

They were standing in the middle of a garden of gumdrop flowers. Little jellybean bushes and lollipop trees dotted the mint green landscape. In the distance was a stream of flowing white chocolate. The sky was covered in pink candy-floss clouds. There was nothing but sweets as far as they could see.

Tedith ran to a lemon drop toadstool, then to a large rock-candy boulder. "Do you think we can eat them?"

"I don't think we should Tedith. I think they are part of a game," Anna said, starting to make sense of where they were.

"A game? What kind of game?"

"A board game."

When the pod operator told Anna to think of a place she wanted to go, Anna searched her memory for a time when she had been happy. Some of Anna's fondest memories were of playing board games with her grandpa, who had a closet full of them. Most of the games were very old, having belonged to Anna's mom when she was a little girl. Grandpa liked to tell Anna how he used to play the exact same game with her mom that he now played with her.

One rainy afternoon last summer Grandpa pulled down 'Candy Land' from the closet shelf and asked her if she would like to play. "Oh, Grandpa, I'm too big for that game," she had told him. Her grandpa shrugged and put the game back in the closet. She now wished she had played it with him. "I sure do miss my grandpa," Anna thought.

"I think we are in Candy Land, Tedith."

"Candy Land?"

"Yeah, Candy Land. I haven't played it in a long time but it used to be one of my favorite games when I was a little girl."

"Well, it looks like a great game," Tedith said, eyeing a red-hot shrub. "Only, I don't know how this is going to help us get home."

"Me either." Anna touched a bubble gum bush. That's when she noticed that she was standing on the beginning square of the game. "Hmmm, maybe, I'm not sure, but maybe we are supposed to play the game," Anna said, looking at the path stretching out before her.

"Play the game?"

"Sure, that must be it. Look, we are standing on the beginning square of a game board. See all those colored squares on the ground?"

Tedith nodded.

"They form a path to the Gingerbread House at the end of the game."

"Okay, but how do you play Candy Land?" Tedith asked, wishing he could eat one of the delicious looking butterscotch flowers.

"Let's see if I remember correctly. When it's your turn you flip over a card." Anna looked around for the cards. "Look there's the stack of cards," Anna said, pointing. "There is a color on the other side of each card. You move along the path to the next square of that color. The one that gets to the Gingerbread House first, wins."

"Are we supposed to play against each other?"

Anna was about to answer when two plastic gingerbread men came strolling out of the nearby peppermint forest. They stood about three feet tall. One was red, the other was blue. They looked just like the plastic gingerbread men that were the game markers in the game Anna played with her grandpa.

The red one waved at them and called out, "Hello there. We are here to play Candy Land with you. Are you ready?"

"Uh, I guess so," Anna said, a little uneasy at the arrival of the unexpected visitors.

"I must warn you, my brother and I are very good. What are your names?"

"I'm Tedith. She's Anna," Tedith called out eager to walk

through a game made entirely of candy.

"Glad to meet you both. They call me Red. My brother's name is Blue." Blue waved to them as he walked over to the first square on the board.

"Now, where is Yellow? Yellow will be turning the cards for us today. Yellow! Yellow, where are you?" Red called out.

Out of the field of suckers came a yellow plastic gingerbread man looking somewhat down-heartened.

"I don't know why I *always* have to be the one who turns the cards. I never get to play," Yellow said, kicking the ground and creating a small cloud of powdered sugar.

"Now Yellow, don't start that again. Blue was the card turner last time, and I turned the cards the time before that. It's now your turn."

"Oh, all right. But I don't have to like it. Who's going first?"

"Anna and Tedith can go first, since they are our guests. You two can play as a pair," Red said.

Tedith quickly joined Blue on the starting square. Anna still not sure about all this, slowly made her way to the first square.

"Okay Yellow, everyone is ready, turn over the first card."

Yellow reluctantly walked over to the stack of cards. He turned over the top card and called out, "Purple!"

Anna and Tedith walked down the path and stopped on the first purple square they came across.

"Blue, you go next," Red said.

Yellow flipped over a card and called out, "Blue."

"Yes," Blue answered.

"No Blue, I didn't call you! I called out the color on the card," Yellow said, obviously annoyed.

"I know, I was just kidding you." Blue giggled then proceed to the first blue square, which was two squares past Anna and Tedith.

"My turn," Red said, as he stepped onto the starting square.

"Green," Yellow called out.

Red passed Anna, Tedith and Blue as he headed to the green square. He was now in the lead.

"Anna and Tedith, your next square is red," Yellow called out, getting more into the spirit of the game.

Tedith and Anna passed a bend and found themselves in the middle of a field of candy hearts with little sayings on them. Like, 'Forget me not', 'Kiss me' and 'Be Mine.'

Yellow continued to call out colors as the players leapfrogged one another down the path of colored squares.

"Anna, what do you think happens if we win the game?" Tedith asked.

"I don't know. I guess it's too much to hope that it will get us to the Crystal Palace."

"Yeah, probably, but maybe we can at least get some candy," Tedith said, drooling over a red licorice tree.

They traveled along Gumdrop Pass and stopped beside a Peanut Brittle house. All the candy was making even Anna's mouth water. She figured a little piece couldn't hurt anything.

As she reached out to break off a chunk of peanut brittle from one of the shutters, a Peanut Brittle man stuck his head out of a frosted sugar window.

"Keep your hands to yourself," he yelled at Anna.

"Sorry," Anna said, quickly pulling back her hand.

He slammed the window, cracking one of the sugar panes.

Both Blue and Red were now several squares behind Anna and Tedith. Ahead of them was the Molasses Swamp. Anna remembered when she played the game with her grandpa that the scariest part of the game was going through the Swamp. She would be glad when they were on the other side. Their turn was next.

"Orange!" Yellow called out. Anna and Tedith walked to the next orange square and found themselves smack dead in the middle of the gooey Molasses Swamp. Long, black, sticky strands of molasses hung from dead trees, giving the swamp an eerie feel. Boiling sinkholes of molasses bubbled and hissed.

"I'm not so sure I like it in here," Tedith said, holding his nose to avoid smelling the sickening burnt sweetness of the swamp.

"I know what you mean. Let's stay close, and whatever you do, don't stray off the path. Who knows what's lurking in the swamp. With a little luck we'll be out of here on our next turn."

Creepy sounds, the kind that make you want to hide under your bed, filled the swamp. Anna tried her best to think only pleasant thoughts, but her fear started to get the best of her. She began to imagine all the terrible things that could be lurking in the swamp. Then an ear-piercing shrill rang out. The swamp immediately fell silent.

"Oh, no. It can't be. Not here." Anna turned around to see three ghostly white figures flying towards them. "Run, Tedith, run."

Tedith began to run down the path. Anna was right behind him. She looked over her shoulder. *The Loyal Forces of the Opposition* were right behind them. Anna grabbed Tedith and jumped off the path into the swamp, careful to avoid the boiling sinkholes. The ghostly threesome flew straight past them. They could hear Donovan cursing them.

Anna and Tedith fled blindly into the dark, gooey swamp. The thick, sticky molasses made it almost impossible to run.

The Loyal Forces of the Opposition turned back toward them. The swamp was too dense for them to fly through so they were now coming after Anna and Tedith on foot.

"We are doomed," Anna told herself. "If only there was somewhere to hide." Then she saw it. "Over here, Tedith." Anna ducked into a small opening in a hollowed-out tree.

Breathing heavily, Tedith jumped in behind her. It was dark, cramped, and stank of burned molasses.

"They couldn't have gone very far. Find them!" Donovan commanded.

Anna saw Donovan's molasses-covered boots as he walked right by their hiding place. She held her breath. Tedith sneezed.

Donovan swung around. "What was that?"

"It came from over here," one of Donovan's men said.

The molasses-covered white boots now stood directly in front of Anna and Tedith. A strong, white-gloved hand reached into the hollow of the tree, grabbed Anna by her yellow t-shirt, and yanked her from their hiding place. He tossed her onto the soft, gooey ground. Anna scrambled to her feet.

"Come out of there," Donavan roared. Tedith slowly climbed out of the tree and stood next to Anna. His orange fur was covered in sticky brown molasses.

The Loyal Forces of the Opposition loomed over them. Anna was now finally face to face with Donovan. She stared into his piercing red eyes. Even though he was dressed in white, there was something very dark about him and his men.

"You two have eluded me long enough. You are now mine," Donovan sneered.

"We have done nothing wrong. Why don't you want us go home?"

"Silence!" Donovan's voice boomed through the forest. Home is the last place you'll be going."

Anna knew she had to do something or they were doomed. She looked around; trying desperately to find some way for them to get away but all she could see was swamp.

"Tie their hands behind their backs," Donovan commanded, sensing Anna would try to escape if given half a chance. One of

Donovan's men held them as the other tied their hands with a thick rope.

"Ouch! Not so tight," Anna protested, refusing to be quiet. Her captors ignored her complaints and pulled the rope even tighter.

"That way." Donovan gave Anna a shove deeper into the swamp.

"Where are you taking us?" Anna demanded, surprising herself at how brave she was being. She didn't feel brave on the inside but she wasn't going to go without a fight.

"It's not *where* I am taking you that's important. It's where I am *not* taking you...I am not taking you home."

One of Donovan's men gave Anna another shove. She fell onto the oozing molasses, just missing a fuming sinkhole.

"Get up," her captor ordered. With every step they took, the swamp became thicker, darker and more threatening.

Anna's mind was racing as she tried to think of some way out. A plan slowly took shape. Donovan was in front, leading the way. Behind him was one guard, then Tedith and Anna, with the last guard behind them. They were sandwiched between the two guards. Anna started to walk slower, pretending that it was more difficult to walk than it actually was. She kept up this charade until the guard behind her had caught up with her and was almost walking beside her. Anna watched carefully; she knew she would only get one chance. When the timing was just right, Anna body-checked the guard sideways. He lost his balance and slipped into one of the boiling molasses sinkholes.

"Ahhhhhh!" the guard screamed.

"Run, Tedith. Run!" Anna called out. They turned around and ran in the direction of the path.

"Go after them!" Donovan shouted at the other guard.

Running in the thick swamp was even more difficult because their hands were tied behind their backs and it wasn't long until the guard had caught up to them. He grabbed them by the scuff of their necks.

"Ouch! Let us go," Anna yelled.

The guard dragged them back to Donovan. Anna kicked and screamed the entire way. The other guard was on the ground, rubbing his leg. He was missing one of his tall, white leather boots. It was in the molasses sinkhole, having protected him from getting burnt when he slipped.

Anna was exhausted. She couldn't fight much longer. She just wanted to go home but home seemed to be the last place she was headed.

"I wish Odin was here," Anna thought.

Almost before the thought was complete, there was a blinding flash of white light. Anna and Tedith's hands were no longer bound; they didn't have a drop of molasses on them, and best of all, *The Loyal Forces of the Opposition* had vanished.

"Odin!" Anna called out in disbelief as she flung herself at him. She hugged him with all her might. "I can't believe you're here."

"Well, you called me, didn't you?"

"What? You came because I wished you were here?" Anna said, releasing Odin from the bear hug.

"Of course. This is, after all, the realm of the imagination. Remember, whatever you imagine comes true. As soon as you imagined me, I appeared. Just like you summoned Donovan and his men."

"But, I wasn't thinking of them when they appeared and I certainly didn't wish for them."

"That's true, so why do you think Donovan and his men appeared?

Anna thought a moment. What was happening right before they appeared? She was thinking about all the terrible things that might be lurking in the swamp.

"Was it my fear?"

"Exactly. Your *fear* of what might be in the swamp drew them to you. You manifested that which you feared the most; Donovan and his men. Just like you manifested me when you thought of me. Most people don't realize what incredible creators they are. People draw to them what they believe and when it appears, they have to deal with it, good or bad. It's one of the many ways that we learn."

Anna kind of understood what Odin was saying, but her head was spinning.

"But what happened to *The Loyal Forces of the Opposition*? They vanished when you appeared."

"Ah, yes. Here you have another universal truth. Two objects cannot occupy the same space at the same time. This is especially true in your heart and your mind. If you are thinking one thing, you have to let go of that thought before you can think of something else. Darkness cannot exist where there is light. Donovan belongs to darkness. I belong to the light. When you thought of me, the darkness vanished."

Anna looked puzzled, so Odin continued.

"Have you ever walked into a dark room and turned on the light?"

Anna nodded.

"Did you ever wonder where the darkness went?" Actually, Anna had never wondered that before.

"Darkness is nothing more than the absence of light. Light consumes darkness. Remember that as you journey home."

Odin stroked Anna's cheek. "My work is done here. It's time for me to go."

"But you just got here," Anna protested. "How I don't know how to get home? I'm supposed to find a Crystal Palace, but instead I find myself in the middle of a board game. I can't do this Odin, I'm scared. I feel safe with you. Can't you please stay with us?" Anna pleaded.

Odin hugged Anna. "Being *safe* my dear, is not the same as being *saved*. Even if I could stay, I wouldn't. It would rob you of all the wonderful things you are to learn and experience."

"Easy for you to say. You're not the one going through them."

Odin threw back his head and let out a big laugh. "True enough, little one, true enough."

"Can you at least point us towards the Crystal Palace?"

"I can't tell you what direction to go. However, it is my experience that when you fall off your path, and fallen off you have and surely will again, it's prudent to get back on as quickly as you can. We all go astray, but try to spend as little time as possible off your path."

"My path?"

"Yes, the path that leads to where you want to go."

Odin patted Tedith on the head. "Take good care of each other."

Before Anna could say another word, Odin twirled around three times and disappeared into a pinpoint of light.

"Wow, did you see that?" Tedith asked.

Anna looked at where Odin had been standing just a moment ago. "I saw it, but I don't believe it. Lately I've seen many things that I find hard to believe. Come on, let's get out of here."

"What do you think Odin meant by staying on the path?" Tedith asked.

"I'm not sure, but Candy Land had a path on it, so I say we head back there."

They made their way through the swamp, careful to avoid the boiling pits of molasses. It was slow going but they eventually reached in Candy Land.

"I wonder where the gingerbread men are." Tedith said, looking up and down the game board.

"They must have completed the game without us. Let's walk to the end of the game. Maybe they are waiting for us by the Gingerbread House."

As they walked down the path, Anna kept her fear and uncertainly in check. The last thing she wanted to do was summon Donovan again. Instead she thought about her mom and her grandma. She had been gone such a long time. By now, the police would be out looking for her. Anna wondered if she would end up with her picture on a milk carton and if her friends missed her. She certainly missed them. She never thought she would admit it, but she even missed school. Even going to summer school would be better than this. Mainly, Anna wondered if she would ever get home again.

"Look Anna, there it is!" Tedith ran towards the Gingerbread House. Anna was two steps behind him.

CHAPTER EIGHT

AUNT B

Tedith reached out and gingerly stroked the wall of the Gingerbread House. "Wow, this is amazing!"

The yummy-looking house was topped with a pink frosting roof. The door had a red translucent candy window in the center and a jujube as a door handle. The fence that surrounded the house was made of tiny ice cream cones that somehow didn't melt.

Anna had once helped her grandma make a gingerbread house at Christmas. It hadn't turned out anything like this, but it sure did taste good.

They approached the front door and were about to knock when

the door flew open. A short, round, very plump woman stood before them. She had pink Texas-sized cotton-candy hair and fingers like miniature Twinkies. She wore a red and white candy-striped dress, white knee-socks and peppermint green shoes that curled up at the tip.

"Hello, hello, welcome, welcome! It's so nice to see you, so very, very nice to see you. I'm Mrs. Beasley, but everyone calls me Aunt B, Aunt B. I'm the proprietor of the Gingerbread House. Come in, come in. You must be so tired, so tired and hungry. Are you hungry? You must be so hungry." Aunt B spoke so fast, and her lips moved so quickly, that she reminded Anna of a Chatty Cathy doll.

Anna opened her mouth to introduce herself, but before she could get a word out, Aunt B's pudgy hands grabbed Tedith's paw and Anna's hand and pulled them into the Gingerbread House. Tedith wiggled back and forth, trying to get out of Aunt B's grasp. There was something about her he didn't like. But then he stopped wiggling and just gawked at the inside of the Gingerbread House. A large fountain stood in the middle of the foyer, flowing with hot chocolate. Miniature marshmallows bopped up and down in the hot liquid. Two candy bar staircases curved upward to a second floor. The walls were covered in royal frosting, studded with jawbreakers and gumballs. The floor was inlaid with Jelly Bellies, in every color and flavor you could imagine.

"Let's get you something you eat. You must be hungry. Very, very hungry. Follow me, follow me."

Anna wasn't sure they should stay, and started to protest, but Aunt B cut her off. "Dinner is waiting, dinner is waiting."

Anna looked at Tedith, who had been dying to eat something ever since they arrived in Candy Land.

Tedith shrugged and said, "I guess it wouldn't hurt to have a small bite to eat."

Aunt B led them down a long corridor, all the time talking non-stop.

"You are going to love it here, love it. You can eat whatever you want, as much as you want, whenever you want. Oh, and there are so many fun things to do. You are going to have such a good time, such a good time. Here's the dining room. Come in, come in."

"Wow!" Tedith exclaimed. The delicious aroma hit Anna first. In the center of a very large room was a massive banquet table overflowing with food. There was an enough food to feed a circus…and everyone in the audience.

On one end of the table were platters of hamburgers, hot dogs and grilled cheese sandwiches. In the center was the biggest bowl of macaroni and cheese Anna had ever seen. There were six roasted turkeys, with all the trimmings. This was just like Thanksgiving, only better. Another tray overflowed with fish and chips. Anna counted eight different kinds of pizzas. There was a stack of submarine sandwiches, piled so high they almost toppled over. The food went on and on, completely covering the enormous table.

A door swung open at the other end of the long room. In marched six identical waiters all dressed in white. They each carried a huge tray brimming with dessert. They were more like soldiers than wait staff, with Aunt B as their drill sergeant. She ordered them to place the trays of food on the table. The first tray held seven different types of pies. Another tray was covered with chocolate cakes. The third tray was filled with ice cream sundaes in every flavor imaginable. The next tray had a vast assortment of donuts and chocolate éclairs. The fifth tray held a mountain of peanut butter cookies that looked almost as good as the ones Anna baked with her grandma. But the last and final tray was the best tray…at least according to Tedith. It held the largest honey pot he had ever seen.

"Eat, eat," Aunt B commanded through a huge crooked grin.

The powdered sugar make-up on Aunt B's face was so thick Anna thought for sure her face would crack under the strain of her enormous grin, but it didn't.

"This is all for us?" Anna asked, over the grumbling of her stomach.

"Oh yes, especially for you, all for you. Eat, eat. I'll be back, I'll be back," Aunt B said as she left the room with the waiters in tow.

"Come on, I'm starving," said Tedith, reaching for the honey pot. He ladled the sweet, golden liquid into a big bowl and dug in. Anna grabbed a plate and piled it high with fried chicken, tacos and lasagna.

She bit into a piece of chicken. "Yum, this is the best chicken I have ever tasted."

"I know," said Tedith through a mouthful of honey. "I've never tasted anything like this."

The two of them ate and ate and ate. Once they had polished off the main course, they turned their attention to dessert. Anna ate a chocolate sundae and two peanut butter cookies, which were second in taste only to her grandma's. Tedith had the same thing he had for dessert that he had for dinner...honey.

Anna sat back after her last bite and groaned, "Ahhh, I'm so full. I couldn't eat another thing if my life depended upon it."

Tedith licked the last of the honey from his paws. "I think I'm going to burst."

As if on cue, Aunt B walked through the swinging door.

"Can't be full already, can't be," she said as she looked at them then at the table still overflowing with food. "You barely touched the food, barely touched it."

"Really Aunt B, thank you, it was all so delicious, but we couldn't eat another bite. What are you going to do with all this left-over food?" Anna asked, looking out at the sea of food still on the banquet table.

"Not to worry, not to worry. More where that came from,

much more. Time to show you your bedroom. Follow me, follow-me."

"Our bedroom?"

"Sure, this way, this way."

They were too full to protest and followed Aunt B's watermelon-shaped behind up the candy bar staircase and down a long lemon drop studded hallway. They passed several gingerbread doors. Anna wondered what was behind them. The house looked like little more than a cottage on the outside, but on the inside it went on forever. Aunt B finally stopped in front of the last door and unlocked it with a key that hung around her neck on a licorice string.

"This is your room, your room. Make yourself at home."

Anna and Tedith walked into a room the size of gymnasium. Along one wall was shelf upon shelf of every board game imaginable. Monopoly and Clue and Battleship. Trivia Pursuit and Mousetrap and Operation. There was even Candy Land!

Along another wall were hula-hoops and yoyos, skipping ropes and pogo sticks. A badminton court and trampoline were in the center of the room. There was even a basketball hoop mounted on the wall. Anna loved playing basketball and last year had even made her school team.

Anna picked up the new basketball lying on the floor and threw it at the hoop. The ball bounced off the rim and, much to her delight, went in. Anna scanned the room. There was so much to see, it was overwhelming.

"Look at this!" Anna gasped as she ran over to a brand new, fire-engine red, 22-speed mountain bike. It was exactly like the one she was hoping to get for Christmas last year, but didn't. "Is this for me?"

"Yes, yes...everything is yours. It's all yours. Stay up as long as you like, have fun, have fun. It's all about having fun!" With that, Aunt B turned and left the room.

Anna hopped on the bike and rode around the massive room.

Tedith climbed a fake tree that had a tree house in it.

The room was a combination of toy store and playland. It was the most amazing place Anna had ever been. Then, Anna saw it. At the far end of the room was a large canopy bed draped in pale blue fabric. She dropped the bike and ran towards it. Anna had always wanted a canopy bed. She lived with her mom in a small inner-city apartment on the sixth floor. They shared the only bedroom. It was so tiny that the two single beds left no room for even a dresser. Anna once told her mom about her dream of having a canopy bed. Her mom just shook her head and told her how sorry she was that she couldn't buy her one. It wasn't only that there wasn't enough room in their tiny bedroom, there also wasn't enough money. Anna's mom did the best she could, but after the essentials were paid for, there was little left over each month. There were many things Anna wanted that she couldn't have.

Anna flung herself onto the oversized bed and gazed up into the blue satin canopy. It reminded Anna of the sky. Tedith joined her. Together they jumped up and down on the soft bed.

"Can you believe all of this? I never imagined there could be a place like this," Anna said as she collapsed on the bed.

"Yeah, this place is the best. Did you see the tree? I've always wanted my own tree house."

"Come on, let's go play."

First they played with the pogo stick and hula-hoop then they played catch with the baseball gloves. Anna loved the smell of the new leather gloves.

"Let's play a board game." Anna ran towards the shelves stocked with games.

"What do you want to play? How about Checkers? No, no. Let's play Snakes and Ladders or maybe we should play Kerplunk. There are so many, I can't decide. You pick."

"I don't care what we play as long as it's not Candy Land. I've had enough of that game for one day," Tedith said. Anna giggled.

They settled on Life, one of Anna's favorites, and set the board up on the nearby game table. They were only a few rounds into the game when Anna started to nod off.

"What time do you think it is?" Anna yawned.

"I don't know but it must be late. It was starting to get dark when we arrived here."

Anna was having a hard time keeping her eyes open. "I'm beat. How about we call it a night?"

"Good idea." They walked towards the bed, stepping over all of the toys strewn on the floor. They climbed into the canopy bed, and almost before their heads hit the pillows they were sound asleep.

Their bedroom door slowly opened. Aunt B tiptoed in. She walked over to the canopy bed, careful to avoid the mind-field of toys. She stared down at Anna and Tedith as they slept peacefully. She had the most peculiar grin on her face. One end of her mouth curled up as the other end curled down. If Anna had been awake to see it, it would have given her the creeps.

Anna rolled over and rubbed her eyes. She yawned and stretched, then suddenly sat up. "Where am I?" Then she settled back down, remembering she was in the Gingerbread House in Candy Land. Anna recalled what a good time she had last night. She couldn't believe their good fortune. Aunt B was so nice and this room with all its toys was amazing. And the food, oh, the food. Tedith was still fast asleep beside her. She tickled him a little. He squirmed. She tickled him again. This time he woke up giggling.

"Good morning, sleepy head," Anna said, smiling at him.

Tedith yawned, "What time is it?

"Hmmm, I don't know. I just woke up. The sun is out," Anna said, noticing the bright yellow light streaming through the bedroom curtains.

Again as if on cue, the door swung open and Aunt B waddled into the room.

"Good morning, good morning. Rise and shine, rise and shine."

Anna and Tedith hopped off the bed.

"Good morning, Aunt B. Do you know what time it is?

"It's 10:45, 10:45."

"10:45?" Anna gulped. At home, Anna's mom wouldn't let Anna sleep past nine, even on weekends. She could hear her mom now, "Wake up Anna. The day's a wasting." Anna wished she were with her mom now. She would even be happy to get up at nine o'clock instead of giving her mom a hard time, which is what she usually did.

"I'm sorry, we really overslept," Anna said, half expecting to get scolded by Aunt B.

"Oh no, you can sleep as long as you want, sleep as long as you want. Who wants breakfast, who wants breakfast?" Aunt B asked, beaming.

Anna couldn't believe how hungry she was after all she had eaten last night.

"Should we wash up before breakfast?" Anna asked.

"No need, no need," Aunt B said, heading out of the bedroom towards the dining hall.

Well that was a first. Anna always had to wash before breakfast at home.

They followed Aunt B into the dining hall. Once again it was overflowing with scrumptious food. There were pancakes and French toast with real maple syrup. Poached eggs, fried eggs, scrambled eggs and boiled eggs. There were pitchers of orange juice, apple juice and even Anna's all time favorite, pineapple juice. There were platters of bacon, sausage and a huge plate of hash browns. There was also a sky-high stack of toast, dripping with melted butter and accompanied by every conceivable jam, jelly and marmalade you could think of. Finally, there was a big pot of honey.

"All this is for us?"

"All for you, all for you. Eat up, eat up." Aunt B left them to enjoy their breakfast.

Anna piled her plate high with all her favorite breakfast foods. Tedith went directly for the honey pot, smearing huge amounts of the wonderful honey onto slices of warm, buttery toast.

"Ummmm, this is so good," Anna said, biting into a fork full of French toast dripping with maple syrup.

When she couldn't eat another bite, Anna pushed herself away from the table. "Ugh, I'm stuffed. I ate too much...again."

The door swung open and Aunt B trotted in. Anna was amazed at Aunt B's uncanny ability to time her entrances so perfectly. She always appeared just when they were finished. It was as if she was an actress in a Broadway play and was following a script.

"Was it good, was it good?" Aunt B asked, grinning at the two of them.

"Oh yes, thank you so much. You have been so kind. We really do appreciate all that you have done for us but we really must be going."

"What's your rush, what's your rush? There is so much to see, so much to do, so very, very much. Come with me, come with me."

Tedith wanted to leave. There was something about this funny little woman that made him uneasy. He couldn't put his paw on it;

maybe it was just that she looked strange. Aunt B was certainly kind enough and had done nothing to raise Tedith's suspicions, but there was still something about her that made him uneasy.

Anna was conflicted. On one hand she wanted to leave so they could continue to look for the Crystal Palace; on the other, she didn't want to be rude or hurt Aunt B's feelings—she had done so much for them already. And besides, Anna was having a great time.

"You'll love it. Promise, promise," Aunt B recited, as if picking up on Anna's uncertainty.

"Well, I guess we can stay, but only for a little bit longer."

Tedith frowned, he wasn't at all sure they should stay.

"Lovely, lovely," Aunt B exclaimed, rubbing her Twinkie fingers together.

Aunt B led them back to the main foyer. As she passed the hot chocolate fountain she reached in, carefully picked up one of the miniature marshmallows and popped it in her mouth. They turned down a long sugar-coated corridor into another wing of the rambling house.

"Come see the fun. Let me show you the fun."

Aunt B stopped in front of the first door they came to and pushed it open. Anna gasped. Behind the door was a huge water park. Several different water slides towered above them, twisting and turning as they snaked their way into a large body of pink water."

"WOW, this is so great," Anna exclaimed. "But why is the water pink?"

"It's not water, not water," Aunt B giggled. "It's cream soda."

"Come with me, come with me."

"Cream soda!" Anna thought, "I wonder if it tickles your nose?"

Aunt B waddled down the hall and held open the next door. Anna and Tedith stared. In front of them was a zoo. Complete with giraffes, lions, elephants, and bears. There was even a hippo. The animals looked real but there was something odd about them.

Anna walked over to the lion's cage to have a closer look. The lion let out a huge roar. Anna jumped back and chuckled. The lion was an animal cracker. They were in the middle of an animal cracker zoo. This place was getting stranger and stranger.

"They are very friendly. You can even ride them it you like, if you like. But please don't eat them." Tedith giggled at the thought of biting into the neck of the cookie giraffe and wondered if they would taste like a cookie or an animal.

"Lots more to see, so much more to see," Aunt B said, as she led them down the hall.

Behind the next door was a full scale amusement park. A wild roller coaster stood in the middle. It was surrounded by a dozen or more attractions, including a Ferris wheel, carousel and bumper cars. They continued to make their way down the hall. Behind each door was something new and amazing. A gigantic snow-covered hill was behind one door. It even had a chair lift to take you to the top so you could toboggan, snowboard or ski. A quick look behind another door revealed a roller skating rink. Behind yet another door was a puppet theatre.

Anna's mouth stayed open down the entire corridor. She could barely believe her eyes. It was all so overwhelming. Finally, Aunt B opened the last door, and the three of them stepped into a bowling alley, with electronic scoring. The only difference from a regular bowling alley was that the bowling balls were brightly colored gumballs and the pins were gummy bears.

"Hey! There you are," someone called out. "We wondered what happened to you." Anna was so bewildered by everything she hadn't even noticed there were others in the room.

"Blue, is that you?" Anna asked.

"Sure, it's me. We are all here."

There, bowling on one of the lanes, were Blue, Yellow and Red, the plastic gingerbread men they had played Candy Land with.

"Glad you are here. Come on, let's play," Blue said, waving them over.

Anna wasn't sure what to do; she knew she should be continuing her journey but she loved bowling. What harm could there be in a game or two? They could always leave as soon as they were finished.

"Go play, go play, it'll be fun, so much fun," Aunt B encouraged.

"Okay but just for a little while," Anna said as she and Tedith joined the gingerbread men. They played several games of gumball bowling. Anna shot her best game ever, 173 points, beating her previous high score by almost 25 points!

The morning flew by. Anna knew they had been there long enough and it was time to leave. She was about to say goodbye to the gingerbread men, when Aunt B came trotting through the door pushing a hot dog cart.

The gingerbread men all ran to greet her.

"Lunch time, it's lunch time" Aunt B announced.

Anna reasoned that they could always leave right after lunch. After all, they did need to eat, didn't they?

Aunt B gave them as many hog dogs as they could eat. Anna liked her dogs with relish and mustard. Tedith was somewhat disappointed that there wasn't any honey and ate his dog plain.

They washed the dogs down with root beer and homemade lemonade. They capped the meal off with ice cream sandwiches.

"So, do you guys live here?" Anna asked, licking the dripping ice cream.

"No, we come and go as we please," said Red, sipping on his

lemonade. "Have you guys tried out the video arcade yet?"

"Uh, no, I don't even remember seeing it."

"It's in the east wing, by the kitchen," Red explained. "It's got all the latest games as well as the oldies but goodies, like Ms. Pac Man.

"Really, Ms. Pac Man?"

Anna loved to play Ms. Pac Man at the rundown arcade by her house. Anna's mom didn't like her going in there, but Anna would save up her loose change and sneak in every now and again.

"Come on, let's go," Blue said as he headed towards the door.

The other gingerbread men ran after him. Without another thought about leaving, Anna and Tedith also ran after them.

The video arcade had every pinball and video game you could think of. There were dozens of them and the best part was you didn't need any money to play. They were all free. The clanking, dinging, beeping and buzzing of the arcades filled the room as they ran from machine to machine playing one or two games on each before moving on to the next. Anna was having so much fun she didn't notice the passing time, and was surprised when Aunt B entered the arcade, announcing it was time for dinner.

Once again, the dining hall held a banquet, with enough food to feed an army. This time the gingerbread men joined them in the feast.

Everyone piled their plates high with their favorite foods from the steaming platters, plates and bowls. Anna dove into a chicken pot pie, followed by a juicy hamburger and French fries. Tedith once again helped himself to the honey. They ate and ate and ate.

Finally Anna pushed her way from the table. "I can't eat another bite," she declared, after her last bite of coconut cake.

"But there are so many dishes you haven't even tried," said Yellow.

"I know, but I'm so full."

"I see you like cake. How about a little chocolate cake?" Yellow said, picking up a big piece with a mischievous smile on his face.

"No, really I can't," Anna said, patting her extended stomach.

"Sure you can," squealed Yellow, as he flung the chocolate cake across the table, hitting Anna on the side of her face.

Anna was shocked. She scraped the chocolate cake from her face.

"Yeah, and you haven't tried the Jell-O," giggled Blue, as a big wad of orange Jell-O hit Anna's arm.

Not to be out done, Anna scooped up a handful of cherry cobbler and squealed as she threw it at Blue.

It wasn't long until the room exploded into a full-blown food fight. A whole lemon meringue pie hit Tedith in the side of his head. He wiped the pie from his eyes, then jumped on the table, picked up a bowl of potato salad and dumped it on Yellow's head. Red was covered in vanilla pudding dotted with green peas.

Blue laughed as he chased Anna around the room pinging her with olives. Everyone was yelling and laughing as they grabbed the nearest food and threw it at each other. Suddenly, the door swung open and in walked Aunt B.

"What do we have here? What do we have here?"

Everyone froze. The room became silent. Anna looked around at the mess and knew she was in deep trouble. Before anyone could say anything, Yellow picked up a handful of spaghetti and threw it at Aunt B. It landed in her pink cotton-candy hair. The tomato sauce dripped down the side of her face. Anna gasped.

Aunt B calmly walked over to the table, picked up a handful of coleslaw, and threw it at Yellow. The room erupted again. The gingerbread men squealed in delight as they flung food, making Aunt B their new target.

It wasn't long until she was covered with food from her head to her peppermint shoes. Anna was amazed that Aunt B seemed to be having as much fun as they all were. She had never been around an adult who would behave in such a manner. The mayhem continued until Anna finally collapsed on the floor, exhausted and happy. Tedith fell on top of her, giving her a sticky hug. Anna couldn't remember when she had had so much fun. The Gingerbread House was the best place she had ever been.

"Bath time, it's bath time," declared Aunt B.

Anna and Tedith were only too happy to make their way back to their huge room, leaving a trail of food behind them.

A huge bubble bath waited for them in their massive private bathroom. They happily soaked in the tub until they were squeaky clean and sweet smelling. Anna slipped into a new pair of flannel pajamas that were laid out waiting for her, while Tedith dried himself with a white fluffy towel. Dead tired, they crawled into the crisp, clean sheets of the big canopy bed. Not even the lure of all the new toys could keep them awake tonight.

"This was the best day of my life," Anna yawned.

"Can you believe this place? I almost split my seams when Aunt B jumped into the food fight. I never knew grownups could play like that," Tedith said, snuggling next to Anna. "Let's visit the Water Park tomorrow."

"Okay, but only one more day. We really do need to keep looking for the Crystal Palace," Anna yawned, then reached over and turned off the light. "Good night, Tedith."

"Good night, Anna. Sweet dreams."

Anna and Tedith awoke well after the sun was up. After another amazing breakfast feast, they spent the morning in the cream soda Water Park with the gingerbread men. Up and down the slides they went, landing in the fizzy cream soda, which did tickle Anna's nose.

Anna's fingers and toes had already turned into pink-colored prunes when Aunt B announced it was time for lunch. After showering, Anna used a hairdryer on Tedith's wet fur; in spite of his protests. When she was finished she couldn't help but giggle at the orange fluff ball that stood before her

Instead of going to the dining hall for lunch, everyone followed Aunt B into the kitchen. The industrial-sized kitchen was a beehive of activity. There were over a dozen white-clad chefs preparing massive quantities of food. Some chefs were baking cakes, pies, cookies, tarts and sticky buns. Another chef was roasting whole chickens on a large spit. Still others chefs stirred large pots of simmering soups, stews and sauces.

"Is all this for us?" Anna asked, bewildered by the magnitude.

"All for you, all for you. Anytime you are hungry, you can come here, come here. Eat all you can, all you can," Aunt B exclaimed. "What do you want, do you want?"

"Gee, I don't know. Hmmm, how about pizza? Do you have any pepperoni—" Before Anna could get another word out of her mouth, a chef in a tall white hat was walking towards her carrying a large bubbling pepperoni pizza. He set it down on a table that had been prepared for lunch.

Blue wanted a t-bone steak. Yellow ate only ice cream for lunch. Red helped Anna with the pizza. Tedith, of course, wanted honey. Aunt B brought them chocolate shakes to wash down their lunch. Even with everyone eating, they barely made a dent in the massive quantities of food. When there wasn't room for one more bite they pushed themselves away from the table.

"Let's go play volleyball," declared Red as they ran to the volleyball court.

Anna happily followed. She reasoned that she deserved a little fun in her life, especially after everything she had been through. Besides what was the rush? The Crystal Palace might be just around the corner. She might as well enjoy the Gingerbread House as long as she could.

One afternoon they played tennis with gumballs and lollipop rackets. They spent another day at the circus; complete with clowns, tight rope walker, and elephants. On another occasion, they spent the morning painting a mural in the art room with fruit-flavored paints. Anna was having the time of her life, and barely noticed how one day effortlessly slipped into the next. There was an endless array of things to see and do.

It was an idyllic life. They woke up when they wanted, played all day long, stuffed themselves on the most scrumptious food and went to bed whenever they felt like it.

Their new friends, Red, Blue, and Yellow were the perfect playmates; always ready for the next adventure. They had discovered a go-cart racetrack behind one of the numerous doors and spent hours racing each other around the track.

Regular mealtimes had become a thing of the past. Any time of day or night, they could go to the kitchen and eat from the huge array of food that had been prepared expressly for them. And if it hadn't already been prepared, one of the chefs was only too pleased to make it for them.

Any thought Anna had of continuing her journey had vanished.

CHAPTER NINE

THE SURPRISE

One morning as they were getting ready for another day of play, Anna noticed that Tedith was unusually quiet. "Come on Tedith, let's get some breakfast. Blue said he would teach us archery today."

"Anna, I know we are having a great time, but don't you think it's time to continue our journey?"

Anna stopped tying her shoelaces and looked at Tedith. "Our journey?" Anna asked, almost more for her sake than Tedith's, as if it would help her come out of a daze.

"Yeah, our journey, you know, going home."

Anna sat down on the edge of the bed. "Wow, I have been

having such a great time that I'd almost forgotten about home."

"I've been reluctant to mention it because we have been having so much fun, but I think we have been here long enough, don't you?"

"I guess so, but it's so wonderful here. I never knew life could be like this, all fun and games. Maybe we could stay just a couple more days," Anna said, reluctant to let go of their comfortable life and venture back out into the unknown where *The Loyal Forces of the Opposition* would surely be waiting for them.

"We still have so much more to do. We barely spent any time at the animal cracker zoo or the amusement park. I told Red I would play jelly-bean bingo with him."

Tedith frowned at her.

"I know, I know. There will always be more for us to do here, won't there?"

Tedith nodded. "Yes, there will always be more to do Anna. At some point we have to leave."

Anna sighed. "Okay, I'll tell Aunt B at breakfast that this will be our last day and we will be leaving first thing tomorrow."

"I know it's hard to leave this place but we can't stay here forever," Tedith said, trying to reassure Anna.

After they had finished getting ready, they joined the gingerbread men in the kitchen, who were already enjoying a breakfast of chocolate chip pancakes. Anna was very quiet during breakfast as she thought about leaving. She didn't know how she was going to tell Aunt B. She had been so good to them; Anna didn't want to hurt her feelings. But Tedith was right; it was time to leave.

"Eat up everyone, eat up. Lots of food, lots of food," Aunt B said as she entered the kitchen.

Anna stared at her half-eaten plate of pancakes. Tedith, noticing her hesitation said, "Anna, isn't there something you want to tell Aunt B?"

All eyes turned towards Anna.

"Ah, yes. Yes there is," she said, trying to muster up enough courage. "Aunt B, you have been really wonderful to us...we are having the time of our lives...we really can't thank you enough, but Tedith and I will be...."

Before Anna could say another word, Aunt B interrupted as if sensing what Anna was about to say, "I have a surprise. A big surprise."

"A surprise! What kind of surprise?" Yellow asked.

"It's for Anna...it's for Anna. Come with me...come with me."

"I love surprises," said Blue as he jumped down from his chair and followed Aunt B out of the kitchen. Yellow and Red were right behind, leaving only Anna and Tedith in the kitchen.

"Anna, you have to tell her," Tedith insisted.

"You saw, I tried to tell her but she wouldn't let me finish. I'll tell her. Really I will, but can't we first see what the surprise is?

Tedith signed. "Alright, but you have to promise you will tell her today that we are leaving tomorrow."

"Ok, ok. I promise. Let's go." Anna rushed to catch up with Aunt B. Tedith lingered several steps behind.

Aunt B lead them to yet another wing of the house, one they had never been in before. The Gingerbread House seemed to go on forever. Anna could only imagine what lay behind the numerous doors they passed. Aunt B finally stopped in front of one of the doors and unlocked it with the key hanging from the licorice string around her neck.

"Go in, go in," she urged.

The ground was covered in sawdust. Thousands of seats looked down on an arena. In the center was some type of obstacle course.

"What is this?" asked Red.

"You'll see, you'll see," Aunt B promised.

A gate opened at the far end of the arena. A majestic horse came prancing towards them. It was pure white with a long flowing mane. Its tail flew proudly in the air as it trotted towards them. Anna stared at the stunning animal. It was magnificent, but there was something different about it. As it got closer Anna gasped. It wasn't a horse, it was a unicorn!

In a flurry, the majestic unicorn came to a stop directly in front of them. It snorted, while tapping its front hoof on the ground. It was the finest animal Anna had ever seen.

"Wow, look at that!" exclaimed Red, as they stared at the grand creature before them.

Anna loved horses. She used to ride Old Ben on her grandparents' farm. He was a chestnut brown horse that Grandpa had 'put out to pasture' a long time ago. Ben spent his days resting and grazing. He was a gentle old soul and was very patient as Grandpa showed Anna how to saddle, mount and ride him. Ben seemed to enjoy the attention. In the beginning, Anna rode Ben just in the corral. Later, when Anna gained more confidence, she and Old Ben would wander through the rolling hills. Occasionally she could even get him to trot. After her grandpa had died, one of the neighbors offered to take Ben, assuring Anna's grandmother that they would give the old horse a good home.

One of Anna's favorite summer rituals while on the farm was going to the Country Fair with her grandparents. One of the things Anna liked best was watching the young girls in the horse show prance around the ring in their smart-looking riding outfits.

Anna dreamed of one day having a horse of her very own that she could ride in the Country Fair. Having her own horse was her most secret desire. She kept it locked deep within her heart. Anna knew if she told her mom, it would make her feel sad that, yet again, there was something Anna wanted that she couldn't provide for her.

"All yours...all yours," Aunt B said, beaming at Anna.

"Really? The unicorn is mine?" Anna asked in disbelief.

"Yes…yes, she is yours. You should name her, name her."

Anna looked deeply into the luminous blue eyes of the regal animal. They seemed to shine and twinkle.

"I think I'll call you Star," Anna said, holding out her hand. The unicorn stepped closer and allowed Anna to rub her nose. Anna was overflowing with joy.

"Take her for a ride, a ride," Aunt B encouraged.

Star was fitted with a fine-looking white leather saddle studded with blue gemstones that matched the color of her eyes. Anna hesitated, but only for a moment, then took hold of the reins, and in one graceful movement mounted Star.

"Me too," called Tedith, who, at least for the time being, was as taken with Star as Anna.

"Well then, come on," Anna said, extending a hand.

Aunt B lifted Tedith up. Off the three of them went around the ring. First walking, then trotting and finally galloping. After circling the ring several times, they stopped next to Aunt B.

"I really don't know what to say. This is the most wonderful gift I've ever been given. Thank you so much…so very, very much," Anna said, almost sounding like Aunt B.

"Star is yours. You must look after her, look after her. Her stable is over there, over there." Aunt B pointed to the opening where Star had entered the arena.

"Oh, I will. I promise," Anna assured Aunt B.

Tedith wanted to say something to Anna about her promise to him that she would tell Aunt B that they were leaving tomorrow, but he knew this wasn't the time. He would have to wait until he was alone with her again.

Anna, Tedith and the gingerbread men spent the rest of day

riding and playing with Star. She jumped so effortlessly over the many hurdles laid out in the arena that she almost seemed to fly.

At the end of the day, Anna led Star to her stable and removed her bridle and saddle as her grandpa taught her. She brushed Star down and fed her. Then Anna kissed her on her nose and told Star she would see her in the morning.

At dinner, the only thing Anna could talk about was Star.

"Did you see how she made those corners and how gracefully she jumped over even the highest hurdle?"

They all agreed Star was the most magnificent animal they had ever seen.

That night in their room Tedith tried convincing Anna it was time to leave, but it fell onto deaf ears. Every time he mentioned it Anna quickly changed the subject. He finally gave up in frustration and went to sleep.

Over the next few weeks, Anna spent every waking hour with Star. She was becoming a proficient horse woman and being with Star was all she wanted to do. Even the lure of what might lay behind the other doors in the Gingerbread House couldn't keep Anna from Star.

On several occasions Tedith tried to talk to Anna about leaving but she would hear nothing of it. Anna was beginning to wonder if Tedith was jealous of all the attention she was giving to Star. Maybe the *real* reason Tedith wanted to leave was so he could have Anna all to himself again.

One evening, after supper, as Anna and Tedith played Snake and Ladders in their room, Tedith decided to really push the point of going home.

"Anna, I know you want to be with Star but don't you think it's time to leave?"

Anna looked up from the game. She was getting tired of Tedith's constant nagging. "We can't leave. You heard Aunt B. Star is my responsibility," Anna said coldly.

"I know Anna but don't you want to go home? Don't you want to see your mom?"

This made Anna cringe. Anna didn't want to think about her mom and she didn't like Tedith using her mom against her. "I don't want to talk about it. This is the happiest I have been in my life and I am not going to ruin it. How do we even know that we can get home? We don't even know if the Crystal Palace is real. And besides, *The Loyal Forces of the Opposition* are out there waiting for us."

"I know Anna, but don't you want to try? Odin said 'if you follow your heart'..."

"Tedith, I don't want to talk about it! I won't leave Star. I'm tired. I'm going to bed." Anna abruptly ended their conversion. She climbed into her canopy bed and turned off the light.

Tedith crawled in next to her. "Goodnight, Anna."

"Goodnight," Anna said with an edge in her voice. She was upset. Why did he have to keep pushing her? Anna lay awake listening to the stillness of the house. She missed her mom terribly but how could she leave Star? She decided not to think about it anymore and fell into a restless sleep.

Anna woke suddenly. She had been dreaming she was back at Imes. Sidea was there and so was Odin. He was drawing something in the air with his walking stick, just like Sidea had done. In the dream, Anna strained to make sense of the drawing, but its meaning was outside her grasp. It was as if it was some secret code. The last thing Anna remembered before she woke up was Odin saying, "Things aren't always what they appear, Anna."

Anna rubbed her eyes and looked out the window. The sky was the color of pencil lead. She looked at the clock by her bedside it was only 3:48 a.m.. Anna tossed and turned trying to go back to sleep. But it was no use, she was wide-awake. She decided to go down to the kitchen to get another piece of the yummy strawberry shortcake she had eaten earlier for dessert.

Anna put on her slippers and tiptoed out of the room and down the candy bar staircase. The house was very quiet. As Anna approached the kitchen, she noticed a light coming from the bottom of the door. It looked like she wasn't the only one who couldn't sleep. Anna was about to push open the kitchen door when she heard a gruff male voice coming from the kitchen. "That's odd," she thought. The only men in the house are the chefs and they don't arrive for work until 6:00 a.m.. Then she heard Aunt B's unmistakable voice. Only there was something different about the way she was speaking. She wasn't repeating her words like she usually did. This sent a shiver down Anna's spine.

"It's working really well. I don't think Anna will ever leave. She loves it here," Aunt B said in a clear, normal sounding manner.

"Good," replied the male voice, "we don't want her to leave…ever."

Anna gasped at hearing this. Where had she heard that voice before?

"She won't," Aunt B said. "One thing is for sure, she will *never* leave Star."

"I must say, that was a stroke of genius. Just when she was about to tell you that she was leaving, you surprised her with Star. Anna has such a sense of responsibility and loyalty that she readily abandoned her heart's longing to go home, to care for a white horse with a horn."

Anna shuddered. There was no mistaking it; Aunt B was talking to Donovan.

"I'll be back in a few days to check-up on things. Keep up the good work."

Donovan opened the back door to the kitchen and disappeared

into the night.

Anna heard Aunt B's footsteps coming towards the door she was standing behind. She quickly darted behind a large rock-candy column. Aunt B swung the door open and walked right past Anna.

Anna huddled on the floor, too shocked to move. Warm, salty tears streamed down her cheeks as reality started to sink in.

"What a fool I have been," she thought. "This whole experience in the Gingerbread House has been the work of *The Loyal Forces of the Opposition*. Everything was designed for the sole purpose of keeping me from going home."

Anna had no idea that *The Loyal Forces of the Opposition* could be so diabolical, using her own wants and desires against her. Anna felt so stupid for allowing herself to be tricked by Aunt B, whom she thought to be one of the nicest people she had ever met. Sure, she was a little strange, but Anna never thought she was wicked. It was still hard to imagine that that funny little lady was working for *The Loyal Forces of the Opposition*. And what about the gingerbread men? Were they also in on this devilish plot?

As Anna sat there, her disbelief and sadness turned to determination. She knew what she needed to do.

CHAPTER TEN

THE ESCAPE

Anna climbed the candy bar staircase two stairs at a time and ran down the sugar-coated hall, that didn't seem nearly as sweet as before. Tedith was snoring loudly as she tiptoed into the room.

"Tedith, Tedith," she whispered as she gently shook him. "Wake, up."

"Anna?" Tedith said, rubbing his eyes with his paw.

"Shhhh, we're leaving."

"What? Now?" He looked over at the window. "It's not even light out."

"Yes, now. Right now," Anna said, changing into the clothes

she had arrived in. "I'll tell you all about it once we are out of here."

Tedith hopped out of bed and followed her out of their gigantic room. Before Anna closed the door, she looked back at the toy-filled room. It was overflowing with all the things she had thought were important.

They quickly made their way down the staircase and past the chocolate fountain. Anna quietly opened the candy-studded door. Even though she now knew they were leaving behind a make-believe world, a world created for the sole purpose of seducing Anna away from her *true* heart's desire, there was a part of her that was sad to leave behind her fun-filled life. But it was only a small part of her. The biggest part of her, the truest part, couldn't wait to get away.

They quickly made their way down the Candy Land path. Although it was still dark, Anna felt lighter with every step she took away from the Gingerbread House.

When they were finally a safe distance away, Tedith asked, "Okay, Anna, tell me. What in the world is going on?"

"You're not going to believe it. I can barely believe it." Anna started, "Aunt B works for Donovan."

"What?" Tedith gasped. Anna was right; Tedith could barely believe his furry orange ears. "That's incredible, but how did you find out?"

"I overheard Aunt B talking to Donovan in the kitchen. I had gone down to get something to eat because I couldn't sleep." Anna then told Tedith everything she had learned.

Tedith shook his head, still in disbelief. "So, it was all a hoax. Aunt B's assignment was to keep us entertained so that we would never continue our journey?"

"Yep. It was nothing but a big charade. It's really strange. Right before I woke up, I was dreaming about Odin. In my dream, he told me that things were not always what they appeared. Boy was he right. I feel like such a fool. If I hadn't woken up and gone down to the kitchen, I might have stayed in the Gingerbread House forever."

Anna looked tenderly at Tedith. "I'm so sorry, Tedith. You tried to make me leave and I wouldn't listen. I was so wrapped up it all the fun, I couldn't see straight. The Gingerbread House contained everything I thought would make me happy. Toys, games, food, and of course, Star."

Tears welled up in Anna's eyes at the thought that she would never see Star again. "I am really going to miss her... I hate how they used her to trick me," Anna said, wiping her eyes.

"It's okay, Anna; you are doing the right thing and that is what is important. You are very brave to leave behind a life of pleasure and fun to venture into the unknown"

Tedith looked up into the pale gray sky. "Now that we are out of the house, what are we going to do? We don't have much time before they discover we are gone."

"I'm not sure. I hadn't thought that far ahead. I only knew we had to get out of there. Let's go back to the start of the Candy Land game, the place where we landed. Maybe we will find something there that will help us get out of here," Anna said.

As they headed down the path towards the start of the game, the first hint of dawn turned everything in Candy Land a light pink hue. Even with the fresh morning light, all the candy they passed had lost its appeal. As they entered the Molasses Swamp, Anna kept her fear in check. The last thing she needed was to draw Donovan to her. They walked through Lollipop Woods and took the pass through the Gumdrop Mountains. When they reached the Peppermint Stick Forest, they could see the start of the game board.

"Come on, let's go," Anna said.

They ran until they reached the first square on the game board. It looked pretty much like it had when they arrived.

"Now what?"

"I'm not sure, Tedith."

Anna walked to the edge of the game board. She hesitated for a moment then knelt down and bent over the edge. Beneath the game board was a vast emptiness. She hadn't realized until now that the game board was floating in space and was actually a planet. A flat planet, but a planet nonetheless; a self-contained world, just like all the other planets in the universe.

Tedith also carefully peeked over the edge. "Whoa! Boy, one step in the wrong direction and…well, I don't know what would happen, but it wouldn't be good."

Anna looked up. The pale pink sky had given way to a light yellow. "Everyone in the Gingerbread House will be awake soon. I'm sure Aunt B will tell Donovan as soon as she discovers we are gone. There has to be some way off Candy Land. If only we could get back to the Amrak Station."

In the distant sky was a bright blue flash.

"What in the honey jar was that?" Tedith asked, covering his eyes.

"I don't know, but it looks like something is headed directly at us."

Anna and Tedith watched in horror as the object in the sky sped towards them.

"Run, Tedith, run. It's going to crash."

They ran towards a huge piece of rock candy, dove behind it and braced themselves for the inevitable crash.

But instead of a crash, they heard what sounded like squealing brakes. They waited a moment then cautiously peeked over the rock candy. In front of them, hovering about five feet off the ground was a flying saucer.

It looked just like the flying saucers in the old black and white science fiction movies Anna watched when her mom let her stay up late on weekends. The ones in the movies had wires holding them up, but there were no wires holding this one up. This saucer was shiny and silver. Blue flashing lights surrounded a large glass dome in the middle.

They watched as a ladder extended from the edge of the saucer to the ground. The glass dome slid open and out popped an orange porcupine-like being. It stood about four feet high and had on a little blue uniform. Its quills were poking out the back of its uniform. It climbed down the ladder and looked around.

"All aboard!" the being called out. Anna and Tedith froze.

A few moments passed and he called out again, "All aboard!"

Visibly annoyed, the porcupine took two tickets from its pocket and looked at them. "Last call for Anna and Tedith."

Anna was shocked to hear their names and whispered to Tedith, "What should we do?"

The orange porcupine shrugged and waddled back towards the flying saucer. As he began to climb the ladder, a faint but unmistakable shrill pierced the silence of Candy Land. The porcupine shuddered and climbed the ladder at a speed that was quite surprising.

Anna knew that if she was going to act, she had to act now. She jumped out from behind the rock candy and ran towards the flying saucer.

"Wait, wait. I'm Anna." Tedith was on her heels.

The being looked down at them.

"Huh! Well, come on if you're coming. We have a schedule to keep and I certainly don't want to hang around here, if you know what I mean."

Anna knew exactly what he meant. They quickly scurried up the ladder and climbed into the flying saucer. Several passengers were already on board. None of them were human, but then Anna and Tedith were getting used to that. The porcupine showed them to two empty seats next to an elf.

"Buckle up. Departure is in five seconds," the porcupine said as he took his seat.

Anna wanted to ask where they were going, but thought better of it. She was so relieved to be leaving Candy Land and *The Loyal Forces of the Opposition* behind she didn't really care where they were going, as long as it was away from here.

There was a pilot and co-pilot in the middle of saucer under the dome. The co-pilot was an interesting mixture of orangutan and zebra.

The engines started to rev up, then the space ship headed straight up like a helicopter. Anna looked out the window. She took a deep breath. It wasn't long before Candy Land was a small square speck far below them.

After several moments, the flying saucer leveled off and the porcupine spoke over the loudspeaker. "Welcome aboard. Our next stop is the main Amrak terminal. Our flight time today will be twenty-four minutes and seventeen seconds. Please observe the 'fasten seatbelt' sign at all times. In a few moments we will begin our beverage service. From everyone at Amrak, we would like to thank you for flying with us today and hope you have a pleasant flight."

Anna could barely believe their good luck. Or was it luck? Perhaps someone had heard her request to get back to the Amrak Station and sent the flying saucer to pick them up. After all, didn't the porcupine have tickets with their names on them? Anna found herself wondering if Odin was behind all of this.

Her thoughts were interrupted by the orange porcupine. He handed her a cup of a blue syrupy liquid and a small cellophane bag of what appeared to be chocolate-covered peanuts. Anna took a sip of her drink and found that it tasted just like chocolate milk. Tedith took a sip of his blue drink and was pleased to find it tasted like honey. What appeared to be chocolate-covered peanuts turned out it be chocolate-covered beetles. They were surprisingly tasty, once you got past the crunch.

The little elf sitting beside Anna was clutching the armrests of his chair. His face seemed to be turning green, but it was hard to be sure since his natural color was green. Little beads of yellow sweat dripped down his forehead.

"Excuse me but are you okay?" Anna asked, genuinely concerned.

"I hate to fly. I really hate it."

"I'm sorry to hear that. Is there anything I can do?"

"That's very nice of you, but no... at least this is one of the new saucers, which cuts the flight time in half. My name it Xel. I'd shake your hand, but then I'd have to let go of the armrest."

Anna smiled. "If you don't mind me asking, why are you going to the Amrak Station?"

Xel looked at Anna a little cockeyed. "You're new to all of this, aren't you?"

Anna blushed and said, "Ah, yes, I guess I am."

"I'm trying to get home."

"You are? Me too."

Xel looked at Anna. "That's what we all want, my dear, to go home."

"Oh," Anna said, feeling a little stupid. "You wouldn't know how to get to the Crystal Palace, would you? That is how I am supposed to get home."

"No, never heard of it."

It wasn't long until the orange porcupine spoke over the loudspeaker, "Please check your seatbelt. We will be starting our descent in a few moments."

"Oh dear, this is the part I hate the most," said Xel, closing his eyes and clutching the armrest so hard his green knuckles turned white.

The flying saucer went into a steep dive-bomb. Even Anna, who loved to fly, grabbed hold of the armrests. Her stomach was in her mouth. Then with a jerk, the flying saucer came to an abrupt stop. Xel opened his eyes and took a deep breath.

"That concludes our flight for today. Please be sure that you take all of your personal belongings with you. On behalf of all our crew, it was our pleasure serving you. We hope you have an enjoyable journey, no matter where your final destination might be."

"Well, I'm glad that's over." Xel took another deep breath. "What realm are you going to next?" he asked as he unbuckled his seat beat.

"Gee, I don't know. Am I supposed to know?" Anna asked, concerned.

"No worries, you can ask one of the Transport Directors in the station. Good luck."

Anna and Tedith climbed down the ladder along with the rest of the passengers. The Amrak Station was even busier than before.

"Look, there's Marlin," Tedith said, pointing to the big turtle on the other side of the station. "Let's go ask him where we go next."

As they walked across the station, they had to stop and wait for a thirty-foot long polka-dotted centipede, while it crossed in front of them.

Marlin was examining his clipboard when they reached him. "Excuse me. I don't know if you remember us, but…"

"Ah yes, Anna and Tedith. I've been expecting you," Marlin said, smiling down at them over his spectacles. "How was the Pink Realm?"

"It was wonderful and terrible all at the same time," Anna answered.

Marlin laughed. "Yes, having everything you want is not always what it is cracked up to be. You know what they say, 'be careful what you wish for, you might get it.' But you two seemed to have made it through just fine. Now, let's see where you are headed next." Marlin consulted with his ever-faithful clipboard. "Looks like you are headed to the Orange Realm. Leaves from Platform Seven in, let's see…in exactly seven minutes."

"What is the Orange Realm?" Anna asked.

"Why that's the realm that deals with emotions."

"Emotions?"

"Yes, you know the things that you feel…happiness, sadness, joy, despair, anger, that type of thing."

Anna looked unsure.

"You'll be fine. Just don't let your emotions get the best of you. Platform Seven," Marlin said with a wink.

Anna wanted to ask him a bunch of questions but noticed that a line of beings waiting to speak with Marlin had formed behind her.

"Next," Marlin said, turning his attention to a flying penguin.

The pod door was already open when they arrived. Tedith poked his head inside. "Hello," Tedith said to the purple aardvark standing by the panel of buttons.

"Come on in. We'll be departing in a few minutes."

They were the only ones in the pod besides the operator. "So is this your first time on the Orange Realm?"

"Yes, it's our first time on any of the realms."

"I remember my first trip there. I landed in a jungle surrounded by wild animals. I was frightened out of my wits. I just had to keep remembering that I was not my fear and that I could keep going in spite of what I was feeling. Remember that you are not your emotions and you will do fine."

The aardvark looked at his watch. "Okay, it's time. It looks like it's just the two of you today."

The operator pushed a button and the glass door to the pod

shut with a loud thud. It sounded so final—like a door closing on a jail cell.

"Do we have to do anything, like close our eyes or imagine where we want to go?" Anna asked.

"No, that's only for the Pink Realm. You will land in the place best suited for you. Ready?"

"Ready as I will ever be."

"Okay, here we go."

The pod rumbled as it started to move upward. Even though Anna didn't have to, she took hold of Tedith's paw. The pod shook as it accelerated. Anna squeezed Tedith's paw tighter. Then everything went black.

CHAPTER ELEVEN

LEVIE

They stood motionless in the dark. The pod was dead still. Tedith was about to say something when the door to the pod abruptly slid open. Intense, bright light pouring in. Then, the heat hit them, like a wave.

It reminded Anna of the school trip they took last year to several artists' workshops. They visited painters and potters and sculptors. All of them were amazingly talented but the one that impressed Anna the most was the glass blower. He worked all day in front of a blast furnace, blowing melted glass into beautiful objects. Anna didn't know how he withstood the heat. Now she didn't know how they were going to stand it. It was oppressive.

The pod operator was nowhere to be seen. Still holding onto each other, Anna and Tedith cautiously stepped outside. The door immediately shut behind them and the pod vanished. They looked out at their new surroundings—sand, nothing but sand, miles and miles of white, hot sand. The red sun beat down on them. Little beads of sweat had already started to form on Anna's forehead.

"Didn't the turtle say this realm had to do with emotions? What does a desert have to do with emotions?" asked Tedith, squinting in the intense light.

"Beats me. I just know we can't stay here. We need to find shelter," Anna said, looking out over the dunes. With no water or shade, Anna knew they wouldn't last long in the scorching heat. But which way should they go? It all looked the same. Anna carefully surveyed the landscape. "What's that?" she said, pointing to a speck on the horizon.

Tedith strained to see what Anna was pointing at. "I see something but it is too far away to tell what it is."

"I hope it's not a mirage." Anna said, squinting at the distant object.

"What's a mirage?"

"It's a trick your eyes play on you in the desert. You think you see something but it's not real. The only way you can tell if it is real or not is to get closer to it. Come on, let's go."

Walking was difficult. The sand was constantly shifting under their feet. Anna now understood the saying, "Like walking on shifting sand." Nothing was solid. You couldn't even rely on the ground to support you.

One moment, the object on the horizon looked like it was getting closer, the next minute it looked like it was further away. Anna didn't trust her senses. How could she? Nothing made sense in *The*

Land Beyond the Clouds. Still, it didn't look like a mirage, but then Anna had never seen a mirage before, so she couldn't be sure.

"This heat is unbearable," Tedith said. "I don't know how much more I can take. I wish I could take off my fur coat."

Anna giggled at the thought of Tedith taking off his orange fur.

They walked a long time in silence. Although it wasn't silent inside Anna—it never was. Her thoughts were her constant companion and now they turned to her grandma, the farm, her friends, and of course, her mom.

Anna would give anything to have her former life back again. Being with her mom in their simple, one-bedroom apartment seemed perfect to her right now. When Anna was home, she wished they lived in a bigger apartment, one with two bedrooms. Why couldn't she be satisfied with what she had? Why was it that she always wanted more?

It seemed to Anna that it didn't matter how much folks had, they always wanted something more. Anna had a classmate, Michelle, whose dad owned a chain of sporting goods stores. They lived in a really big house, in an upscale neighborhood. Anna went there once for a pool party. Michelle had her own bedroom, tons of clothes, a playroom in the basement, and went on vacations to Hawaii and Italy. They even had a housekeeper. Anna told herself if she had all that, she wouldn't want anything else. But Michelle wasn't satisfied, she wanted more; she wanted her own bathroom. As she showed Anna her bedroom Michelle complained that she had to share a bathroom with her brother, who was always hogging it. Anna poked her head in the bathroom. It had two sinks, a huge walk-in shower, with several shower heads, and a whirlpool tub that looked like it could hold four people. The bathroom was bigger than the kitchen in Anna's apartment. Anna couldn't believe that Michelle wasn't happy with what she had.

But sometimes you don't know how good you have it until you

don't have it. Now that Anna didn't have her one bedroom apartment, it was all she wanted. Anna no longer cared if she had to share a bedroom with her Mom. She wanted her life back, exactly the way it was.

"Are you okay?" Tedith asked, noticing the pensive look on Anna's face.

"Yeah, I was thinking about my life back home and how I wanted things to be different. If I get home, I'm going to be more grateful for what I have." Anna paused, "Tedith, do you think my mom has stopped looking for me?"

Tedith turned around, and looked directly at Anna. "Never, Anna. Your mother will never stop looking for you."

"I wish I hadn't climbed Jacob's Ladder. I never should have followed that beam of light into the forest. My mom is always telling me I'm too adventurous for my own good and that I should settle down."

"What are you talking about? Your adventurous spirit is one of the things I love most about you. It's part of what makes you who you are. You are always ready to try something new, always willing to take a chance and see what's around the next corner."

"But look at what I have gotten myself into. I might never get home."

"You don't really believe that, do you?"

Anna sighed, "I'm not sure anymore."

Tedith was worried about his friend. She seemed to be losing faith. Maybe it was just that the heat was getting to her. One thing was for certain, they couldn't go on for much longer.

They stopped at the top of the next dune. The object on the horizon was still a tiny speck.

As they began walking down the dune, Tedith lost his footing and tumbled down, head over tail. Anna ran after him.

"Are you okay?" Anna asked, brushing the sand off of him.

"Yeah, but I'm exhausted. I'm not sure how much longer...Ahhhhhh!" Tedith screamed.

Anna turned around, "Ahhhhh!" she also screamed. A startled camel, not five feet from them, stumbled backwards, almost losing its rider. It was hard to tell whether the camel, Anna or Tedith, was more shocked.

"Easy, Pasha, easy," the rider said through a white cloth that protected their face from the sand and sun.

The camel immediately calmed down at the sound of the rider's voice.

"Down, Pasha," the rider commanded.

The camel knelt down and the rider, wearing a turban and long, flowing turquoise robes, jumped off.

"I didn't mean to startle you. It's not often one sees people on foot out in the desert. I am Naia." The rider said, removing the face cloth.

Anna was surprised to see an attractive woman standing before them. She had almond eyes the color of sand and translucent bronze skin.

"I'm Anna," she said, noticing that Tedith was hiding behind her. "It's okay Tedith, you can come out. You just startled the camel."

"Pasha wouldn't harm a fly," Naia reassured Tedith, who cautiously stepped out from behind Anna.

"If you don't mind me asking, what are you doing in the middle of the desert?"

Anna told Naia all about the Amrak Station and how the pod disappeared as soon as they stepped out of it.

"Well, you certainly picked an interesting place to land."

"I didn't pick it. The doors of the pod opened and there we were standing in the middle of a desert."

Naia smiled. "We all pick our own path. We just don't always remember the path when we encounter it. Well, you can't stay out here. Climb up," Naia said, pointing to Pasha's hump.

"Really?"

"Sure, I'll take you to Levie."

"Levie?"

"Yes, Levie. It's that distant speck on the horizon." Naia pointed to the object Anna and Tedith had been walking towards. At least they now knew it wasn't a mirage.

Anna examined the camel. Naia smiled.

"Have you ever been on a camel before?"

Anna shook her head.

"Well, there is nothing to it. Put your foot in the stirrup and climb onto the saddle."

Anna tentatively approached the camel. She put her foot in the stirrup and swung her leg over the big beast. Naia was right. It was easy, just like mounting Star.

"Come on little fella," Naia said.

Tedith wasn't sure about all this, but let Naia pick him up anyway and hand him to Anna.

Naia climbed in front of them and took hold of the reins. "Up, Pasha, up." With a loud snort the camel rose from his knees and instinctively headed towards their destination.

A camel's walk is unlike most other four-footed animals. It takes a step with *both* left legs, plants them firmly, and then takes a step with *both* right legs. This produces a side-to-side rocking motion similar to being on a boat, which makes some people feel seasick. Luckily, Anna wasn't prone to seasickness, so the camel's walk didn't bother her. Tedith however, was another story. After a short distance, the swaying motion made him feel queasy. Even under his orange fur, Naia could see he was turning green.

"Hang on there, little one. Focus on the horizon and you will be fine," Naia advised as she handed Anna a flask of water. "Not too much at once. Take small sips." Anna took several small sips and passed the flask to Tedith. In spite of his queasy stomach, he was able to hold down some water.

Anna found the rhythmic motion of the camel very soothing. It wasn't long before Naia looked back to see that Anna had nodded off. Tedith, on the other hand, was having a hard time holding on.

The camel made slow but steady progress. After several miles, Naia turned around and gently shook Anna awake. Anna gasped. Only a few dunes away was a town made entirely of tents, in every size, shape, and color imaginable. Some were the size of a small elephant and others as large as Anna's school.

"As you can see, we are just about there," Naia said to her two unlikely companions.

Tedith would have been overjoyed at this news if he wasn't feeling so sick.

"What is this place?" Anna asked.

"Levie? It's the main town in these parts. People go there to get supplies, sell their wares and meet up with friends."

"The Crystal Palace wouldn't be in Levie would it?" Anna asked.

"The Crystal Palace?"

"Yes, that's how I am supposed to get home."

"No, Levie doesn't have a Crystal Palace, at least not that I know of. I could take you to see Madame Jano. Everyone goes to her for advice. Maybe she can help you find it."

"That would be great. Thanks."

As they reached the outskirts of Levie, Naia directed Pasha into what appeared to be a boarding stable for camels.

"Down, Pasha," Naia commanded. Tedith almost fell off as he

dismounted. He was so relieved to be back on solid ground once again, even if it was sand. Naia handed Pasha's reins to a young man dressed in a traditional robe and turban. She spoke to him in a language Anna had never heard before.

"They'll take good care of you here fella. I'll see you in a few days," Naia said as she stroked Pasha's neck.

"This way." Naia led them through the stable and into a tiny tent-lined alley.

The alley led to a large crowded marketplace. Merchants with pushcarts called out their ware, "Baskets, baskets, beautiful baskets."

Small tent covered stalls, overflowing with their goods encircled the marketplace. Some were stocked high with fruits, nuts, and vegetables. Others sold cookware, brooms, and clothing.

On one corner, a street magician performed tricks with a shabby little monkey. Dogs ran freely in and out of the crowded marketplace, barking and chasing each other. Everyone was dressed in long robes. Most of the men wore turbans. Some of the women had veils covering their faces. Anna felt quite out of place in her sneakers and jeans. Being accompanied by a talking orange teddy bear didn't help her to blend in either, but no one seemed to take notice of them.

Naia maneuvered through the crowds with the confidence of someone who had done this many times before. Anna and Tedith had to walk smartly to keep up.

Although Naia was being incredibly helpful, her mind was someplace else. Clearly, something was troubling her. She wanted to help Anna and Tedith, but she worried that it would keep her from the reason she had come to Levie in the first place.

Naia turned onto a side street which wasn't nearly as congested as the marketplace. After several twists and turns through the maze of tents, she stopped in front of a bright red tent.

"This is where Madame Jano lives. Before we go in, I must tell you that…"

"Who's there?" called out a voice from the inside the tent. Naia hesitated.

"I said, who's there. Make yourself known," the voice demanded.

Naia pushed back the blue flap that acted as the door and ushered Anna and Tedith inside. The coolness of the tent was a welcome relief from the sun and dust. The room was sparsely furnished. A round table surrounded by four red velvet chairs stood in the middle of the tent. In the center of the table was a large crystal bowl filled with water. The only other item in the room was a handsome bird on a tall perch. Anna wasn't certain but she thought it might be a falcon. "That's strange," Anna thought, "I was sure the voice was coming from inside the tent, but no one is here."

"For the last time. Who is there?" repeated the voice.

There it was again. Where was the voice coming from? It certainly sounded like it was coming from the tent.

"Madame Jano, it's me, Naia."

"Naia, my dear, well why didn't you say so. It has been far too long," the voice said in a much softer tone. "Come here, my dear, so I may see you."

Naia sat down in one of the red velvet chairs and peered into the bowl of water.

"Ah, there you are," said the voice from the crystal bowl of water. "My, you are as lovely as ever. To what do I owe my good fortune?"

Anna was astonished. Just when she thought she was getting used to this strange world, something else amazed her.

"I have brought a couple of fellow travelers with me in the hope that you might be able to help them on their quest home."

"I will do what I can. Please have them come over here so I

may see them."

Naia motioned for Anna and Tedith to join her at the table. They sat down on the chairs but didn't look into the bowl.

"Well, let me have a look at you," the voice from the bowl ordered.

Cautiously they leaned over the bowl.

"Madame Jano, this is Anna and Tedith," Naia said.

"Come a little closer so I may see you," Madame Jano said.

Anna bent closer and looked directly into the bowl. A grand woman, with shocking red hair looked back at Anna from her watery world.

"Hello, Anna," Madame Jano said, smiling.

"Hello, Madame." Anna tried her best to conceal how surprised she was to be speaking to someone in a bowl of water. Not wanting to be left out, Tedith peered into the bowl.

"Ah, and you must be Tedith."

Tedith became uncharacteristically shy and didn't say anything until Anna nudged him.

"Yes, Madame, I'm Tedith."

"It's very nice to meet you both. Any friends of Naia, are friends of mine."

"Now, how can I assist you?"

"I want to go home..."

"Don't we all, my dear, don't we all," Madame Jano said longingly.

"Well, I was wondering if you could tell me how I can get to the Crystal Palace."

The majestic bird let out a loud squawk from his perch where he had been carefully watching everyone.

"Hush now, Oran. We have company. Hmmm, the Crystal Palace, you say. That's an interesting way to get home."

"Yes, so I have been told."

"Well, let's see what we can find out for you. Please place your right hand in the water." Anna cautiously put her hand in the bowl. Everyone was very quiet. Anna felt silly sitting there with her hand in a bowl of water. Then, she felt Madame Jano take hold of her hand, which freaked Anna out even more. She wanted to pull her hand away but she held steady.

After what seemed like an eternity Madame Jano said, "I see that you still have much to do before you can go home. Deal with what is in front of you, even if you don't know how it will assist you. Trust your path, trust yourself and no matter what happens, keep going until you are home." There was a long pause then Madame Jano said, "That's it, my dear. You can remove your hand from the water."

Anna was visibly disappointed. She thought she would learn something new, something that would help her. Instead she received the same cryptic advice she had gotten from Odin and Sidea. "But... what am I to do, where am I to go?"

"It's often not so much about what you do, as it is about how you do it," Madame Jano said.

"But I will get home won't I?" Anna asked.

Before Madame Jano could answer, Naia interrupted. "Thank you, Madame Jano. I fear we have taken up enough of your time."

Anna wanted to stay and ask more questions. But Naia was obviously in a hurry and was now making it clear that it was time to leave.

"Remember, you are always welcome here, all of you. Good luck, Anna. I envy you and the journey you have ahead of you," Madame Jano said.

"It was nice to meet you and thank you for your help," Anna said, although she wasn't sure anything Madame Jano had told her was helpful.

Naia held open the tent flap. Anna squinted as they stepped outside into the bright sunlight.

"Well, it's been nice meeting you both, but I need to get going. I am sorry but this is where we must part company," Naia said, as the matter that brought her to Levie weighed heavy on her heart. "What will you do?"

"I don't know. I guess we'll just keep looking for the Crystal Palace. Thank you for all of your help," Anna said, her own heart heavy with the thought of what might be waiting for them.

"Yeah, thanks Naia. It was nice to meet you. Come on Anna, let's go," Tedith said.

Naia stood and watched them walk down the tent-lined street. She knew she had to be about her business and had already spent more time helping Anna and Tedith than she had wanted but she also knew she couldn't leave them alone to fend for themselves. Levie was no place for the likes of them.

"Wait," Naia called out. Anna and Tedith turned around. "If you like, you can stay with me for a few days. My family keeps a small tent in Levie."

"Really?" Anna asked, grateful once again for Naia's kindness.

Naia smiled a weary smile. "Come. It's this way." She led them through the maze of tents. Naia hoped she wasn't making a mistake inviting them to stay with her and that it wouldn't interfere what she had come to do.

It wasn't long until they stood before a blue tent. "Here we are," Naia said as she pulled back the flap.

The inside held an assortment of dusty, mismatched furniture. "You can use the pillows over there as a bed." Naia said, pointing to a large pile of multi-colored pillows.

"Thank you, Naia. We will do our best to stay out of your way," Anna said, sensing Naia's preoccupation. There was always more to someone than you could see and Anna didn't want to be a burden to Naia, who had already helped them so much.

"Make yourselves at home. Come and go as you like. I'm not sure when I will be back," Naia said as she turned to go.

As soon as Naia was gone, Tedith said, "I'm hungry. I wonder if there is anything to eat." He wandered over to a little kitchen area and opened a small cupboard. The only thing inside was a container of rice.

"How about going out and getting some food? We still have two gold coins left from selling the beanie."

"I'm not sure, Tedith. We really should continue to look for the Crystal Palace before we get sidetracked again."

"Well, we can do both. We can pick up some food and ask around. Besides, it's getting late and it will be dark before long and we shouldn't go to bed hungry."

"Okay, but keep an eye out for anything that you think might lead us to the Crystal Palace."

They wandered through the tent-lined streets towards the marketplace. It was easy to find, as every now and again there was a little sign pointing the way to the marketplace. By the time they arrived the crowds had thinned out and the merchants were starting to close up their stalls.

Anna surveyed the remaining vendors for one that was still open. "Over there."

They passed the magician with the little monkey as they headed for a green and white-striped tent, where a merchant was selling fruits and vegetables. His back was to them as they approached.

"Excuse me, sir," Anna said.

The man turned around, revealing a face etched with wrinkles and a mouth full of rotting teeth. A black patch covered one eye and a faded red turban was tightly wrapped around his head. He closely examined them with his one good eye.

"Ah, I was wondering if we could buy some food." Anna inquired hesitantly.

Without a word, the merchant placed a few pieces of fruit and a handful of nuts into a paper bag and handed it to Anna. He held out his bony hand to be paid. Anna handed him one of the gold coins. He bit into it without taking his good eye off of Anna. When he was convinced it was real, he turned his back on them and continued to tend to his produce.

They wandered back through the marketplace as the setting sun turned everything a burnt orange. The heat of the day was starting to give way to cooler night air. Tedith reached into the bag and pulled out a piece of fruit shaped like a pear but was bright blue. He took a big bite.

"Yuck!" Tedith spit out the nasty fruit along with a small white worm. He threw the fruit in the trash then took a fig from the bag and bit into it. "That's better."

"We should head back, before it gets too dark to see where we are going," Anna said, aware of the quickly fading light.

As they passed the magician once again, the little monkey grabbed the fig from Tedith. "Hey," Tedith called out, "That's mine, give it back."

The monkey quickly popped the fig in his mouth then hid behind the magician.

Anna snickered. "Come on Tedith, let's go."

"But…" Tedith began to protest.

"There is more in the bag. Let's go."

They left the marketplace the way they had entered it and walked down the tent-lined street. There were four orange tents on the first corner they came to.

"Uh, I think we go this way," Anna, said, pointing to the right.

"Really? I thought we came from over there," Tedith said, pointing to the left. "Or did we go straight?"

Anna looked down each of the streets. They looked much the same. "I'm pretty sure we go right." But once they had started walking down the street, Anna was anything but sure. At the next corner they turned left. They walked pass a few more streets then turned right. Nothing looked familiar.

As darkness slowly descended on Levie oil lamps began to glow from the inside of the tents, illuminating their way.

They wandered down street after street, hesitating at each crossroad, trying to decide which way to go. When they finally came to a dead end they had to admit that they were hopelessly lost.

"Now what?" Tedith asked, looking up into the star-filled sky.

"There is not much we can do but keep on walking. With a little luck maybe we will stumble upon Naia's tent," Anna said, shivering. The temperature had plummeted now that the sun had gone down. Anna stuck her hands in her pockets to keep them warm. She found her lucky stone and rubbed it.

They turned around and continue to walk through the maze of tents. With nothing to guide them they had no idea if they were headed in the right direction. If they didn't find the tent soon they would have to find a place to spend the night.

"What's that?" Tedith asked, noticing a movement in the distant.

Anna strained her eyes to see. "I think someone is coming towards us."

A lone figure dressed in a black robe was walking quickly towards them. He was obviously in a hurry so they moved aside to let him passed. He was about to walk right by them when Anna called out, "Excuse me but we are lost." The man stopped and stared at them with eyes the color of night. "Would you know how to get to Naia's?"

The stranger remained quiet but his eyes were still locked on them. He gave Anna the creeps. When it was obvious he wasn't going to answer them Anna said, "Well, sorry to have bothered you. Come on, Tedith."

The stranger continued on his way and had almost vanished into the night when Tedith quickly turned around and called out, "Do you know how to get to Madame Jano's?"

The lone figure abruptly stopped and walked back towards them. Anna was frightened and thought about running.

"This way," the stranger hissed as he walked right by them. Tedith and Anna followed him as he wove his way through the maze of tents. He walked very fast and Tedith had to run to keep up. The stranger finally stopped in front of now familiar, red tent.

"Thank you sir. Thank you so much."

Without a word, the man turned abruptly and disappeared into the night.

"Who's there?" a familiar voice called out from the tent. "I know someone is out there. Make your presence known."

"It's Anna and Tedith, Madame Jano," Anna said, walking through the flap of the tent. A loud squawk from Oran, greeted them.

"Lord Almighty! What are you two doing out this time of night? Come here so I can see you," Madame Jano ordered.

"We got lost trying to get back to Naia's tent from the market," Anna said, peering into the bowl.

"Gracious me, you look half frozen. Lift that yellow flap by Oran."

As Anna lifted the flap Oran let out another squawk. He wasn't very fond of visitors. Behind it was a tiny bedroom, obviously meant for guests, since Madame Jano had no use for it. "There should be some blankets on the bed. Wrap yourself in them."

Anna and Tedith were only too happy to oblige.

"You'll have to spend the night. You will never find your way back in the dark. We'll figure out how to get you back to Naia's tomorrow."

Tedith and Anna were dead tired. "Thank you Madame Jano. We really appreciate it."

"You two crawl into bed. I'll see you in the morning."

The two weary travelers climbed into the feather soft bed. As Anna drifted off to sleep, her thoughts turned to Naia. She wondered what had brought her to Levie; it certainly seemed to be important.

They awoke to Oran squawking. Anna yawned and stretched. Tedith reached for the bag of food that had gotten them into this mess. He avoided the blue fruit and popped a few nuts into his mouth.

The rustling of the paper bag had gotten Madame Jano's attention. "Are you two awake?"

"Yes," Anna said as she hopped out of bed and walked towards the table. Anna peered into the bowl and was more than a little surprised to see Madame Jano's bright red hair rolled-up in curlers.

"Good morning," Anna said suppressing a giggle.

"My, I thought you would never wake up. Naia is going to be worried sick over the two of you."

"Great," Anna thought, "I've made another person worry about me."

"How do we..." But before Anna could finish, the flap to Madame Jano's tent flap flew open and *The Loyal Forces of the Opposition* stormed in.

CHAPTER TWELVE

THE FORTRESS

Madame Jano was furious. "Who's there?" she demanded "Quiet!" Donovan commanded.

Anna took hold of Tedith's paw and backed up against the wall of the tent.

"So, Anna, we meet again. Take them!"

Before they could react, Donovan's men had Anna and Tedith in their clutches. They struggled to get away but the men were too strong.

Madame Jano continued to protest, but there was nothing she could do from her watery world.

"It's no use, Anna," said Donovan. "This time there will be no escape. Let's go."

Anna's only thought was to get away. She bit the hand of her captor.

"Ouch," he called out, shaking his injured hand, "That will be enough from you." He grabbed her even more fiercely.

They dragged Anna and Tedith out of the tent, mounted three white stallions, and rode off in a cloud of dust.

"Oran, quickly, follow them! Tell me where they take them," Madame Jano instructed.

Oran flew out of the tent and straight up into the blue sky. Higher and higher he went until he spotted the three horses galloping towards the edge of town. He located a pocket of hot air and glided effortlessly. He was careful to keep his distance. The men were shrewd and Oran didn't want them to sense his presence.

Based on the direction they were traveling, Oran knew exactly where the men were headed—and it wasn't good.

The men continued to gallop at breakneck speed. Oran wondered what *The Loyal Forces of the Opposition* could possibly want with a girl and an orange bear.

He watched as the riders approached a massive, wood barricade. A dozen or more soldiers, proficient in armed combat, were perched along the top. The barricade surrounded an imposing stone fortress with four towers, one on each corner. It was well known that the fortress was occupied by *The Loyal Forces of the Opposition*. To the best of Oran's knowledge, no one had ever escaped from the fortress. Oran feared for the girl and bear as he flew closer to get a better look.

Two large wooden gates opened as the horses approached the barricade. Once inside, the riders dismounted. They handed Anna and Tedith over to two soldiers. Oran could see that Anna was still struggling to get away. She kicked the shins of one of the soldiers. He let out a loud yelp and rubbed his leg. The girl had gumption. Oran had to give her that, even if her days were short-numbered. He watched as they carried Anna and Tedith into the stone fortress, suspecting this would be the last time he would ever see them. Oran circled the fortress a couple times, but he had learned as much as he could and headed back to Madame Jano.

Naia was at Madame Jano's when he arrived.

"Oran, quickly, tell us what did you learn?" Naia pleaded.

Oran flew to his perch. "It's not good news. They took them to the fortress."

"I was afraid of that," Naia cried. "We've got to get them out."

"Naia my dear, you know that fortress is impervious. There is nothing we can do. I am afraid their fate is sealed," Madame Jano reasoned.

"But we have to do something. Good Lord, she is only a young girl!"

Madame Jano sighed. "I understand Naia but what would you have us do? The fortress is well-guarded and we don't even know where in the fortress they are being held."

"I don't know what we should do. I just know we have to try something. Oran, can you find out where in the fortress they are being held?"

"I can't get into the fortress undetected. A falcon would be too suspicious."

They sat in silence, searching their hearts and minds for something, anything, that could save their new friends.

"Although a falcon would be too suspicious, a mouse wouldn't be," Madame Jano said, breaking their silence.

"A mouse?" Naia looked puzzled.

"Brilliant, Madame Jano, just brilliant!" Oran exclaimed. "But do you think he'll do it?"

"You know Snidley. He's squeak is worse than his bite. He'll complain, but he'll do it."

"Could someone please tell me what is going on? Who is Snidley?" Naia asked.

"Snidley is an old mouse." Madame Jano explained, "He scurries from tent to tent looking for scraps of food. Most people chase him out, but Oran and I put cheese out for him. At first, he would take the food and run off, but now he stays for a while and chats with us. Mainly he complains about his aches and pains and how badly the world is treating him. He could easily enter the fortress undetected, and with a little luck, locate Anna and Tedith."

Naia's eyes lit up immediately. "Where do we find Snidley?"

"We don't find him. He finds us."

Oran flew over to a large wooden storage box and pulled out a huge piece of cheese, much larger than the one they usually left out for Snidley. Oran set it down by Madame Jano's table and flew back to his perch.

They watched and waited. In less than a minute, a little grey mouse peeked under the edge of the tent. His nose was twitching a mile a minute as he attempted to pinpoint the exact location of the cheese that his keen sense of smell assured him was there. Then he spied it. It was huge, almost as big as he was. He couldn't believe his good fortune. He spotted Naia watching him, which made him hesitate, but only for a moment, before he scurried to the cheese.

Madame Jano had an acute sense of hearing and could hear Snidely munching away. "Hello Snidley. How are you?" she asked.

"I've been better. My arthritis is acting up," Snidley said as he continued to devour the soft creamy cheese.

Naia smiled at hearing this.

"Snidley, this is our friend Naia," Madame Jano said.

"Hi," Snidley said, reluctant to interrupt his eating for idle conversation.

"Snidley, there is something we want to talk to you about."

"What do you mean there is something you want to talk to me about? I knew this big block of cheese was too good to be true. I knew there had to be a catch," Snidley mumbled through a mouthful of cheese.

Madame Jano continued, undeterred. "Donovan and his men are holding a couple friends of ours in the fortress. We need you to find out where."

Snidley stopped in mid-bite.

"You've got to be kidding. There is no way I am going anywhere near the fortress. You must be crazy."

"Now, Snidley, no one is going to notice a little mouse. You'll be in and out in a blink of an eye."

"Uh-uh, no way. Why should I risk my life? I don't even know your friends."

"How about we make a deal. If you do this for us, I will give you a life-long supply of cheese."

Snidley's ears perked up.

"Think of it, Snidley," Madame Jano continued, "all of your favorite cheeses, Cheddar, Swiss, Gouda..."

"No Blue Cheese, I hate Blue Cheese," Snidley piped in.

Madame Jano smiled, "Okay, no Blue Cheese. So you'll do it then?"

"I didn't say that. It's awfully dangerous and my back leg has been acting up. Besides, how would I get there? It's a long way for an old mouse."

"I'll take you," volunteered Oran, "you can fly on my back. I'll drop you off right outside the barricade."

"You? No way! You only want to get me outside so you can eat me," Snidley said.

Oran swooped down from his perch and landed a couple of inches from Snidley. "If I wanted to eat you I would have done it a long time ago," Oran said, looking him straight in the eye.

Snidley gulped. He had to admit Oran had a point.

"I don't know. I don't like excitement. I like things calm. Too much activity gives me a headache."

Naia bent down and stroked the little mouse. "Please, Snidley, my friends are in grave danger and we really need your help."

Snidley liked the touch of the beautiful woman. It was rare that genuine kindness was extended to him.

Snidley softened. "Oh all right, but I want the cheese waiting for me when get back."

"Great, then it's settled," said Madame Jano.

"What are you going to do once you know where Donovan is holding them?" Snidley asked.

"I'm not sure. While you are gone, we'll think of something," Madame Jano said.

"Climb aboard," Oran commanded.

"What, now? I haven't even finished my cheese," Snidley protested.

"There will be a storehouse of cheese waiting for you when you return."

"Oh all right," Snidley said as he took one more big bite.

Naia gently picked up the mouse and placed him on Oran's back. "You are looking for Anna and Tedith, a young girl with an orange teddy bear.

"You're kidding, right? All of this for a girl and a teddy bear?" Snidley blurted out, still chewing the cheese in his mouth. "Okay, okay, never mind, just tell me what you want me to do."

"When you find them, tell them we sent you and that we are going to do what we can to get them out. Get as much information as you can. Not just where they are holding them but also the location of the entrances, how many men are guarding them, anything you think would help us rescue them."

"Okay, just make sure the cheese is waiting for me by the time I get back and remember…no Blue Cheese." Snidley swallowed his final mouthful of cheese, wondering if it would be his last. "Well let's go if we are going, before I change my mind."

"Okay hold on," Oran instructed. Snidley grabbed Oran's feathers tightly.

"Good luck and be careful," Naia said as Oran flew out of the tent towards the fortress. It wasn't long until they were high above Levie. Snidley held on for dear life and tried not to look down.

"Not so fast," Snidley complained.

Oran ignored him and caught an air current that lifted the two unlikely partners even higher.

"There it is," Oran said, indicating the fortress in the distance.

"I don't know. I don't think I can do this. I've never been very brave. Maybe we should turn around."

"You'll be fine. No one is going to pay any attention to a mouse."

Oran landed on the ground just outside the wooden barricade. It would have been too suspicious landing in the courtyard.

"You'll have to find a way through the barricade and into the fortress. I'll be flying nearby waiting for you to come out. When I see you, I will come down to get you. It shouldn't take you long. Go in, find them and come right back."

"Okay but don't go very far," Snidley said as he slid off Oran's back. He watched as Oran soared into the clear blue sky, hoping it wouldn't be the last time he saw him.

The barricade that surrounded the fortress was made from massive logs, erected vertically and fastened together with thick rope.

A sharp point topped each log. They formed an impressive defense.

Snidley scampered along the edge looking for a way in. The logs were packed together so tightly that there wasn't enough room for even a little mouse to squeeze through.

"Oh dear, oh dear," Snidley mumbled to himself as he scurried along.

Then he saw a narrow opening between two logs. He tried to squeeze through but his pot belly got stuck.

"If only I hadn't eaten all that cheese," Snidely thought. He began to gnaw on the wood surrounding the opening. If he could make it a little bit bigger, he was sure he could fit through. After several minutes, the opening was just large enough for him and his belly to slip through.

There, in the middle of a courtyard, loomed the imposing stone fortress with its four impressive towers. Soldiers, each with a threatening looking sword, were stationed on either side of the fortress's only entrance. Other than the soldiers, the courtyard was deserted. Snidley scurried to the edge of the massive building, a few yards from the entrance.

He glanced up and saw Oran circling high above. This was somewhat reassuring but Snidley still wasn't sure he was up to the task. He sincerely hoped they hadn't put their faith in him for no good reason.

Now that he was at the fortress he had no idea how he was going to get inside. There would be no gnawing through the fortress's stone walls to get to the other side.

Snidley's doubt was growing. As he considered his predicament, the mammoth doors to the fortress swung open. Snidley watched as two soldiers marched out.

"Shift change," one of the soldiers said to the two standing guard.

As the new soldiers took their places Snidley saw his opportunity. He ran towards the open door. One of the soldiers was blocking his way, so he ran right through his legs.

"Hey," the soldier yelled spinning around. He drew his sword and ran after Snidley.

"Leave it," commanded the other solider "It's only a mouse. It's harmless."

Snidley continued to run down a long corridor. "That was close," he thought. When he was sure he was out of harm's way he stopped to catch his breath and survey the fortress. It was enormous, especially for a little mouse. How was he ever going to find Anna and Tedith in such a huge place?

"I've got to think. If I were Donovan, where would I hold them? Hmmm, I guess I would hold them in a dungeon; that is if I had one. If Donovan does have a dungeon there would have to be stairs leading down to it."

Snidley scurried down the main corridor of the fortress looking for stairs that might lead to a dungeon. He passed several large heavy wooden doors, all of which were shut.

"Oh dear, oh dear," he moaned. "Maybe the stairs are behind one of these doors, but which door?"

Snidley approached the end of the main corridor, which connected to a smaller hall. His doubt was growing; there was still no sign of a stairway or a dungeon.

Snidely scurried around the corner…and froze.

A large raggedy, calico cat was washing himself halfway down the hall. Slowly, Snidley turned around. As quiet as a church mouse, he tiptoed back the way he had come. He looked back down the hallway as he was about to turn the corner. The cat looked up. Their eyes locked. The cat let out a harrowing meow then took off down the hall like his tail was on fire. Snidley ran back down the main corridor as fast as his little legs would carry him, which wasn't very fast. The cat turned the corner and was quickly gaining ground. Snidley knew the end was near. When the cat was right behind his prey he pounced. Snidley dove at the crack under the nearest door. He slid on his belly into a room, just in time to hear an earsplitting cry as the cat slammed into the door.

"What was that?" asked a loud voice from the far end of the room.

"I think it was the cat, probably chasing a mouse," another voice answered.

Snidley quickly ran to the nearest piece of furniture; a gaudy gold leaf stool. From the safety of his hiding place, he surveyed the room. The massive room was lavishly furnished with ornate fabrics and fancy carved furniture that was more befitting of a palace than a fortress in the middle of the desert.

Three men gathered at the far end of the room. One was sitting on a large throne-like chair. The other two stood in front of him. The men talked in hushed tones among themselves. Snidley wished he could hear what they were saying. He cautiously darted from table to chair to couch, so as not to be detected. He hid a few feet from the men behind a floor-length, silk-embroidered curtain.

Snidley peered out from the edge of the curtain. All of the men were dressed in identical pure white uniforms. The only thing that differentiated them was that the man on the throne was wearing a crystal medallion on a white gold chain around his neck.

"So Anna and Tedith are securely locked away?" asked the man on the throne.

"Yes, Donovan."

Snidley gasped at the sound of his name. Of course, Donovan was legendary in these parts, but Snidley never thought he would meet up with him.

"Good. I think it's time to pay them a little visit. Let's go."

The three men headed for the door. Snidley knew an opportunity when he saw one. After the men closed the door Snidley ran to the door and cautiously slid under the crack. Luckily, the cat was nowhere in sight, probably off licking its wounded pride.

Careful to keep his distance, Snidley followed the men as they made their way to the other side of the fortress. He tried hard to remember the direction so he could tell Madame Jano and Naia.

The men finally stopped in front of a door, which looked exactly like all the other doors they had passed. One of them took out a large brass key from his uniform and put it in the lock.

Behind the door was a spiral staircase. However, it didn't lead down to a dungeon, but up. It went up one of the fortress towers.

Snidley looked at the soaring staircase and groaned under his breath. "I'm too old for this," he thought. The men climbed the stairs rapidly. Snidley was afraid of losing them, but he couldn't keep up and had to stop several times to catch his breath. When the men reached the top, he could hear them talking but couldn't make out what they were saying. He continued to climb as quickly as he could. He was only four steps from the top when the men started their descent.

Snidley jumped out of the way right before one was about to step on him. Luckily, the stairwell was dimly lit and they didn't see him.

Snidley climbed the few remaining stairs. There, huddled in a corner, was a young girl with a small teddy bear who was trying to comfort her. Snidley waited until he heard the door at the bottom of the stairs being closed and locked before approaching them.

Tedith jumped, "A mouse!"

"It's okay, my name is Snidley. Madame Jano and Naia sent me. Are you two okay?"

"Well, we're not hurt, but we are far from being okay. Naia and Madame Jano sent you?"

"Yes, they sent me to find out where you are being held in the fortress. Once I tell them, they are going to rescue you." Snidley explained.

Anna didn't say anything.

"Gee," Snidley thought, "that's gratitude for you."

"Did you hear me? They are going to rescue you," Snidley repeated, puzzled by their lack of response.

"I'm sorry. That's wonderful, really it is. It's only that we won't be here long enough for them to rescue us. Donovan came here to tell us that he is moving us to the Pit of Doom. He proudly boasted that no one has ever escaped from it. I imagine it's where we will live out the remainder of our days. He's sending soldiers up right now to take us there," Anna explained, barely able to hold back her tears.

"It's okay, Anna. Snidley is here now. He'll help us find a way out," Tedith said reassuringly.

Snidley was shocked to hear this. "Wait a second. I would like to help, really I would, but I'm a little mouse. I can't help you escape. The only thing I agreed to do was find out where you were in the fortress Donovan was holding you. Madame Jano and Naia are going to help you."

"Well, there's got to be something we can do. We can't give up," Tedith said, scratching his furry little head as if that would help him think of something.

"The first thing we need to do is get you out of this tower," Snidley said, stating the obvious.

"Yeah but the door at the bottom of the stairs is locked," Anna said.

"Okay, if not the door, what about the window?" Snidley pointed to a small window high on the wall.

"Anna, lift me up so I can see what's below," Snidley instructed.

Anna gently picked up the little mouse and, standing on her

tiptoes, reached up and placed him on the windowsill.

"What do you see?" Tedith asked.

"It's straight down; a long way down. Even if we had a rope, the soldiers would be sure to see us climbing down."

Snidley noticed Oran flying high overhead. He waved at him but Oran was a long way off, there was no way to get his attention. Anna picked Snidley up off the ledge and placed him gently on the floor.

"Maybe there is some way to unlock the door. Perhaps—" Snidley stopped in mid-sentence. "Who's there?" Snidley demanded, his nose twitching as he sniffed the air.

Tedith looked at Anna and twirled his fingers around the side of his head to indicate that he thought Snidely had a few screws loose.

"I said, who's there? I know you are there, so come out."

Much to Anna and Tedith's surprise, a brown mouse came out from a small crack in the stone wall.

"Who are you?" Snidley barked.

"I'm Rosie, I live in the fortress," said the nervous little mouse. She was not used to talking to strangers, or anyone for that matter.

"I'm Anna, this is Tedith and Snidley," Anna said, trying to make Rosie feel more at ease.

"What are you doing here?" asked Rosie.

"We are prisoners. Donovan..." Anna began to explain.

"We don't have time for this. We need to figure out how to get out of here. The soldiers will be here any minute." Snidely wasn't used to being around girl mice, especially cute ones, and didn't quite know how to act. "Now, where were we? Oh, yes, perhaps there is some way to unlock the door." Snidley paced up and down.

"Perhaps I can help," Rosie offered shyly.

Snidley looked at her suspiciously. "Really? How?"

"See that stone in the wall?" Rosie said, pointing to one of the stone blocks. "Three from the bottom."

Anna walked over to the wall and placed her hand on one of the stone blocks. "This one?"

"No, the one to the right of it," Rosie directed.

Anna placed her hand on the stone Rosie indicated.

"Push on the top right corner of the stone."

As Anna pushed, a portion of the wall swung open, revealing a passageway.

They all stared in amazement.

"Wow!" exclaimed Tedith, poking his head into the passageway.

"The fortress is full of secret passageways," explained Rosie. I've lived here all my life, so I know them all."

"Where does this one lead?" Snidley asked, seeing that he had been wrong about Rosie.

"It leads to the kitchen. If you like, I'll show you the way. It's pretty dark in there."

"What are we waiting for?" said Tedith.

When all four of them were in the passageway, Rosie told Anna which stone to push. The opening in the wall closed behind them.

"Be very quiet. The passageway runs right by the main rooms and even though the walls are made of stone, a loud sound can still be heard on the other side," Rosie cautioned.

They quickly followed their unlikely rescuer through the dark passageway.

At one point, they could hear muffled voices coming from the other side of the wall. They tiptoed past them. After a few more twists and turns Rosie stopped.

"The kitchen is on the other side." Rosie poked her head through a little crack in the wall. "It's all clear. Anna, push the top left-hand corner of the stone directly in front of you...the fourth stone from the ground."

Anna pushed the stone and, as before, part of the wall swung open, allowing them to enter the kitchen.

Tedith immediately began scouting for food. He found some bread and broke off a piece for each of them as Rosie told Anna how to close the opening.

"Now what? I hate to be the bearer of bad news, but we are still in the fortress and it won't be long until they discover you aren't in the tower," Snidley said.

"Snidley is right," Tedith said. "We need to find a way out of the fortress and through the wooden barricade."

"I have an idea," Rosie offered. She scurried across the kitchen and slipped under the crack in an old wooden door.

"What is she doing?" Snidely asked.

Before anyone could answer, Rosie slipped back under the door and ran over to them.

"Every day, there is a food delivery from town. I just checked, the wagon is still here. If you are careful you can hide in the back of the wagon. It'll take you back to Levie."

"Rosie, you're brilliant!" exclaimed Tedith.

Rosie blushed. "You should go now." They followed her to the old wooden door. Rosie slipped under it and immediately returned. "The coast is clear. Climb in the back of the wagon and cover yourself with the tarp."

Anna took a deep breath and opened the door a crack. The wagon was about twenty feet from the door.

"Thank you so much Rosie. Really, you're the best."

"That's okay, I was happy to help. Besides, it was nice to have someone to talk with. It's kind of lonely here," Rosie said, looking shyly at Snidley.

"Okay, well, we need to go. Thanks." Snidley said, realizing he was blushing.

"I'll go first," said Anna, making a run for the wagon. She climbed in the back and hid under the tarp. She waved for Tedith. Anna reached down and helped him into the wagon. Then she waved for Snidley.

"Next time, be sure to bring mangos. Donovan won't be happy if you forget them again," a voice said from around the corner.

"Of course, of course, I won't let it happen again," the merchant replied.

Snidley ran towards the wagon. "Hurry," Anna thought.

Then, he suddenly stopped and turned back towards the open door. Anna wondered what he was doing.

"Do you want to come with us?" Snidley asked Rosie.

"Really?"

"Sure, I have a nice place. You can live with me. That is, if you want to," Snidley said, in an uncharacteristically soft tone.

Rosie lit up. "I'd love to. I've always wanted to leave this place."

Together they ran to the wagon. Anna scooped them up just as the merchant turned the corner.

Hidden under the protection of the tarp, they heard the merchant climb onto the wagon. "Giddy-up," he said as he gently shook the reins.

The wagon moved forward with a jolt. The heavy doors to the fortress opened for them to pass through. They entered the courtyard. They were almost clear, they just had to get through the main gate of the barricade. The wagon abruptly stopped.

"I need to inspect your wagon," a soldier said.

The merchant jumped down from the wagon and walked towards the back. Anna held her breath. It was over, there would be no escaping now.

Snidley began to squeak very loudly. He then ran out from

under the tarp onto the ground and right over the soldier's boot.

"Hey, that's a mouse. You're bringing mice in here. I hate mice. Get out of here," yelled the solider, as another soldier opened the gate.

The merchant quickly climbed back onto the wagon and drove through the gate. Anna couldn't believe it, Snidely had saved them. He sacrificed himself to save them. What a brave little mouse.

They had gone about a half mile when a faint but unmistakable shrill rang out. Donovan had once again discovered that Anna had slipped through his fingers.

Anna shivered thinking about how close she and Tedith had come to being thrown in the Pit of Doom. The air under the tarp was musty and stale. The road was bumpy and the going was slow but Anna didn't care. She was grateful to be free. She worried about Snidley though. How heroic he had been.

Finally, they heard the sound of people mingling in the marketplace. It was like music to Anna's ears. The wagon came to a stop. After they heard the merchant get off Anna peeked out from under the tarp and watched him enter a yellow tent.

The stowaways slipped undetected from the back of the wagon and quickly got lost in the crowded marketplace. Anna slipped into one of the narrow streets and was thankful they could finally talk.

"That's a relief but we are not out of danger yet. I am sure that Donovan won't give up that easily. We need to get to Madame Jano's tent. Maybe she can help us get out of town," Anna said. "But which way? This town is a maze. It could take hours to find her tent."

"I know," Tedith said. "Rosie, Madame Jano said she was going to have a big pile of cheese waiting for Snidley. Can you smell it?"

Rosie put her nose in the air. It started to twitch. "This way."

They followed her as she scampered down the tent-lined streets. After several turns Rosie stopped in front of the now familiar red tent. Anna flung open the flap.

"Anna, Tedith! How in the world did you escape?" Naia cried out, hugging them as if they were her own children. "We were worried sick about you. But wait, where's Snidley?"

Anna was about to explain how Snidley sacrificed himself for them when Oran flew in the tent with Snidley clutching tightly to his feathers. He landed on the ground. Snidley slide off and Oran flew to his perch.

"What in the world happened?" Naia said surprised to see all of them.

Before Anna could explain, Madame Jano asked, "Did you find out where the Pit of Doom is?"

"What?" Naia swung around in disbelief. "What is going on?"

"Everyone calm down," Madame Jano said. "Let me explain. The Pit of Doom is where Donovan takes his captives. The fortress is just a holding place, until he moves them to the Pit, which is believed to be somewhere in the desert. But no one has been able to find out where it's located, at least not 'til now. Isn't that right, Anna?"

Anna confused, just nodded.

"What most of you don't know, is that the reason Naia is in Levie is to locate the Pit of Doom. Her brother was captured and taken there a few days ago. Isn't that right, Naia?"

"Yes, but how did you know?" Naia asked.

"There is much I know, my dear."

Naia turned to Anna. "Anna, is it true? Do you know where the Pit of Doom is?"

"Yes, I suppose I do," Anna said.

Naia looked at her in disbelief. People had been searching years for its location. Now, this young girl has found it. All along, Naia thought she was helping Anna and Tedith and it turned out that Anna was helping her.

"When Donovan came into the tower to tell us he was going to move us to the Pit, he boasted that the Pit everyone was looking for was right under their noses. Everyone thinks the Pit is in the middle of the desert, but it isn't. The entrance to the Pit is in the middle of the marketplace. It's in a green and white-striped tent. The same tent Tedith and I bought food from. A man with one eye runs it. The entrance to the Pit of Doom is in the back."

Naia began to cry as she hugged Anna and Tedith again. "You have provided a tremendous service. Not only can we now free my brother but we can also free everyone that is being held captive. Madame Jano, did you know that Anna would find the Pit of Doom?" Naia asked.

"I saw that she had the opportunity to do so. I'm pleased that she did. Snidley, you have been awfully quiet. What do you make of all this and who is your friend?" Madame Jano asked with a watery smile.

"This is Rosie, and ah, well, she's come to live with me," Snidley said, blushing.

"Rosie, it's very nice to meet you. You have a very brave boyfriend, who is also very rich, I might add. He has a whole storeroom of cheese, as I am sure you can tell from the delicious aroma. Anna, as for you, I believe your work is done here."

"Yes, I guess so but I'm still no closer to finding the Crystal Palace or getting home."

"You may be surprised at how far you have come. But you should go now. Donovan will surely be looking for you and I imagine this will be one of the first places he checks."

Anna did not like hearing this. She didn't want to venture out into the desert again but she knew Madame Jano was right. Donovan would be back shortly."

"It was really nice meeting you all." Anna and Tedith hugged Naia goodbye. "Goodbye, Snidley. Take good care of Rosie. Thanks Madam Jano. Bye Oran."

Oran let out a weak squawk. Everyone was sad to see Anna and Tedith leave. They started to walk towards the flap of the tent.

"Wait, not that way. Use the back door," Madame Jano said.

"The back door? There's a back door?" Anna asked, puzzled.

"Yes, it's the white flap over there."

Anna lifted the flap. She and Tedith were back at the Amrak Station.

CHAPTER THIRTEEN

PUZZLING

The tent flap turned into a solid wall as soon as it closed behind them. The now familiar hustle and bustle of the Amrak Station surrounded them. Departure announcements echoed throughout the large station. Beings of all shapes and sizes rushed to catch their flights. Transport pods departed full and arrived back at the station empty.

"Hey there's Marlin. Let's find out where we are going next," Tedith said.

Anna didn't share Tedith's enthusiasm. She was growing weary of all this and wondered if finding the Crystal Palace would really get her home. Unfortunately, she had little choice but to continue. She half-heartedly followed Tedith across the crowded station, careful to dodge a pair of arguing striped armadillos.

Marlin looked up from his trusty clipboard as they approached. "What? You two again? Back so soon?"

"A lot happened in the short time we were away," Tedith said.

"Ah yes, better that way than to have it drag on for eons." Marlin turned to his clipboard. "Let's see…ah yes…you are off to the Blue Realm. How are your school grades Anna?"

"What a strange question," Anna thought. "Pretty good, mostly A's and B's."

"Good, because you're going to need all your wits about you for this realm. It's pretty heady."

"Is the Crystal Palace on the Blue Realm?"

"You never know my dear. You never know. Your transport pod doesn't leave for forty-five minutes," Marlin said, checking the large clock on the station wall. "Why don't you wander over to the cafeteria and grab a quick bite to eat. I imagine at least one of you is hungry," Marlin said, patting Tedith on the head. "You still have a gold coin left don't you?"

"Uh, yeah we do," Anna said, wondering how he knew about the coins.

"Good, you'll find the cafeteria between Platform Five and Six."

"You'll be departing from Platform Eleven. Listen for the announcement."

"Thanks Marlin."

The smell of food guided them to the cafeteria. They grabbed a tray and waited their turn in line. A black and white-checkered turkey stood in front of them. Anna was shocked to see the bird piling his plate with roasted turkey and stuffing. Wasn't that like being a turkey cannibal?

163

Anna looked over the selection. Remembering how the food in Candy Land had tempted her, Anna decided on something simple; a bowl of chicken noodle soup and an oatmeal cookie. Tedith, as always, was happy with a big helping of honey. Anna unwrapped the bandana and gave the last gold coin to the cashier; a portly blue giraffe in a pink hairnet. It was exactly enough. Anna hoped they wouldn't need any more money during the rest of their journey.

The cafeteria was very crowded. Anna's mom would say, 'they were packed in like sardines.' Anna surveyed the crowded room looking for a place to sit. She could barely believe her eyes.

"Look who's here!" She ran over to a booth in the corner where Odin was dunking French fries into brown gravy and popping them into his mouth.

"Anna, Tedith, fancy meeting you here," Odin said with a mischievous smile. "Won't you join me?"

"But Odin, what are you doing here?" Anna slid into the booth opposite him.

"Why having lunch of course," he said with a wink.

"Oh Odin. Seriously, did you know we were going to be here?"

Odin just smiled. "So how goes the journey?"

"You can't imagine the things we've seen and the situations we've found ourselves in. I didn't think we were going to make it through some of them, but we did." Anna sighed deeply and continued, "But in spite of it all, we aren't any closer to getting home and I still don't have a clue where to find the Crystal Palace or what about it will get me home."

"You are doing splendidly my dear. You'll find your way. Have faith in yourself and your path."

Anna wished she shared Odin's positive outlook. "It seems that everywhere we go, Donovan and his men are waiting for us. We barely escaped them last time. If it weren't for the help of Naia and Madame

Jano, we'd be in the Pit of Doom right now."

Anna was frustrated, tired, and wanted the whole thing to be over. "I don't know why I have to go through all this. I don't want to be here anymore. I want to be home," she sulked.

"But you are not home, you are here."

"I know I am here but I want to be home, with my mom."

Odin looked deeply into her eyes. "If you aren't where you are, you are nowhere."

Anna sighed. "Please Odin, no more riddles."

"Think about it Anna. If you aren't where you are, where are you?"

Anna looked at him like he was touched in the head.

Odin continued. "You are nowhere. You can't be anywhere other than where you are. Can you?"

Anna nodded as what Odin was saying started to sink in.

"If you can accept where you are, you can get to where you want to go; but only if you are willing to start where you are. 'Wanting' to go home, won't get you there Anna. Dealing with where you are, will."

Before Anna could say anything, a voice over the loudspeaker announced, "Blue Realm leaving from Platform Eleven in five minutes.

Anna didn't want to leave, but she knew Odin was right. If she wanted to get home, she had to deal with where she was. "That's us. I guess we'll be going. Will we see you again?" Anna asked, knowing she probably wouldn't get an answer.

"Trust yourself Anna. Handle what is in front of you and you'll be home before you know it."

Anna and Tedith reluctantly hugged Odin goodbye and made their way back through the station.

Several beings were already waiting in line when they arrived at the platform, including a yellow-bellied being that was as big as a hippo. Anna wondered how they would all fit in the pod.

The door to the pod opened. "Blue Realm, all aboard."

Anna and Tedith were the last to get on, right after the yellow-bellied being. The operator shut the doors. They could barely breathe it was so tight.

"Welcome," said the purple aardvark from his cramped corner, "I will be making several stops on the Blue Realm. I'll let you know when it's your stop. Anna and Tedith, you'll be the first two to get off."

Anna was grateful to hear this. Her face was squished against the arm-pit of a hairy crocodile.

The pod took off as if it were a rocket, and, thankfully, stopped after only a couple of minutes. The pod doors slide opened, Anna and Tedith tumbled out into pitch blackness. Before they could even thank the operator, the pod was gone.

"Wow is it ever dark. I can't even see my paw in front of my face."

Anna took a couple of steps. "Ouch," she cried out, rubbing her head. She explored, with her hands, the object she had banged into. It was flat, smooth, and long.

"I think it's a wall. Let's follow it, see where it goes." They ran their hands along the wall for several feet in one direction until they reached a corner. They continued to follow the wall, turning each time they came to a corner.

After the forth corner Tedith said, "We are back where we started."

"Yeah, we must be in a box."

"Well, there has to be some way out of here."

"I didn't feel anything resembling a door along the walls. Did you?"

"No, nothing."

"Maybe we should check the floor," Anna said as she got on the ground and began feeling her way along the smooth floor. After searching for a few minutes, Anna's hand hit a small object protruding slightly from the floor.

"I found something." Anna continued to explore the object with her hand. "I think it's a handle. Help me pull on it."

Anna and Tedith pulled up on the handle. A trap door opened and bright light streamed into the box.

Anna poked her head in through the trap door.

A roar of applause greeted her. "Bravo, bravo. Great, really great. Good work!" A roar of applause greeted her.

Below them was a room full of beings with very long necks covered in rings, heads as small as tennis balls, bulging eyes and long floppy ears. Their bodies were quite short but their arms and legs were long and slender.

Four of them moved under the trap door and stretched out a large tarp.

"Jump," one of them called out.

"What do you think, Tedith?"

"Well, they look friendly enough, besides this seems to be the only way out of the box."

"It's alright, you'll be fine," one of the beings yelled.

"On the count of three…" Tedith took hold of Anna's hand.

"One, two, three."

They landed safely in the middle of the tarp.

"Welcome. We are so glad you're here. I'm Rubon. You're Anna and Tedith, are you not?"

"Ah yes," Anna said, still amazed that people seemed to not only know who they were, but were expecting them.

"Good, good. You're right on time. We received a memo this morning telling us of your arrival. Did Marlin brief you about our lovely realm?"

"Well, he told us that we would have to have our wits about us," Anna said as she climbed out of the tarp.

"That's right. This realm will test your mental agility. You already passed the first test by getting out of the box. And I must say you did it in record time, beating the last record by twelve seconds. So, we are expecting big things from you on this level. You will encounter two more puzzles. There is no time limit. Complete them at your own pace. Of course, the sooner you complete them, the sooner you'll be ready for the next realm."

"But what about the Crystal Palace and getting home?" Anna asked, annoyed with all the distraction.

"I'm sorry, but I can't help you there."

Anna sighed, wondering if she would ever get home. "Okay, what do we have to do?"

"Now, now, it's not going to be that bad. Who knows, it may even be fun," said Rubon with a wink. For a moment, he reminded Anna of Odin, who always seemed to be winking at her.

"When you are ready, go through that door." Rubon pointed to a white door at the far end of the room. "The rest will be up to you."

As they made their way towards the door, an avalanche of good wishes accompanied them.

The door slid opened as they approached. Anna hesitated.

"It's okay, you'll be fine."

Anna took a breath and they walked through the open door. The door slid shut behind them.

They seemed to be in an outdoor corridor. The walls on either side of them were about six feet high. Above them was blue sky.

"Well, at least we don't have to figure out which direction to go. There is only one way to go," Tedith said, marching down the corridor.

The corridor made several turns until they encountered a wall that forced them to turn left or right.

"Which way?"

"Let's go right," Anna said.

It wasn't long until they came to a dead-end.

"It looks like we should have gone left," Anna said, turning around.

They twisted and turned their way along the corridor until another dead-end stopped them. They turned around and continued until the encountered yet another dead-end. Finally, after the umpteenth dead-end, Anna had enough and flopped onto the ground.

"This is useless. We are in a maze. We are walking in circles."

Tedith plopped on the ground next to Anna.

As they sat in silence Anna's thoughts turned to her mom and grandma. It must be very hard on them. First, Grandpa and now me. Anna had no idea how long she had been away. She didn't even know if her birthday had already passed. Anna's mom told her she could have a birthday party this year, which was a real treat. She never had a party before. Anna ached to go home, but first she had to deal with getting out of the maze.

Anna looked up into the clear blue sky. "I don't see how we are going to get out of here, no matter how much we walk."

Tedith jumped to his feet. "That's it. We aren't supposed to walk our way out of here. We are supposed to use our noodle to get out."

Anna looked at him somewhat hopefully. "You know what? I think you are right. Up until now, we have only been using our feet. We have to use our heads to get out of here. But how do you figure your way out of a maze?"

"I don't know but there must be a way." Tedith scratched his furry orange head hoping it would stimulate his brain cells.

A striking red bird flew overhead. It looked so carefree. As Anna watched the bird soar through the air, an idea started to take shape.

Their problem was they were on the ground. If they were in the air, like the bird, they could clearly see how to get out of the maze. It was all a matter of altitude. The higher you go, the more you can see. It was the difference between being on a mountain and seeing for miles, or being in a valley and seeing only what's in front of you. Being in the maze was like being in the valley. If they could somehow get higher they could see how to get out.

"Tedith, I've got an idea." Anna picked up her little orange friend and hoisted him high above her head. "Grab hold of the edge of the wall and pull yourself up."

Tedith grabbed hold and triumphantly pulled himself up.

"Wow, Anna I can see for miles!" Tedith exclaimed.

"That's what I was hoping, but can you see how to get out of the maze?"

Tedith studied the many twists and turns of the maze. "I think so, this way."

Tedith walked steadily along the top of the wall as Anna followed him on the ground below.

First, he turned left, then right, and then another right. After a dozen or so more turns Tedith said, "I can see the opening. It shouldn't be long now."

Sure enough, after a few more turns, Anna emerged from the maze. She reached up. Tedith jumped into her arms and gave her a little bear hug.

"That was great, Anna. You really used your noggin on that one."

"I couldn't have done it without you. We make quite the team. It would be terrible if I had to do all of this on my own. Thanks little buddy." Anna put Tedith down and surveyed their surroundings. The landscape was unremarkable except for one thing. On a hill, at the crest of the horizon, was an unusually-shaped building. Anna instantly recognized it from a school project she did on Japan. It was a pagoda.

It soared into the blue sky. Anna counted sixteen stories. Each story was topped with a gently arched roof that was slightly smaller than the one below it. There were detailed carvings on the corners of each roof, but they were too far away to see them clearly. What was most striking about the pagoda wasn't its size; it was that the pagoda was made of gold!

"Wow!" Tedith exclaimed, "Do you think it's real gold?"

"I don't know. Let's go find out."

They walked along a small, crushed stone path, through a meadow of sweet grasses blowing gently in the wind. The pagoda shone brilliantly as the sunlight hit it.

Even before they reached the building, Anna could sense the power of the pagoda. It seemed ancient and wise, like it might hold some secret or special knowledge.

As they approached, the carvings on the corners began to take shape. They were dragons, more specifically, heads of dragons. Anna did the math in her head. There were sixteen roofs, with four dragons per roof, which meant that there were sixty-four dragons. The size of each dragon-head corresponded to the size of the roof, with the largest dragons being on the first floor roof and the smallest being on the top roof.

Like the building, the dragons were made entirely of gold, except for their amazing eyes, which were the largest rubies Anna had ever seen. Even the smallest dragons had ruby eyes the size of ping-pong balls. However, what really fascinated Anna was that each dragon held a gold bell, encrusted in emeralds in its mouth.

Anna and Tedith stopped at the opening of the pagoda and

looked up in wide-eyed wonder.

"Why do you think there are bells in the mouths of the dragons?" Anna asked. "Do you think it has anything to do with the next puzzle?"

"I don't know but the pagoda sure is beautiful." Tedith reached out and touched the wall of the shiny gold building.

Anna was starting to get the hang of how things worked in *The Land Beyond the Clouds*. She realized that it wasn't so much about figuring out the future, it was more about dealing with what was in front of her. It took trust to believe that by handling the present, the future would take care of itself. The pagoda was what was on her path, so it was what she needed to deal with.

"Come on, let's go inside."

Anna and Tedith stepped through the arched entrance and waited for their eyes to adjust to the dark, cool interior. A staircase, leading to the other stories, ran along one wall. A large stone pedestal stood in the center of the pagoda. The pedestal had eight sides, which Anna recalled from geometry, was an octagon.

"What do you think the pedestal is for" Tedith asked as they walked towards it.

As soon as they reached it, a brilliant beam of light streamed down from above, onto the pedestal. The light startled Tedith and he stumbled backwards landing on his furry little behind. Anna stepped away from the pedestal to help Tedith and the room returned to darkness. "You okay, Tedith?"

"Yeah, I'm okay." Tedith said, more embarrassed, than hurt.

They approached the pedestal again. This time they were ready for the bright, white light.

The octagon was carved from a solid piece of white, almost translucent marble. Seven crystal prisms sat on the top of the pedestal. Each one reflected the light shining from above onto the walls of the pagoda. In science class last year, Anna had learned about prisms, so she wasn't surprised to see the reflection of light on the pagoda walls, but something wasn't right.

"That's strange," Anna said, studying the reflections.

"What is?" Tedith asked, walking over to one of the reflections on the wall.

"Well, in school when we shone a light on a prism, it reflected *all* the colors of the rainbow. Each of these prisms reflects only *one* color."

Tedith reached out and touched the red reflection on the wall in front of him. His orange fur glowed as it mingled with the intense red light.

Anna went to investigate the reflections for herself. Once again, as soon as Anna stepped away from the pedestal, the room went dark.

"Tedith, come over here and stand by the pedestal so I can take a closer look."

The room came to life again as soon as he approached the pedestal. Anna went up to the purple reflection and stuck her hand in it. Other than turning her hand purple, nothing special happened.

"Do you think the third puzzle has something to do with the reflections?" Tedith asked.

"That's what I am thinking, but what could it be?" Anna studied her purple hand.

"Maybe we are supposed to touch all the reflections," Tedith offered.

"Maybe." Anna wasn't convinced but decided to try anyway. She walked around the pagoda, touching each of the remaining colors; red, green, yellow, blue, dark blue and orange. As she suspected, nothing happened.

"Hmmm, maybe the puzzle has something to do with where the colors are. There are four on one wall, two on another wall and one color on the last wall. Each wall has half the number of colors of the previous wall. Maybe it has something to do with math." Math was not one of Anna's better subjects, so she decided to try something else.

Tedith put his paw over one of the crystals on the pedestal. Instantly, the orange reflection disappeared. "Do you think it could have something to do with making the reflections disappear?"

"I don't know but let's find out."

Both Anna and Tedith blocked the reflection of two crystals with their hands.

"The crystals are too far apart to cover all seven," Anna said, trying to maneuver her hands and arms in such a way that they covered more of the crystals.

"Wait, I have an idea." Tedith ran out of the pagoda and within seconds returned with four very large leaves from one of the nearby trees.

"You take these two and we will make a tent over the crystals."

They carefully positioned the leaves over the crystals, blocking all of the light. But, as before, nothing happened.

"Dang, I thought for sure that was it," Tedith said, obviously disappointed.

Anna carefully studied the pedestal and reflections. "We've got all the colors of the rainbow, right?"

"Yeah, if you say so," Tedith said, not exactly sure what colors make up a rainbow.

"Maybe the puzzle is about putting the colors together so they form a rainbow."

Tedith started to get excited. "You might be onto something, but how do we do that?"

"We've been focusing on the reflection, but maybe the crystals hold the key."

Anna gently lifted the crystal that reflected red light and placed it next to the crystal that reflected yellow. Red and yellow reflected onto the wall, overlapping a little. Then she picked up the green crystal and placed it next to the other two. She continued until all the crystals sat in a row. Now, on one wall, was one beautiful reflection, containing all the colors of the rainbow. As beautiful as it was, nothing happened.

"Something is not right," Anna said, examining the reflection. "I know! They are in the wrong order! The colors of a rainbow are always in the same order. But what order? I wish I had paid more attention in class."

Anna started to rearrange the crystals. Orange, blue, purple, red, yellow, green, dark blue. Nothing happened. Then she tried, blue, yellow, dark blue, green, purple, red, orange. Still nothing.

After several more combinations, Anna threw up her hands in frustration. "This is impossible. We could be here all year. Do you know how many color combinations there are?"

"No, how many?"

"I don't know exactly, but I know there are thousands of combinations," Anna sighed. "And we don't even know if this is the right puzzle."

They pondered the pedestal for a little longer.

"Maybe we should go see what is on the other floors of the pagoda. Maybe the puzzle is on one of the other floors."

As Anna turned towards the staircase she noticed there were letters carved into each side of the marble pedestal. One letter on each side. R, O, Y, G, B, I and V. The last side had an image of the sun carved into it, completing the eight-sided octagon.

"Look at these carvings, Tedith. Do you think they have anything to do with the puzzle?"

"Beats me." Tedith ran his paw over the sun carving.

Anna studied the carvings. "Well, there are seven letters and there are seven colors. Do you think that is a coincidence? Maybe the letters have something to do with the colors."

Tedith jumped in, "Maybe they tell the order of the colors. Let's see. 'R,' is red…'O,' is orange…'Y,' is yellow." Anna started to get excited. "'G,' is green…'B,' is blue, 'I,' is…wait, what color is 'I'? There isn't a color that begins with 'I.' And what about 'V'? There isn't a color that starts with 'V' either. Darn, I really thought we were on to something."

They stared at the crystals and the colors for a long time.

"I don't know, Anna, maybe the puzzle doesn't have anything to do with the crystals after all. Maybe the puzzle isn't even in the pagoda."

"It's gotta be this." Anna continued to study the problem. "Wait, I think I've got it. The dark blue color isn't dark blue at all."

"It isn't?"

"No, it's indigo, which is another name for a very dark blue…and purple isn't purple, it's violet! R-O-Y-G-B-I-V. The letters really are the order for the colors of the rainbow! Hurry, let's line up the crystals."

They carefully rearranged the crystals to correspond to each letter. Red, then yellow, then green. The colors glowed on the wall, as they overlapped a little with the colors beside them, just like how a rainbow's colors blend together. Tedith placed the blue and indigo crystal next. Anna picked up the violet crystal, the final piece needed to complete the rainbow.

"Okay, buddy this is it…"

A high-pitched shrill pierced the air. The sound shook Anna to her core. She dropped the crystal. It hit the cold, hard floor. It shattered into a million pieces.

"Donovan!" Anna scooped up Tedith and ran.

The pagoda once again returned to darkness as soon as they stepped away from the pedestal.

Anna headed for the staircase. However, instead of going up, she hid under it. It didn't provide much cover but it was better than nothing. Anna couldn't believe she had broken the crystal. How were they ever going to complete the puzzle now?

She peeked out to see Donovan's shadowy silhouette in the entranceway.

He slowly walked towards the pedestal. "Oh no," Anna thought. "As soon as he reaches the pedestal the room is going to be flooded with light and he is sure to see us."

Donovan was only a couple of steps from the pedestal. Anna crouched further behind the stairs, hoping against hope, that he wouldn't see them.

As Donovan reached the pedestal bright light flooded the room. As soon as the light hit Donovan, he screamed out as if in pain, as if the light was burning him. He stumbled backwards and fell to the floor. The room went dark.

"Curse you, Anna. I know you are in here." Donovan staggered to his feet.

Anna knew they couldn't stay there. Even in the dark, if Donovan got close enough he would see them.

Anna had no idea what to do, especially since they no longer had the crystal to complete the rainbow. She put her hand in her pocket and rubbed her lucky stone. If she ever needed luck it was now.

Donovan was making his way around the pagoda and was quickly closing in on their hiding place. If they were going to escape, they had to act now. She grabbed Tedith and ran, not towards the entrance, not up the stairs but towards the pedestal.

As soon as they reached the pedestal, the room once again flooded with light. Donovan cried out and covered his face as if hiding from the light. Anna placed her lucky stone next to the other crystals. "I only hope my stone is more crystal than stone," she thought.

Nothing happened. Donovan was starting to recover. Anna was about to run towards the entrance when a magnificent rainbow appeared on the wall. It glowed and slowly grew until the entire room was engulfed by its radiant colors.

Then the bells in the dragon's mouths began to chime in unison. They rang out in an ethereal, lyrical rhythm.

Donovan collapsed on the floor, covering his ears as if protecting himself from some terrible noise. The rainbow covering the walls started to swirl, the colors engulfed Anna and Tedith in a vortex. It felt like being in an eye of a hurricane, everything was still and strangely peaceful. The vortex lifted Anna and Tedith upwards. There was nothing Donovan could do but watch as Anna and Tedith once again slipped through his grasp. The vortex lifted them towards an opening at the top of the pagoda. As soon as they reach the opening, there was a flash of the brilliant white light. It was so bright that Anna and Tedith couldn't see anything beyond the light.

The light began to fade. Anna could feel that she was on solid ground once again. As her eyes recovered from the bright light she could see some colors, then some shapes. Where were they? No, it couldn't be. They were standing in the middle of the Amrak Station.

CHAPTER FOURTEEN

WAFER TOWN

Anna and Tedith jumped out of the way, just in time to avoid being hit by a vehicle piled high with luggage.

"Hey!" Tedith called out after the driver, "Watch where you are going. Where did you get your license, in a box of *Cracker Jacks*?"

"Come on, Tedith. Let's get out of the traffic lane." Anna led Tedith to a bench along one wall.

"Boy, that last realm was a real trip. I wonder how many more of these realms we have before we find the Crystal Palace."

"I don't know. It seems like there are an infinite number of realms. Worlds upon worlds, each one more bizarre than the last."

Anna surveyed the station, which seemed to be busier than usual. "There's Marlin. Let's go find out what time our next pod leaves."

Anna had slowly resigned herself to the fact that the only way home was through these weird worlds. She just hoped that there wouldn't be many more of them.

On their way across the station, a pink furry being approached them. "Excuse me, could you tell me which way the cafeteria is?" Anna tried not to stare but she wasn't doing a very good job. "Uh, uh," Anna stuttered as she realized the being wasn't made of pink fur, but of long pink, spaghetti-like noodles.

"Did you hear me?" the being asked, batting its long pink noodle eyelashes.

"Ah, yes, pardon me. It's over there between pods five and six."

Anna and Tedith watched as the spaghetti-being walked towards the cafeteria, leaving a slimy trail behind it, not unlike the type snails leave.

"Speaking of food," Tedith said as his tummy began to rumble, "It has been quite some time since we've had something to eat."

"I know, but we don't have any money left. Maybe there will be something to eat on the next level."

When they reached Marlin, he was talking to a small saucer hovering a few inches from his nose. Anna and Tedith realized that he wasn't talking to the hovering saucer but to the saucer's occupants. There were four tiny beings inside, each not much bigger than a grain of rice. Marlin turned to his ever-ready clipboard.

"Sinsand, Sinsand…Ah, yes, here you are. You are headed for the Pink Realm, it leaves from Platform Nine in, let's see…." He turned to the big clock that hung in the middle of the station, "it departs in twenty-two minutes."

The little folks said something to Marlin that Anna couldn't hear and flew off.

"Now, who do we have here? You two, back again?" Marlin said with a smile.

"Yes sir, it was another short journey but we didn't find the Crystal Palace," Anna said obviously disappointed.

"Well who knows, it might be on the next realm. Now, let's see where you are off to next." Marlin consulted his clipboard. "Uh, the Purple Realm. You're in luck. It leaves at 8:00 p.m. tonight." He glanced at the station clock, "Only ten hours and forty-three minutes from now."

"What? It doesn't leave for almost eleven hours?" Anna protested.

"Actually, you should consider yourself very lucky. This transport pod only departs once a year. It could have been worse, a lot worse."

"Wow, I guess so," Anna said. Anna's mom had tried to explain 'context' to her. Anna didn't really understand but now it made sense. Sometimes if you only have a little information, like, the pod leaves in eleven hours, it can seem like a long time. But when you have all the information, like, the pod leaves only once a year, you realize waiting eleven hours is a relatively short wait, not a long one.

"Do you have any suggestions as to what we can do until the pod leaves?"

"There is always the reading room. They have an excellent selection of newspapers and journals from all over inner-galactic space. They even have some books from my favorite author, RJ or, you could hang out in the cafeteria. They make an excellent chocolate lava cake," Marlin said.

"We don't have any money," Tedith said, holding his stomach as if that would stop it from grumbling.

"In that case, you could always go into town. There is a soup kitchen there. I am sure they would be happy to give two weary travelers a bite to eat."

"Really, you think so? Do you think they will have honey?" Tedith perked up.

"I'm not sure about the honey but I'm quite sure that you will be able to get something to eat. It's a short walk from the station. Leave through the main entrance and turn right. There is a path that takes you to the edge of town. From there it's only a couple of blocks. You will have plenty of time to get there and be back before your pod leaves."

They thanked Marlin and headed for the main entrance of the station. The large glass doors slid open as they approached. They entered a barren landscape of rocks, boulders, and some straggly vegetation. It was completely different from the landscape that was there when they had first entered the station so long ago.

As they began to walk along the path towards town, a loud sucking sound came from behind them. They turned around to see the Amrak Station being sucked into a tiny speck. The speck hovered in the air for a moment then vanished with a loud pop.

In horror, Anna ran to where the Amrak Station had once been. "Oh, no! How can a station vanish into thin air?"

Tedith was speechless. He watched Anna darting to and fro, as if somehow running around would make the station reappear. Finally, Anna stopped and stood silently beside Tedith.

"What are we supposed to do now?" Anna asked as she stared at the place where the Amrak Station once stood.

"I don't know. Maybe someone in town will know what happened to it." Tedith tried to sound reassuring.

"I hope so. We have to find it before our pod leaves."

The disheartened travelers headed towards town. Ugly trees loomed over the path. They passed a couple of pitiful looking avocado trees. They were throwing rotten fruit from their branches at each other and arguing over which avocados were best for making guacamole.

"Hey," Tedith yelled as he ducked just in time to avoid being hit by a particularly nasty piece of fruit.

The trees were so unpleasant that Anna was sure their guacamole would taste bitter.

When they first started their journey, yelling trees would have stunned Anna but she was getting more and more used to the strangeness of this land. Anna wasn't sure how long they had been gone. Time had a very different quality in *The Land Beyond the Clouds*, but she knew they had been gone a very long time.

Tedith's stomach continued to grumble as they walked towards the town.

"Uh, Anna, I mean, I know that we have to find the station, but do you think we could stop in the soup kitchen for a quick bite once we get into town?"

Anna couldn't help but smile at her little friend. No matter what predicament they found themselves in, Tedith could always eat. She was so grateful for him. She didn't know how she could have made it this far without him.

"I suppose so, but let's make it quick. Who knows how long it will take us to find the station."

"Look Anna, a sign."

Anna read it out loud. "Welcome to Wafer Town. Population 555 and ½. I wonder who the 'half' is." Anna continued reading. "In accordance with city ordinance 447392-B, scissors, hole punches, and matches are not permitted within town limits. How strange. Why do you suppose those item are prohibited?"

"Beats me. Do you think they call it Wafer Town because they make wafers here, you know, the little sweet ones your grandma keeps in the cupboard? Come on let's go. I can almost smell the soup kitchen from here," Tedith said as he ran ahead.

"Wait-up," Anna called out but it was no use. There was no stopping him when a meal was close at hand.

Anna noticed that a man was walking on the path towards Tedith. As soon as Tedith saw the man he stopped dead in his tracks.

"Good day, young fellow," the man said as he passed Tedith. Too dumbstruck to say anything, Tedith just stared at the man as he walked towards Anna.

What had made Tedith stop so abruptly? Anna wondered. Then she saw it.

The man on the path was of average height, had brown hair and wore a nicely-fitting suit. He looked normal in every way, except that he was flat. Flat as a pancake. Flat as an oatmeal cookie. Flat as a tire. When he turned sideways, he was so thin he almost disappeared. Although the man was nicely dressed on the front, his back was plain brown cardboard. The man was made out of cardboard! Little tabs on his clothing were folded over his shoulders and along his sides to hold his suit on, exactly like the cut-out dolls Anna had at home.

The cut-out man stopped and talked with Anna. Tedith couldn't hear what they were saying.

After the man had walked on, Tedith ran back to Anna. "Did you see that? He's made of cardboard."

"I know, amazing isn't it?"

"It sure is. What did he say to you?"

"I asked him if he knew where we could find the Amrak Station. He had never heard of it."

"Oh, that's too bad. Did you ask him anything else?"

"Nothing in particular. He was very nice," Anna teased, knowing what Tedith was getting at. "Oh all right. I asked him if he knew where we could find the soup kitchen. He told me it was at the

184

intersection of Paper and Pulp. At least now we know why it's called Wafer Town. People are as thin as wafers. It also explains why scissors, hole punches, and matches aren't allowed."

The town looked regular enough. There was a bank, grocery store, gas station, and a few houses with white picket fences and colorful flower beds. They saw several more cut-out people. Each was as thin as the last. They asked everyone they passed if they knew where the Amrak Station was. No one had even heard of it. Anna was getting worried. She had no idea how she was going to find the station. Anna knew she needed to trust and that somehow it would all work out, but it wasn't easy.

Anna heard Tedith's tummy growl and her thoughts turned to the soup kitchen. She wondered if it would be like the one where her grandpa volunteered. One Thanksgiving he took Anna there to help serve food. It was a real eye-opening experience for her. Entire families came to have a meal. After that, Anna became more thankful for what she had. Even if she did live in a small one-bedroom apartment in the city, they always had enough to eat.

Anna and Tedith soon arrived at the intersection of Pulp and Paper, but the only thing on the corner was a grand building with a large staircase and impressive white columns. An elegantly dressed cut-out woman, carrying a small cut-out poodle, walked down the staircase.

"Excuse me Madam, we are new to town and are looking for the soup kitchen," Anna said.

"Why, you are standing in front of it, my dear," she said, pointing to the grand building.

"This is the soup kitchen?"

"It certainly is."

The poodle started barking at Tedith. Tedith hid behind Anna. Ever since his run-in with Old Jed on the farm, Tedith stayed clear of dogs.

"Thank you Madam. If I could trouble you with one more question. You wouldn't know where the Amrak Station is, would you?"

"The Amrak Station? No, can't say that I have ever heard of it."

Tedith tugged at Anna's sleeve. "Come on, let's go in." The sooner he got away from that yappy poodle, the happier he'd be.

"Well, thank you."

"You are welcome my child. I hope you enjoy your lunch."

They walked up the grand staircase. A doorman in a blue uniform opened the ornately carved wooden door and bowed to them. Inside, a lavishly decorated foyer, complete with crystal chandelier, welcomed them. Soft classical music played in the background. Anna was pretty sure the music was Mozart's. He was Grandpa's favorite composer and he used to play his music all the time.

"Good day, Miss, I am Jeeves. I will be your Maître d'. How may I assist you?" Jeeves was wearing a black paper tuxedo and spoke with an English accent.

"Ah yes, ah, we were wondering if we could get something to eat?" Anna still couldn't believe this was a soup kitchen. The only other soup kitchen she had been at was in a humble church basement.

"But of course. Do you have reservations?"

"Reservations? No. No we don't." Anna nervously twirled her hair.

"Not a problem. Will just the two of you be dining with us today?"

'Ah, yes it's only the two of us."

"Very well Miss. Right this way."

"Excuse me sir but I think there might be a mistake. We were told this was a soup kitchen and, well, we don't have any money."

"Money? I see you are not from here. We don't use money in Wafer Town. Everything is free. Now, may I show you to your table?"

"I guess so...I mean yes, thank you."

Anna and Tedith followed cut-out Jeeves to a handsome wood-paneled dining room. Rich, blue velvet curtains hung from the windows. Each table was elegantly set with fresh flowers, crisp white linens, silver, crystal, and fine china. Elegantly dressed cut-out people occupied several of the tables. Anna had never been in such a fancy restaurant. She wanted to hide. She felt very much out of place in her jeans and sneakers. And of course, there was the small matter of her being round while everyone else was flat.

"Your table Mademoiselle." The Maître d' pulled out a chair. Anna had seen this in movies and quickly sat down. "Um, thank you."

Without missing a beat, Tedith hopped into the chair opposite Anna and seemed quite at ease. He was happy simply knowing that he would soon be fed.

"Your waiter will be here momentarily." He handed them menus embellished with gold. "I hope you enjoy your meal."

Tedith opened his menu and started to giggle.

"What's so funny?" Anna asked.

"You'll see."

Anna opened the menu. It was divided into three sections; appetizers, entrees and desserts. Under each section were a dozen or more selections, all of them soups! At least that explained why it was called a soup kitchen. Anna recognized many of the soups, such as Chicken Noodle, Cream of Mushroom, Tomato, and Beef Barley. They even had Ox Tail soup, which Anna hated but was one of her grandma's favorites. But, for all the soups Anna did know, there were twice as many that she had never heard of before. Such as, Hairy Owl Foot Soup, Toad Heart Warts Soup, Cream of Bees Knees Soup, Pickled Hummingbird Wing Soup, and Black Stone with Sauerkraut Soup.

"They certainly have the largest selection of soups I have ever seen."

"Wow, I don't believe it!" Tedith cried, almost jumping out of his chair.

"Shhhh, Tedith," Anna said, embarrassed as she noticed people watching his outburst.

"Look at the dessert section. They have honey soup on the menu! In fact, they have five types. Rose Petals with Honey, Chocolate Chip Honey, Honey Bubble Gum, Honey Soup with Peanut Butter, and Kittah Honey Soup. Hmmm, I wonder what that one tastes like. Can you believe it? What should I have?"

"Please Tedith, keep your voice down, people are looking," Anna pleaded, sinking lower in her chair.

Anna was taught that it wasn't polite to make a scene or to draw attention to herself, but Tedith couldn't contain himself. He had hit the jackpot, or more accurately, the honey-pot.

A tall, cardboard waiter sporting a black paper moustache and tuxedo approached them.

"Good afternoon Mademoiselle, I am Marco and I have the honor of serving you today. Do you have any questions regarding the menu?"

"This is our first time here and, ah, well, I'm not very familiar with all your soups," Anna said as she twirled her brown hair.

"We do have some extraordinary creations. May I suggest that Mademoiselle start with the Peapod and Cricket soup? It's a nice light soup with a little crunch. As a main course, I highly recommend the Kitchen Sink Soup. It's our specialty. People come all the way from Cardboard City for this soup. It's truly exceptional."

Anna crinkled her nose. "A soup made from a kitchen sink?"

The waiter laughed. "No, it means it has everything in it *but* the kitchen sink. For dessert, the Chocolate Mousse Soup is a must for a first-time visitor."

"Okay, that all sounds fine," Anna said, not quite knowing what she was getting herself into.

"And for you…" Marco began.

"I know exactly what I want," Tedith interrupted. I want to start with Chocolate Chip Honey Soup. For my main course I'll have Honey Bubble Gum Soup and for dessert I'll have the Honey Soup with Peanut Butter."

Anna started to turn red.

"…But all of those are from the dessert section," Marco said, a little flabbergasted.

"I know, isn't it great? Three different honey soups. I can't wait." Tedith was positively beaming as he handed the menu back to the waiter.

"Very well, your first course will be out shortly."

"Tedith…" Anna began but then couldn't bring herself to reprimand him. He was so happy.

It wasn't long until Marco returned, carrying a silver tray with two bowls of steaming soup. "I hope you enjoy the first course."

Tedith tucked his linen napkin under his chin and dug into the bowl of sweet honey.

"This is amazing soup. It is warm and smooth with the perfect amount of stickiness," Tedith said licking his spoon.

Anna was delighted at how good her first soup was as well. She even liked the crunch of the crickets. As they finished their last spoonfuls, Marco arrived with the main course.

Anna wasn't sure about this course, the Kitchen Sink Soup. It looked more like a chunky stew than a soup. She tentatively took a spoonful. The flavors exploded in her mouth. One moment it tasted like chicken noodle soup. The next moment it tasted like a rich Clam Chowder. Then it tasted like Tomato Soup. The riot of flavors somehow blended together perfectly. Anna could see why it was the house specialty. It was truly delicious.

Anna was finally feeling more at ease when their dessert course arrived. It made her smile from ear to ear. In front of her was bowl of warm white chocolate soup, in the middle stood a small dark chocolate moose. It wasn't chocolate *mousse* soup—it was chocolate *moose* soup. She bit off the antlers. Tedith was lost in his honey and peanut butter soup which he was sure came from heaven.

"Excuse me Mademoiselle," Marco said as he approached the table. "Is your name Anna?"

"Ah, yes it is," Anna replied, looking puzzled.

"You have a phone call."

"There must be a mistake. No one knows I am here. Are you sure it is for me?"

"The caller said I would know you because you would be with an orange teddy bear."

Anna looked puzzled. "Well I guess that would be me."

"Maybe it's about the Amrak Station," Tedith said hopefully.

"Please follow me Mademoiselle."

He led Anna to a guest phone in the foyer.

Anna hesitantly picked up the phone and said, "Hello."

A high-pitched, shrill blasted out from the receiver. Anna dropped the phone and ran into the dining room.

"Tedith we have to go."

"But I haven't finished my dessert."

Anna grabbed Tedith by the paw and pulled him from his chair. She didn't care if she was making a scene.

"Hey, what are you doing?" Tedith protested.

"I mean it, Tedith, we have to go *now*!"

Marco, seeing the commotion, came towards them. "Is everything alright?"

"I'm sorry but we have to go. The meal was wonderful, really," Anna said as she made her way towards the door.

"What's wrong?" Tedith demanded, once they were outside.

"Donovan. It was Donovan on the phone."

"No!" Tedith gasped. "How did he know we were here?"

"How does he *always* know where we are? We have to find the Amrak Station."

"How are we going to do that?"

"I don't know Tedith. I only know we can't stay here."

Across the street, standing by a bus stop was a cut-out man and woman with two children."

"Maybe the bus those people are waiting for goes to the Amrak Station," Anna said, crossing the street, desperate to get away before Donovan arrived.

"Look Ma, a round person," one of the kids said, pointing at Anna as she approached.

"Hush Scout, it's not polite to point."

"Excuse me. I see you are waiting for a bus. Do you know if it goes to the Amrak Station?"

"Amrak Station you say?" the man asked thoughtfully.

"Yes, have you heard of it? Do you know how to get there?"

"I heard a story once about the Amrak Station. But it was so strange; I thought it was only a story. I didn't think that it was real. You sure it's real and not some imaginary place?"

"It's quite real. We've been there several times."

"How about that, it's a real place. Well, I'm sorry but I can't help you. I always thought it was some make-believe place."

The bus pulled up to the curve, the door opened and the cut-out family climbed aboard.

"You getting on?" the bus driver asked Anna and Tedith.

"This bus doesn't go to the Amrak Station, does it?" Anna asked.

"Amrak Station? No, this bus goes to Metro Station in

Cardboard City. Are you getting on? I have a schedule to keep."

"Come on, Tedith, we can't stay here." They hopped on the bus, grateful that they didn't have to pay bus fare.

CHAPTER FIFTEEN

CARDBOARD CITY

Anna started to relax the further the bus got from the soup kitchen. The road was bumpy. It twisted and turned though a barren countryside.

Scout ran up and down the aisle of the bus. His parents tried to restrain him but he was not one to be easily restrained. The only other passenger on the bus was a cut-out teenager with a nose ring and green spiked hair that stood-up as if it was guarding the head it was growing out of.

Anna worried that they wouldn't find the Amrak Station in time; let alone locate the elusive Crystal Palace. There seemed to always be another obstacle in their way. Why did getting home have to be so difficult?

"Excuse me," Anna said to the bored looking teenager sitting across from them, "Do you have the time?"

He glared at Anna as if to say, 'How dare you speak to me?' He rolled his eyes and finally looked at his paper *Mickey Mouse* wristwatch. "It's ten minutes after twelve."

"Thanks."

"That means we have less than eight hours to find the station. I only hope someone in Cardboard City can tell us how to find the Amrak Station. I wonder how much longer until we arrive."

Tedith hopped down from his seat. "I'll go to ask the bus driver."

Anna watched as Tedith talked to the driver. She could tell something was wrong by the look on his face as he walked back down the aisle.

"What, what is it? What did the bus driver say?"

"It's another four hours, or more, to get to Metro Station, depending on traffic."

"What? Four hours? But..." Anna then stopped herself. There was no sense shooting the messenger.

Anna calculated the time in her head. They would have less than three hours to find the Amrak Station once they arrived in Cardboard City.

Anna began to doubt her decision to get on the bus. Maybe they should have stayed where they had last seen the Amrak Station. For all she knew, the bus was taking them farther away, rather than closer. On the other hand, she had to get away from Donovan. In life, it can be so difficult to know if you are making the right decision. Maybe there aren't right and wrong decisions. Maybe it just doesn't matter what you choose. Maybe all roads lead home and some are just longer and harder than others.

Anna resigned herself to the fact that there was nothing to do but see what happened when they arrived in Cardboard City.

After what seemed like an eternity of being jostled on the bumpy road, the bus turned onto a large super-highway. Cardboard City loomed in the distance. It seemed to spring out of nowhere, an island of skyscrapers, in a sea of barren land.

Anna lived in Canada's largest city, Toronto, but she had never seen anything like this. It reminded her of pictures she had seen on TV of New York City.

It wasn't long until the bus entered the city—block after block of buildings, cars, people, and noise. They made their way through the city at a snail's pace. Anna had never seen traffic like this. The foot traffic was equally heavy. Cut-out people were rushing to run errands, meet friends, or just go home, something Anna wished she could do. Everyone seemed to be in a hurry.

The bus stopped several times and each time cut-out people got on the bus. Every driver of every car seemed to be yelling or honking.

Anna wasn't a big fan of cities. She liked the country where her grandma lived much better. But, perhaps the city would have its advantages. Donavan might have a harder time finding them among all these people. And surely they would be able to find someone or something that could tell them how to get to the Amrak Station.

"Do you think we should get off?" Tedith asked, looking at the gridlock of traffic.

"No, not yet. The bus driver said this went to Metro Station. If anyone will know about the Amrak Station it should be someone at another station," Anna said, hoping she was right.

It seemed to take forever but the bus driver finally yelled, "Metro Station, end of the line, everyone off."

Anna and Tedith departed along with everyone else and found

themselves in front of a very large train station. It was old but quite striking.

Inside the station, people were rushing to catch their trains. Departures and arrivals were called over a loudspeaker, not unlike the Amrak Station. The big clock at the end of the station read 5:47 p.m., which gave them a little over two hours to find the Amrak Station.

Anna started to ask everyone they passed about the station. No one knew what she was talking about. Anna then noticed an information booth and headed towards it with Tedith in tow. If the people at the information booth couldn't help her, no one could.

"Amrak Station? Nope, can't say that I have ever heard of it. Let me check our master list. It contains all of the stations. "Amrak...Amrak, there is an Amtrak, is that it?"

"No, it's Amrak, A-M-R-A-K," Anna said impatiently.

"No, there is nothing here by that name. Sorry."

Anna and Tedith walked over to a bench and plopped down. As they watched people rushing to their destinations, Anna wished she could hop on a train that would take her to the Amrak Station, or better yet, take her home. Why did she have to go through all of this?

"What now?" Tedith asked, finally breaking the silence.

"We have to keep looking," Anna said.

"But look where? We've asked dozens and dozens of people but not one of them has a clue. I don't think asking more people is going to help us find the station."

Anna knew that Tedith was right. One of her mom's favorite sayings was, 'The definition of insanity is doing the same thing over and over and expecting different results.' They had to try something else. The only problem was Anna couldn't think of anything else.

"Come on, let's get out of here. One thing is for sure, we're not going to find it sitting around here."

The sun was low on the horizon. The tall buildings cast long shadows over the city.

"Which way?"

"I'm not sure it makes much difference," Anna said, looking up and down the street. "Let's go this way."

They made their way through a maze of people as they headed up the street.

After walking a half a dozen blocks, Tedith started to get frustrated. "Anna what are we doing? Where are we going?"

"I don't know Tedith. I was hoping to see something that would help us."

"My feet hurt." Tedith complained as he sat down on a large stone staircase that led to an imposing stone building.

Anna looked up at the building and the large carved stone sign above the entrance.

"Oh my goodness, that's it!" Anna scooped up Tedith and ran up the stairs two at a time.

"Hey," Tedith called out, "what's going on?"

Anna, too concerned about the ticking clock, ignored Tedith's protests and continued towards the building.

"I'm sure we will find our answer in here." Anna put Tedith down in front of two large commanding doors.

"Where are we? What is this place?" Tedith asked, following Anna into the building. Anna didn't need to answer. Tedith knew exactly where they were as soon as they entered.

"Wow, look at all these books!"

Even Anna was stunned into silence by the sheer scale of the library. She had never seen anything like it. Anna loved libraries but never imagined one could be so large. In the main room alone, you could have fit four or five of Anna's local libraries, and that was just on the first floor. The library had seven floors. "There must be a squillon books here," Anna thought.

"Where do we start?" Tedith asked, feeling more optimistic.

"Why the librarian, of course," Anna replied, confidently.

Anna had started her love affair with books when she was quite little. Her mom read to her almost every night. When she turned five, her mom got Anna her very own library card. Every other Tuesday after dinner they would walk to the bookmobile. At seven o'clock on the dot, the bookmobile would pull into a parking lot of an old strip-mall. Anna would sit on the floor in the children's section, flipping through the books while looking at the pictures and making up her own stories. Then, when Anna could read, she graduated to the thicker books, the ones that had more words than pictures. Her library card allowed her to take out three books at a time, which didn't seem nearly enough. Now, Anna regularly visited the library in her school as well as the public library which was a short bus ride from home. Anna was a furious reader and like her mom, she always had 'a book on the go'.

Anna loved the smell of libraries and this one was no exception. There was something quite reassuring about the somewhat musty smell of books.

Self-assured, Anna walked up to a tall middle-aged woman, who was sorting books behind a counter. She looked not unlike the librarian at school, except of course, she was made of cardboard.

"Excuse me, could you tell me where I might find books on stations?" Anna asked.

"Stations? What type of stations?" The librarian inquired, as she set down the stack of books she was sorting, and looked at Anna over the top of her paper reading glasses.

The question caught Anna off guard. "Ah, ah…"

"Train stations?" the librarian asked, trying to be helpful.

"No, no…it isn't a train station."

"What about a subway station. Is it a subway station?"

"No…it's not a subway station."

"Then is it a gas station or a weigh station?"

"No, it's...well, it's kinda hard to describe. It's a transport station. It's where beings go when they want to get to the next realm. It's full of glass pods."

"Glass pods?" The librarian looked at Anna as if she was a little crazy. "Can't say that I have ever heard of a transport station, but perhaps you will find what you are looking for in the transportation section. Do you know the Dewey Decimal System?"

Anna nodded.

"Good. Books on transportation start at 385, third row of books on your left, half-way down the aisle, on your right."

"Thank you." Anna blushed.

According to the large clock suspended from the massive ceiling, it was now 6:27 p.m., giving them only one and one half hours to locate, and get back to, the Amrak Station.

The transportation section had shelf upon shelf of books on every conceivable mode of transportation. There were the obvious categories, like boats, trains, trucks, and airplanes. Then there were books on more obscure modes of transportation such as hot air balloons, blimps, and hovercrafts.

There were hundreds of books to choose from. "I certainly hope I can find it in time," Anna thought.

Anna finally settled on three heavy 'general transportation' reference books and brought them to a large oak table, where a cut-out man was intensely studying one of the many books he had in front of him on 18th century composers. He looked up occasionally to jot down a note on the writing pad beside him.

Anna opened the first book to the table of contents and skimmed it for anything closely resembling transport stations. Nothing jumped out at her, so she turned to the index at the back of the book. It was twenty pages long. She carefully reviewed the index but nothing even remotely similar to the Amrak Station was listed. She then randomly flipped through the book, but nothing caught her eye. She repeated this with the two other reference books.

While Anna searched the books, Tedith sat quietly next to her, flipping through a dog-eared Dr. Seuss book he had picked up in the children's section. Before Tedith had been lost, Anna used to stuff him in her backpack and take him to the library with her. Of course, he wasn't alive then so he couldn't help himself to the books. He liked it when Anna would read out loud. Now, reading to himself was even better.

There was nothing of help in any of the books Anna had brought to the table. She returned them to their proper places on the shelf then carried several more reference books back to the table.

As she flipped through these new books, Anna kept glancing at the clock and the minutes ticking away. She was beginning to think coming into the library wasn't such a good idea after all. It might have been wiser to keep looking for the Amrak Station in the city. Anna made several more trips to the transportation section. Each time she returned with a stack of books which she carefully reviewed.

The lights in the library started to flash on and off. Anna looked up from her book and frowned.

"It means the library is closing in ten minutes," said the man who had been sharing their table.

Anna looked at the clock, 7:20 p.m.. "Wow, it's that time already?"

"Afraid so," the man said as he packed his papers into a leather briefcase.

"Now what, Anna? It's getting dark outside and we don't have any place to stay and nothing to eat."

"I don't know Tedith, I just don't know."

Anna wasn't ready to give up her search. There had to be some way to find the station in time.

"Excuse me, I couldn't help but overhear you say that you don't have any place to stay. A flat in the building I live in has just become available. It's a small one bedroom, fully-furnished apartment, quite charming actually. If you are interested I could take you there," the cardboard man said, putting on his paper hat.

"That is very kind of you but we can't afford an apartment," Anna said, looking into the kindly face of the man.

The man smiled, "Sure you can, it's free. Everything is free."

"Oh, I knew that was true in Wafer Town. I didn't realize that Cardboard City was like that as well."

"Yes, it makes life easier in some ways and more difficult in others," the man said thoughtfully.

Before Anna had gotten caught up in Candy Land, she would never have thought that having whatever you wanted would make life difficult, but now she knew how it could be true.

The lights in the library began to flicker again.

Anna sighed. She didn't want to admit it, but it was very unlikely that they would find the Amrak Station before the pod departed. They had only an hour left and they were no closer to finding the Amrak Station now than when they had begun. This meant they would need someplace to stay until they found the station.

"Well, I guess it would be okay to at least look at the apartment," Anna said reluctantly.

"Okay, let's go, before they kick us out of here." The man smiled. "By the way my name is Tom, Tom Bayer."

"Nice to meet you, Mr. Bayer. I'm Anna and this is Tedith."

"Please call me Tom."

"My building is only a few blocks from here," he said as they followed him out of the library. Anna wished she could bring some books with her but she didn't have a library card.

Although nightfall had quickly descended on Cardboard City, it still glowed from the many lights.

"This way," Tom said, turning left down the street. "So where are you two from?"

Anna hesitated. She wasn't sure how much she wanted to tell him. She finally said, "Toronto."

"Hmmm, never heard of it." Tom could tell something was bothering Anna and didn't want to push. He figured she'd tell him if she wanted to.

They walked in silence for a few blocks until Tom turned down a residential, tree-lined street, which seemed somewhat out of place in the middle of the city. It was also surprisingly quiet which was a welcome relief from the noise of the city.

"Here we are." Tom stopped in front of a lovely old brownstone. An alley cat was licking its paws on the stoop.

"Did you see that?" Anna said, staring at the cat.

"See what?' Tom asked.

"That cat just winked at me."

"I don't think cats can wink Anna, but who knows, stranger things have been known to happen."

Anna thought, "You can say that again. This whole place is stranger than fiction."

"Our little building has four apartments, one on each of the three stories and one in the basement, where the landlord, Mr. Zimmerman, lives. I live on the second floor. Miss Tercinne lives on the ground floor. She's a schoolteacher. The vacant unit is on the top floor. There isn't an elevator, but I can't imagine that will be a problem for you two."

Tom stopped by the front door and rang the buzzer for apartment 'A.'

"Yah, who is it?" a gruff voice called over the speaker.

"It's Tom, Mr. Zimmerman. I have someone here that is interested in the vacant apartment."

"What? At this time of night?"

Tom refused to respond to the rudeness of Mr. Zimmerman and waited silently.

"Oh, alright, I'll get the key and meet you there."

"Don't mind him. He's a little rough around the edges, but his bark is worse than his bite."

Tom opened the door with his key. Inside was a small, sparkling clean lobby. The floors were shiny black and white checkered linoleum tile. An oak staircase led to the other levels. On the wall was a row of mailboxes with the names of each tenant next to the apartment number. Anna noted the names of people who were to become her new neighbors. Apartment 'A,' Mr. Zimmerman. Apartment 'B,' Miss Tercinne. Apartment 'C,' Mr. Bayer. And finally apartment 'D'... Anna's mouth dropped open.

"Our names are already on a mailbox. Apartment 'D', Anna and Tedith." Anna said in amazement. "How can that be?"

Tom glanced over and smiled. "I guess it goes to show that you are supposed to live here after all.

"....but...how is that..." Anna stopped and sighed. There was little sense in trying to figure things out. So many things didn't make sense.

"That is where Miss Tercinne lives," Tom said, pointing to a door with a big 'B' on it.

Anna and Tedith followed Tom up two flights of stairs and waited in front of apartment 'D.' They could hear Mr. Zimmerman's footsteps and his grumbling from the stairs below. He was out of breath by the time he reached them.

Mr. Zimmerman looked Anna and Tedith over and grunted as he opened the door to the apartment.

Anna immediately took to the apartment. It had been recently renovated and everything was clean and fresh. It had high ceilings and shiny hardwood floors. There was a lovely bay window with tiny lead-cut glass. A small, eat-in kitchen was off to one side of the main living area. The bedroom was just big enough for a double bed and a dresser. The simple furniture looked brand new.

"I run a quiet building. No loud noise or music after 8 o'clock and ya gotta sign a one year lease."

Anna gulped as the reality of the situation sank in. It was now ten minutes after eight and the transport had left without them. They never should have left the station. Now they wouldn't get to the next realm until next year. That is, if they could even find the station. Anna was lost in her thoughts when Mr. Zimmerman's gruff voice snapped her back to reality.

"Well, ya want it or not?"

"I guess so—I mean, yes, thank-you, we'll take it. Can we stay tonight?"

"Tonight? Yah, I guess so. I'll bring the lease by tomorrow. Here are the keys." Mr. Zimmerman let himself out and grumbled all the way down the stairs.

"Well then neighbor, welcome. You should find everything you need, but if there is anything I can do, just let me know."

"Thank you Mr...I mean Tom. Tedith and I really appreciate it."

"No problem. I'll leave you to settle in. Goodnight."

Anna shut the door behind Tom.

"Wow, our own apartment, how great," Tedith exclaimed, jumping on the couch.

Anna sank into the easy chair. Tears began to stream down her face.

"Oh Anna, it's not that bad. You'll see, we'll find the station and in the meantime we have this really nice place to live."

"I know, Tedith," Anna said, trying to put on a brave face. "But a year is an awfully long time and I miss my mom so much."

"It'll go by quickly, you'll see. We have a whole city to explore and everything is free. Heck, we could go out to eat every night if we wanted to. Speaking of which, I'm hungry. I wonder if there is any food in here."

This made Anna smile. Leave it to Tedith to think of his stomach at a time like this. "Well, let's have a look."

Not too surprisingly, the cupboards and fridge were full of food.

"Oh boy, I'm going to have a honey sandwich."

"I think I'll join you."

CHAPTER SIXTEEN

THE SEARCH

It didn't take long for Anna and Tedith to settle in. They spent their days looking for the Amrak Station and exploring the many sights and sounds of Cardboard City

It finally became abundantly clear to Anna that she wasn't going to find the station by asking everyone she met. So she abandoned that strategy and concentrated on searching for the station on her own.

Anna kept a vigilant eye out for *The Loyal Forces of the Opposition*, but so far, there hadn't been any sign of them.

In the several weeks that they had been there, Tom had become a good friend. Tom was a professional musician; he played clarinet for the Metro Philharmonic Orchestra. He invited Anna and Tedith to a few of his performances. At home Anna mainly listened to pop music. Until she heard the Philharmonic, Anna had no idea that music without words could be so moving.

As Anna's friendship deepened with Tom, she felt she could confide in him and one evening she told him their whole story. How she had gotten to *The Land Beyond the Clouds*, how she was supposed to find the Crystal Palace and how she and Tedith had missed their transport pod to the next realm.

Tom just shook his head in disbelief. He assured her that he would do whatever he could to help her get home. True to his word, he joined them whenever he could in their search for the station. Tom had lived in Cardboard City his whole life and knew it like the back of his hand. Not only did he give Anna information that might help her find the station but also restaurant recommendations, directions to various sights, and shopping tips. He even told Tedith where he could get the sweetest honey.

Next to visiting the library, Anna liked visiting the museums the best, especially the Modern Art Museum. Tedith loved the stores the best, especially since he could go into any store and take whatever he wanted. At first Tedith took home almost everything he saw. It wasn't long before their little apartment was overflowing with kitchen gadgets, bath products, lawn ornaments—even though they didn't have a lawn—and honey pots in every shape and size. Luckily, the novelty of having everything he saw had started to wear off and Tedith could now go into a store without having to bring half of it home with him.

One evening, Tom invited them to his apartment for dinner. Anna heard it was polite to bring a gift. She had searched high and low for something that she thought he would like. At 6:00 p.m. on the dot Tedith rang the Tom's door bell.

"Welcome," Tom said as he opened the door. "Come on in."

They stepped into a disheveled living room. A misshaped couch stood along one wall, a coffee table was piled high with books. The walls were covered in watercolor paintings from a local artist that Tom fancied and in the middle of the living room floor was a small putting green. A vast array of golf clubs were scattered about. However, the main feature of the room was a state-of-the-art sound system. It was so large you could hardly move without bumping into it. Anna often heard music coming from Tom's apartment. Sometimes the floor to her apartment even vibrated.

"This is for you." Anna handed him the gift.

"Why thank you," Tom said, tearing off the wrapping paper.

"Wow, this is great." Tom quickly went over to his stereo and put the CD in the player. "I thought I had all of his recordings but I don't have this one. Thanks."

Tom adjusted the stereo. The sweet sound of Mozart's music filled the room.

"Can we help with anything?" Anna asked.

"No, you two make yourself at home. Dinner is almost ready."

Tom returned to the kitchen.

Anna looked for a place to sit, but except for the chairs around the dining room table all other seating was covered in sheet music. Anna walked over to a fish bowl by the window. It had two cardboard gold fish in it. Unfortunately, one was floating belly up at the top of the bowl.

"Dinner is served," Tom called out, carrying a big pan of lasagna to the table.

"It looks delicious," Tedith said.

Before they could take their seats the door bell rang.

"I wonder who that is. I'm not expecting anyone." Tom opened the door.

"Francesca! When did you get back? How was your trip? Come in, come in."

"I just got back. I had a great time but it was too short," said a pretty cut-out woman with thick brunette hair and an Italian accent.

"Yes, vacations always are," Tom agreed. "Well, you look great. Excuse me. Where are my manners? Francesca, this is Anna and Tedith, our new neighbors. Miss Tercinne is the schoolteacher I told you about."

"Buona sera, very nice to meet you both. How do you like our little apartment building?"

"We really like it."

Francesca noticed the set table. "I'm sorry. I am interrupting your dinner. Perhaps we can get caught up later, Tom."

"Nonsense, we haven't even started. There is more than enough. Please join us."

"Are you sure I won't be intruding?"

"Not at all. You can tell us all about your travels."

While they enjoyed dinner, Francesca told them all about her trip to Frenchville. To Anna it sounded a lot like Paris, even though she had never been to Paris. Heck, until now Anna had never been anywhere further than Ottawa.

"So Anna, tell me about yourself. What brings you and Tedith to Cardboard City?" Francesca asked as they began to eat dessert.

Anna hesitated.

"Go ahead Anna, tell Francesca. She might be able to help."

Francesca listened in amazement as Anna told her story.

"My goodness, so much for such a young girl. And this station, what's it called, Amrak? It disappeared into thin air and you haven't been able to find it?"

"Yes, and we've looked every place we can think of, asked dozens of people and have made several trips to the library but there is still no sign of it."

"And what about school?"

The question caught Anna off guard. "What do you mean?"

"We'll if you really are going to be here a year, you really should continue your schooling. What grade are you in, sixth?" Anna nodded.

"I am sure I could talk to the principal and get you enrolled in the school where I teach. The new school year starts next week."

"Oh, I don't know. I really should spend my time looking for the station. I have to find the Crystal Palace or I will never get home."

"That is all well and good but you shouldn't neglect your schooling. You wouldn't want to be held back a year when you get home would you?"

"I guess not." Anna wasn't at all convinced that going to school was a good idea.

"And we can all look for the station during the evenings and weekends."

"Yeah, but..."

"Anna, I really think this would be best. You can't spend all of your time wandering around the city."

"Okay. But…"

"Great, then it is settled. I will call the principal and get you enrolled," Francesca said, smiling.

Anna shrugged.

"It won't be that bad, Anna. I'll be with you and like Francesca said, you really should keep up with your schooling," Tedith said, sensing Anna's uncertainty.

"I'm sorry Tedith, but you can't go with Anna to school. Teddy bears are not allowed," Francesca said.

"Then I can't go," Anna said, defiantly. "Tedith and I are in this together. Where I go, he goes. If he can't go to school, I'm afraid I can't go either."

Francesca was about to object but she could see that there would be no changing Anna's mind on this matter.

"Okay. I'll see what I can do. I'll ask the principal for an exception."

The next evening, Francesca told Anna that she had talked to the principal, who had agreed to let Anna and Tedith attend school. Francesca gave them a list of supplies that they needed to get before school started.

Tedith was thrilled. He thought going to school would be great. Anna was less than enthusiastic. She was afraid going to school would be a waste of time. But she reasoned with herself that she could always drop out anytime.

Anna and Tedith spent the next few days gathering their school supplies, and wandered the city in the hopes of stumbling upon something, anything that would lead them to the Amrak Station. At one point, while they were in a stationary store, Anna had a sense that someone was watching her. She didn't see anyone but still worried that someone was following her.

On the first day of school, Tedith was finishing his breakfast of Rice Krispies with honey when there was a knock on the door.

"Come in," Anna called out.

"Hi," Francesca said as she opened the door. "Are you two ready?"

Anna nodded. She still wasn't sure that going to school was the right thing to do, but she also knew she could leave if it didn't work out. She did have to admit that Tom and Francesca had been great to them. They spent all of their spare time looking for the station.

Tedith, on the other hand, was just plain excited. He had always longed to go to school. He hated it when Anna left him on her bed each day as she went off to school. There was no one to play with. He sat there all day, bored, just waiting for her to get home. This was going to be great. He was sure of it.

"Can I bring my honey pot with me?"

Francesca laughed. "You won't need it Tedith. There will be lots of honey in the cafeteria."

Tedith beamed. A cafeteria! This was going to be even better than he had thought.

As they walked the four blocks to school, they noticed that the weather had started to turn. There was a little nip in the air, the first sign of autumn. The leaves would soon be changing color.

"Based on your special circumstances, the principal, Ms. Howard, has assigned you and Tedith to my class, Room 202. Isn't that wonderful?"

Anna shrugged. The first day of school was always awkward, especially in a new school. Anna wouldn't know anyone. Thank goodness Tedith would be with her.

They walked into a room that looked like every other classroom Anna had ever been in. A chalkboard ran along the front of the room. In the center of the room, twenty or so desks were arranged in a semi-circle.

"Why don't you take those desks?" Francesca pointed to two desks close to the front of the room.

It wasn't long until the room began to fill with the children who were to become Anna's classmates. Anna tried to be inconspicuous. Everyone was flat and made of cardboard except her and Tedith. Anna even sucked in her already flat stomach, in an effort to fit in better with the other students.

Tedith didn't seem to notice. He was too busy drawing pictures with the colored pencils and paper he had brought with him.

The children were all talking and giggling, getting caught up on what they had done during the summer.

A bell rang.

"Everyone take a seat, it's time to start," Francesca said, in her best schoolteacher voice.

After the room settled down, she wrote her name on the blackboard.

"Good morning, I'm Miss Tercinne and this is Grade 6. If you're not supposed to be in Grade 6, you have my permission to leave now." The class giggled. "I would like to welcome two new students to our school. Tedith and Anna, please stand up. Tedith jumped to his feet. He loved being the center of attention. Anna, on the other hand, preferred to stay in the background. She blushed as she slowly rose to her feet.

"I expect you all to make them feel welcome."

A hand shot up in the air. It belonged to a boy with wiry paper hair and a sharp cardboard nose.

"Yes Warren, what is it?"

"She's round and he is a teddy bear." The class erupted into laughter, which was exactly what Warren was hoping for. Anna turned an even deeper shade of crimson and sank into her seat.

"Okay, that will be enough. Everyone calm down."

Francesca then glared at Warren. "Why Warren, how very observant of you," Francesca said sarcastically. "Hopefully, you will be able to turn your keen intelligence into higher marks this year." The class snickered.

"Alright, everyone settle down. Get out your English books and turn to page twenty-one."

The morning went quickly as they studied grammar, one of the few subjects Anna didn't like.

The bell rang for recess. "I'll see you all back here in fifteen minutes." Francesca said.

The schoolyard was abuzz with activity. Children were playing tag, skipping rope, bouncing balls, and swinging bats. Not only did

Anna not know anyone, but as Warren so accurately pointed out, she was the 'round' kid in a schoolyard of wafer-thin kids. She stayed close to the brick schoolhouse, twirling her hair, trying not to stand out more than she already did.

A large rubber ball landed by Anna's feet. A girl, with a mane of long, curly hair the color of pumpkin came chasing after it. Anna picked up the ball and handed it to her. Anna had noticed her in class. She had never seen so many freckles of one face and thought it would take a long time to play 'connect the dots.' She reminded Anna of a noble lion.

"Hi. I'm Debbie, where are you from?"

"Ah, Toronto."

"Never heard of it. Wanta play?"

"Sure."

"Me too!" Tedith piped in.

The three of them played dodge ball as if they were old friends. It wasn't long until the bell rang, calling them back into class.

"That was fun! Wanta have lunch together?"

"That would be great." Anna began to warm up a little more to the thought of being in school.

The rest of the morning went by uneventfully. Anna was afraid she wouldn't be able to keep up but the school work wasn't difficult. She glanced over at Debbie several times. Each time she was biting her nails. Anna was afraid she would be down to her knuckles before lunch.

The bell rang and the class quickly filed out. Debbie waited for Anna and Tedith in the hallway. "This way." Debbie led them down the halls.

"You got any brothers and sisters?" Debbie asked, as they stood in the cafeteria line.

"No, it's only me and my mom. How about you?"

"Yeah, I got a brother and three sisters. They're a real pain. They are always taking my things and picking on me." Anna was surprised to hear this. She always thought it would be great to have a brother or sister; someone to play with and share your secrets. It was lonely at times, being an only child. I guess everything has its good and bad points.

It was now their turn to order. "I'll have a hamburger, French fries and gravy, and a cream-filled chocolate donut," Debbie told the lady standing behind the cafeteria counter who was wearing a paper hair net. "Wow," Anna thought, "I guess one of the advantages of being a cut-out person is you could eat whatever you wanted and not put on weight."

"I'll have the same," Anna said, smiling at Debbie. "This school thing isn't all that bad after all," Anna thought.

Not surprisingly, Tedith ordered honey sandwiches for lunch— four of them.

Over the next few weeks, Debbie and Anna became inseparable friends, spending every recess and lunch together. Debbie showed Anna the ropes and introduced her to a few of her other friends.

Debbie took a real liking to Tedith. She would tickle and tease him and even smuggle honey-sesame treats into class for him. You weren't supposed to eat in class, but Francesca turned a blind eye as Tedith munched away, while trying his best to hide it. Anna was actually enjoying school, except for Warren, who teased Anna every chance he got.

Every day, right after school, Anna and Tedith would run off in search of the Amrak Station. Tom and Francesca often joined them in their quest. Debbie usually wanted to play after school but Anna told her she couldn't. She was always vague as to the reason why, just saying that she had other things she needed to do.

Francesca asked several professors she knew from the local

university about the Amrak Station. Tom called the transport commissioner of Cardboard City, but even he hadn't heard of it.

Sometimes Francesca wondered if Anna hadn't made the whole thing up, but she couldn't explain why Anna was round when everyone else was flat. Obviously, she had to be from somewhere else. But from where? And how could a station vanish into thin air?

One day during lunch, Debbie was very quiet, which wasn't like her at all. She was always talkative and ready to play.

"Is something wrong?" Anna asked, concerned about her friend.

Debbie shook her head from side to side.

"Come on Deb, if there is something wrong, you can tell me," Anna encouraged.

"Yeah, right. Like you tell me everything? Every day you run off right after school and all you say is, 'I have things to do.' Whenever I ask about your mom or your old school, or even where you live, you change the subject. It's like you've got some sort of secret life. I don't even know why you are round and everyone else is flat. Not that it matters, I mean, I don't care that you are different, I would just like to know why."

Anna thought about what Debbie had said. "You're right. There is a whole bunch about me that you don't know. Are you sure you want to hear about it?"

"Of course I do. I'm your best friend, aren't I?"

Anna couldn't deny that. Debbie was her best friend and she deserved to know the truth. Anna started at the beginning and in one breath told Debbie all about Jacob's Ladder, Odin, *The Loyal Forces of the Opposition*, the elusive Crystal Palace and how the Amrak Station disappeared into thin air. She ended with how she met Tom and started going to school.

Debbie listened carefully; most of the time with her mouth

wide open. Anna was afraid Debbie was going to catch a fly. Even after Anna had finished her story, Debbie was too shocked to say anything.

"Debbie? Debbie, are you all right?" Anna shook her a little.

"Yeah, yeah I'm fine… it's…well, I mean, I had no idea."

"I know. That is why I didn't tell you. It's unbelievable…it's also very scary. What if I can't find the station? I'll never get home…or see my mom again." Anna started to choke up.

"It's okay, Anna, I am sure you will find the station before the next train leaves."

Anna smiled. "It's not a train. It's a pod, a transport pod."

"Whatever it is, I am sure you will find it."

"That's what I thought in the beginning but I am not so sure anymore. We have been here for almost nine months and there is no sign of it anywhere."

"What about this Odin guy? Maybe you should contact him."

"I don't know how. He shows up when he shows up. I haven't seen him in quite some time. I like him and everything but even when he appears he's not particularly helpful. Usually he says a few cryptic sentences, that I don't understand, then disappears."

"What does he say?"

"Well, let's see. He told me that everyone has to find their own way home and that there are as many paths home as there are people. I mean, what am I supposed to do with that? He also told me to follow my heart because it would lead me home. And if I fall off my path, to get right back on." Anna sighed. "I'm sure he means well, but I don't know what to do with what he tells me. For all I know, he is sending me on a wild goose chase."

They sat silently pondering Odin's words when the bell rang, signaling the end of the lunch.

When they returned to class, Warren was holding court. He had captured a frog, a cardboard frog, but a frog nevertheless, and was jabbing it with a pencil to make it jump.

Anna was horrified. "Stop that, stop it right now." Anna ran up to Warren and scooped up the frog, surprising everyone, including herself with her bravery. Warren was the class bully and almost no one stood up to him.

The little frog was trembling; it was no more than a baby.

"Give me back my frog," Warren yelled, as he lunged at Anna, who quickly moved out of the way.

Anna ran to the back of the room with Warren in hot pursuit. He chased Anna as she held the frog around the classroom. The students were in an uproar, cheering Anna on.

"What is going on in here?" Miss Tercinne hollered as she entered the chaotic classroom. Everyone froze.

"Warren was jabbing a frog with a pencil and Anna rescued him," one of the students explained.

"Warren, is that true?" Miss Tercinne asked, already knowing the answer.

"I don't know what the big deal is. It's only a frog."

"This is the last straw, Warren. You have done nothing but disrupt this class from the moment you stepped into it. You have detention for a month, and if I ever even hear about you being cruel to an animal again, you'll be suspended. Do you understand me?"

Warren was going to object but he could see how angry Miss Tercinne was and decided to keep his mouth shut, for once in his life.

"Answer me, Warren. Do you understand me?"

"Yeah, I understand you."

Miss Tercinne then turned her attention to Anna. "Let me see the frog."

She gently took the frog from Anna and examined it. "It looks okay, just shaken up. Poor little fella. Warren you should be ashamed of yourself."

Anna, you and Debbie take the frog to the creek behind the playing field and release it. Tedith, you can go with them. Come right back, we have math next."

Anna gingerly took the frog from Miss Tercinne.

"Can you believe Warren? How could he be so mean?" Debbie asked when they were outside of the class. "You were really brave to take him on."

"I can't bear to see animals being hurt." Anna stroked the little frog.

They walked through the sports field towards the small creek. The little frog kept looking at Anna as they walked.

"It's strange but this frog looks familiar to me," Anna said, staring at the frog.

"Like you have seen it before?" Debbie asked.

"No, not like that, but it reminds me of someone."

The frog then winked at Anna.

"Did you see that?" Anna exclaimed.

"See what?" Tedith asked, trying to get a closer look at the frog.

"It winked at me."

Debbie laughed and said, "Frogs can't wink."

"I swear, when I said it reminded me of someone, it winked at me."

"Okay, if you say so." Debbie was not convinced.

They reached the tiny creek, which wasn't much more than a slow trickle of water.

"There you go, little fella." Anna placed him on a rock by the water. "You're safe now. Go on."

The frog didn't budge.

"Do you think it's hurt?" Tedith asked.

"I don't know. Go ahead, little guy, it's alright," Anna said, in her most convincing voice.

"Ribbit, ribbit," the frog replied.

"Well at least he can talk," Debbie said. "Maybe we should get a stick and give him a little shove."

"Okay, but let's be gentle, he's been through enough." Anna reached down and picked up a stick. She tenderly touched the frog with the end of it.

The frog started to twitch, then jerk back and forth. With each jerk, the frog became larger and larger.

"Holy-moly," cried Debbie at the ever expanding frog.

They watched as the frog grew bigger and bigger until it was the size of large dog. Then it started to puff out like a balloon someone was blowing up. Its skin was stretched so thin they were sure the frog was going to explode.

"Run for cover," Debbie yelled.

They jumped behind a rock and waited for the frog to burst. Instead, it floated a few feet off the ground. It was a giant frog balloon.

"Ribbit," the frog said again.

"Geez-Louise! I thought the frog was going to bust for sure," said Debbie, coming out from behind the rock.

"This is freaky." Tedith stepped towards the frog to have a closer look.

Anna was the last to emerge from behind the rock.

"Tedith, no!" Anna yelled, as Tedith reached out to touch the frog but it was too late. The frog exploded as soon as Tedith touched it.

Odin stood before them, smiling, as if what had happened was the most natural thing in the world.

"Anna, Tedith, so nice to see you again. This must be Debbie. It's a pleasure to make your acquaintance."

"Odin! You scared the daylights out of us," Anna said, not sure if she was more relieved or mad at him for appearing this way.

Odin just held open his arms and without thinking Anna flung herself at him and started to cry.

"It's okay, little one. It's okay," Odin said, stroking her hair.

Anna couldn't contain herself. "It's just that we left the station 'cause we were hungry, and the station disappeared, and there was this soup kitchen, and Donovan, and everyone is flat, and we got on a bus, and we missed the transport pod, and now I'm in school, and the station is nowhere to be found and…and…" Anna sobbed.

"There. There. Everything is fine," Odin said.

"It's fine? How can it be fine? If I don't find the station I'll never get home."

"I see. Well then, you really are in a pickle, aren't you?" Odin smiled.

"…but you just said everything is fine."

"Well, I think it's fine, but obviously you don't, so it mustn't be fine."

"See, like I told you, he is always talking in riddles," Anna said, turning to Debbie who was still standing there too stunned to move or talk.

"Hello, Tedith, it's good to see you. How are you?" Odin patted Tedith on his head.

"Hi Odin, I'm great. Did you know you can get whatever you want here and it doesn't cost anything? And the honey, oh the honey, I never knew bees made so many kinds. I must have had twenty different types so far and I still haven't even come close to trying them all. We have this great apartment and I'm going to school. Can you imagine me in school?" Tedith could barely contain his excitement.

"Well, Tedith, it appears you are faring far better than your young mistress here."

Anna wiped her eyes. "I'm sorry, I don't mean to complain, but

I don't know what to do. We've been looking for the station for months and there is no sign of it. No one has ever heard of it. I don't think there is any hope we are ever going to find the station, which means we are going to be stuck here… forever."

"I see. And you have looked everywhere for the station?"

Anna nodded.

"…and it is nowhere to be found?"

Anna nodded again.

"Well then, I guess I would have to agree with you. It doesn't sound like you are going to find the station. It all sounds quite hopeless."

Anna could barely believe her ears. "Does that mean we are stuck here?"

"I didn't say that. I said that it doesn't sound like you are going to find the station."

Anna looked at him slyly. "What are getting at?"

"Well, if it were me, I would ask myself what it is that I really want."

Anna frowned as she pondered what Odin was saying.

"Well, what I want is to find the Crystal Palace," Anna said.

"Is it?" Odin asked.

"Well, no. What I *really* want is to go home." Anna was starting to understand what Odin was saying. "I have been spending all my time looking for something that I *think* will get me home. Instead of focusing on getting home, I have been focusing on the station. I got so caught up in getting back to the Amrak Station that I lost touch with what I really want, which is to go home."

"My, my, you are a clever one. Maybe you are learning something at that school you are attending after all." Odin smiled. "Well, I see I am done here. Debbie, it was a pleasure to meet you," Odin said, bowing slightly towards Debbie.

Debbie, still too stunned to say anything, only nodded.

Anna was about to protest. Even if she now knew to focus on 'getting home' and not the Amrak Station she still didn't have a clue what to do next. But before she could say a word, Odin touched Anna on the tip of her nose with the crystal on the end of his walking stick.

Just before Anna and Tedith vanished, they heard Debbie call out, "Have a light-filled journey."

CHAPTER SEVENTEEN

ZEEBEE

Tedith was jumping up and down. "Look where we are! That Odin, he sure is a tricky one. How do you think he does that?"

"I don't know. I'm just happy he does," Anna said. "It's kinda weird though. As soon as I understood that I was focused on the wrong thing—the station, instead of going home—we were back in the station."

"Yeah, maybe sometimes you don't actually need to *do* anything. Maybe you only need to change what you are *focusing* upon."

Anna turned to her little friend. "Why Tedith, that is awfully profound of you."

Tedith blushed. "Now what? According to Marlin our pod leaves only once a year, which means we still have to wait for more than three months."

"I don't know. I hope there is someplace to stay in the Amrak Station because there is one thing for sure, there is no way we are leaving the station again," Anna said, quite determined. "Oh no…"

"What? What's wrong?"

"I just realized we didn't get a chance to say goodbye to Tom or Francesca. And what about Debbie? We left her standing there. We probably will never see any of them again. I never thanked them for everything they did for us."

Anna really did want to get home but she also realized there were people in that strange world she was going to miss.

"I'm sure they will understand, especially when Debbie explains to them what happened."

"Yeah, I guess so. It's still sad. I'm going to miss them."

"Yeah, me too. Look there's Marlin," Tedith said, pointing to the ever-present Transport Director. "Let's tell him we are back. Maybe he knows where we can stay until our pod leaves. There is also the problem of food. What are we going to eat? Food isn't free here."

Tedith was right. They were going to need a place to stay and food.

They walked the short distance to Marlin. He was explaining to a family of orange-bellied tadpole-like beings where to catch their next transport pod.

"Anna and Tedith. How nice to see you so soon."

"Soon?" Anna said surprised." We have been gone for almost nine months."

"Really, has it been that long? Time does fly here around here. So tell me how did you like the Purple Realm."

Anna looked puzzled. "We haven't been on the Purple Realm

yet. Don't you remember? We were hungry so we left the station to get something to eat. And well, it's a long story but we missed our transport pod. Now we have to wait another three months for the next pod. The only problem is we don't know where to stay or what we are going to..."

Before Anna could finish, Marlin started to laugh, one of those great big belly laughs.

Anna was annoyed. She couldn't imagine what was so funny. They had wasted months being lost and not making any progress in getting home. Anna thought it was just plain rude for Marlin to be laughing at their misfortune.

Marlin took off his glasses and wiped away his tears of laughter. "Excuse me, I don't mean to laugh, but you were on the Purple Realm the entire time. You have successfully completed that Realm."

Anna was astonished. "But, we never took a transport pod."

"Yes, the Purple Realm is a sneaky one. You can get into it many different ways. When you left the station, did it disappear?"

Anna nodded. "Yes, as soon as the door shut, the station disappeared. I was horrified."

"Well, from that point on, you were on the Purple Realm. You are back here, so that means that you now ready for the next realm. " Marlin beamed at them.

"Really, you mean all that time in Wafer Town and Cardboard City wasn't wasted?"

"Wasted? No, not at all, you were right where you were supposed to be, doing exactly what you needed to do, and learning what you needed to learn," Marlin assured Anna.

"Wow Anna, did you hear that? We completed the Purple Realm and all this time we thought we were lost. Thanks Marlin, that's great." Tedith gave Marlin's kneecaps a big hug.

"You are most welcome."

Marlin flipped through his clipboard. "Let's see. You will be visiting the Gold Realm next. Your pod leaves from Platform Eleven at 11:11 a.m., exactly three hours and thirty-three minutes from now. While you wait, may I suggest you visit our reading room? We have a lovely selection of books and magazines. Take the spiral staircase next to Platform Eleven to the second floor."

"Thanks Marlin," Anna said.

"I hope you have a wonderful journey. Who knows, this might be the realm where you find the Crystal Palace."

As they walked towards the reading room, they passed the usual assortment of beings. They didn't seem to be so strange to either of them now. It's funny how things that are so strange to you when you first encounter them seem perfectly ordinary once you have been around them awhile.

Tedith's stomach rumbled as they passed the cafeteria. He looked up at Anna sheepishly. "I can't help it. It smells so good."

"I know, but those four honey sandwiches you had for lunch are going to have to keep you going for a while longer. Besides, we don't have any money. Come on, let's go see what they have in the reading room. Maybe they will have that issue of National Geographic you like so much—the one about honeybees."

When they got to the top of the spiral staircase, Tedith jumped on the banister and slid all the way down, landing on his behind with a gentle thump. Anna looked down at him and shook her head.

"I'm coming," Tedith said, scurrying up the steps.

"Only Tedith," Anna thought, "can find fun in something as simple as a set of stairs."

The reading room had a large assortment of magazines and a few rows of books. In the center of the room was a large table with wooden chairs. Nestled around a coffee table were four worn but comfortable-looking easy-chairs.

Anna wandered over to the young readers section and browsed through the titles, most of which she had never seen before. She selected a couple of books and settled into one of the easy-chairs. Next to her was an interesting being, covered with eyes. Anna wondered if the eyes he was sitting on were closed; she certainly hoped so. She also wondered if he could read faster because he had so many eyes.

Anna opened the first book, *The Adventures of Spudkinakins*, and began to read. Tedith had a cookbook and was drooling over a photo of a triple chocolate layer cake.

As Anna read, her eyes started to get heavy. She liked to read in the comfort of her bed before she went to sleep. Anna's mom would often find her fast asleep with a book in her hands, with the bedside light still on.

Anna tried to keep her eyes open but the words on the page were lulling her to sleep. It wasn't long until she nodded off.

The soft sound of flutes playing filled the air. Anna gently stirred from her slumber. The music was wonderfully soothing, like angels playing for all who could hear. Anna was so taken by the lovely sound it took her a moment to realize she was no longer in the reading room. She jumped to her feet and ran around in a panic calling "Tedith! Tedith!"

"I'm over here."

Anna was relieved to see Tedith running towards her. "What happened? Last thing I remember was reading."

"I don't know. One minute I'm looking at a picture of butterscotch pudding and the next minute I hear you calling me."

"Oh dear, what have I done?"

The music faded as Anna took in her surroundings. They were standing on the side of a mountain and there were mountains and valleys as far as the eye could see. Wildflowers covered the ground, filling the air with a delightful fragrance that wasn't quite jasmine, and wasn't quite honeysuckle. It was something even more exquisite.

Anna sensed there was something special about this place. The air was clearer, the sun was warmer, and the colors were brighter. Everything was vibrant and alive.

It wasn't simply how the place looked but how it felt. It reminded Anna of how she felt when she touched the first rung of Jacob's Ladder, so very long ago. She had no idea when she took that one step, that it would lead her on this most incredible journey.

She wondered if she had known, if she would have climbed the ladder. The answer didn't manner. What did matter was that she was where she was and that she had to keep going. She desperately wanted to get home. She no longer cared that she lived in a tiny apartment or that money seemed scarce. There were more important things, like her mom and school and her friends.

"Look!" Tedith said, pointing into the distance, "Over there."

Far in the distance, over many valleys and mountain peaks something sparkled in the bring sunlight.

The sight of it took Anna's breath away. "It's the Crystal Palace."

"It is?"

"Yes, I'm sure of it. It's identical to the one I saw when Sidea asked me to close my eyes. But wait. If that's the Crystal Palace then we must be on the Gold Realm. This world is amazing. You fall asleep on one level and wake-up on the next. I thought I had messed up again."

Anna gazed at the palace and it seemed to beckon her. She watched as the sky thickened and the Crystal Palace disappeared in a shroud of clouds. Anna hoped that wouldn't be the last time she saw it.

"But how are we going to get there?" Tedith asked. "It must be a squillon miles away!"

"I don't know, Tedith, it certainly is a long way off, but we haven't come this far to give up now."

"Look at all those mountains. How are we ever going to get over them? And what about food, we don't have any food."

"Tedith, don't tell me you are turning soft on me." Anna said, feeling a renewed sense of optimism. "I don't know how we are going to make it. I only know that we are. Grandpa used to say, 'The longest journey begins with the first step.' So let's get started. Based on the position of the sun it must be early afternoon. Let's see if we can make it to the bottom of the mountain by dusk."

They meandered down the gentle mountainside through the meadow of flowers for the better part of two hours. Even though going downhill was easy they were still a long way from the bottom of the mountain.

"Let's stop here and rest," Anna said as she plopped on the ground.

Tedith was only too happy to stretch out on a cushion of flowers. Even though the sun was warm, there was a nip in the air. And although the wildflowers were lovely, they were beginning to fade. Anna suspected that they were approaching autumn.

"How long do you think it will take us to get to the Crystal Palace?" Tedith asked, chewing on a piece of long grass.

"A long time. We are only part-way down the first mountainside and there must be a dozen more mountains between us and the Crystal Palace."

"I'm thirsty," Tedith said.

"I know; me too. Maybe we will find some water at the bottom of the mountain."

A pair of green eyes was watching them from the cover of the long grass. It slithered towards the two unsuspecting travelers.

Anna shrieked, as a pure white snake emerged from the tall grass.

"Oh excuse me, I didn't mean to scare you," the snake said in the most polite fashion.

Anna was too flabbergasted to speak. The snake was as long and thick as a fire hose. Its white scales glistened in the sunlight. It was actually quite beautiful, once you got over the fact that it was a snake.

Sensing that it wasn't welcome, the snake turned and began to slither away.

"No, wait. I'm sorry. You caught me by surprise. Please stay."

The snake turned back towards them. "I'm Zeebee," the snake said, giving a little bow. Tedith chuckled. He had never seen a snake bow before.

"If you don't mind me asking, what brings you to these parts? We don't get many visitors."

"We are trying to get to the Crystal Palace," Anna replied.

"I see. Trying to get home, are you?" Zeebee asked, much to Anna's surprise.

"Why yes, how did you know?"

"It's the only reason to go the Crystal Palace."

"Really?" Anna questioned, twirling her hair. It wasn't often one spoke with a snake and she found it to be a bit unnerving. "I thought the Crystal Palace was unique to my journey."

Zeebee laughed, which sounded more like a hiss. "It is. Just because the path is the same doesn't mean the *journey* is the same."

Anna felt as if she was listening to Odin, who always talked in riddles.

"Ever notice that two people can do exactly the same thing and have two completely different experiences? Consider riding a roller coaster. One person can feel exhilarated, while another person can feel like throwing up."

Anna didn't care about any of that. She just wanted to get to the Crystal Palace.

"Anyway, I'm afraid you not only have a very long journey ahead of you, but you are not going to be able to start until spring."

"Spring! What do you mean?"

"The snows will be coming in a few weeks, making the mountain trails impassable. After the snow has melted, in the spring, the trails will be clear enough to travel. Don't worry. I have a place you can stay for the winter."

Anna couldn't believe her ears. "But, we have come so far and our destination is in sight. I don't want to wait until spring. I want to go…now. Isn't there any other way?"

Seeing Anna's distress Zeebee cautiously added, "Well, there is a way you could make it before winter sets in but..." Zeebee hesitated.

"But what?" Anna insisted.

"It's not a good idea. Forget I ever mentioned it."

"Please tell me," Anna pleaded. "I really want to get home. Please Zeebee."

Zeebee took a deep breath. "Okay. There is a short cut through the mountains, but it means going through the *Valley of Quilrum* and over *Soopoil Ridge*."

"…and that's not good?" Anna asked, not sure she wanted to know the answer.

"No, that's not good, not good at all. Very few make it through even one of them. And, to be perfectly honest, I have never heard of anyone making it through both of them. Donovan rules both those areas."

Anna shuddered at the sound of his name. "You know about Donovan?"

"Everyone knows about Donovan in these parts. He has a very strong foothold in the Gold Realm. This is his last chance to stop beings from getting home. He does everything he can to prevent them from reaching the Crystal Palace."

"What makes the valley and ridge so dangerous?"

"No one really knows. They say it's different for everyone. I only know that those who attempt the shorter route are rarely seen again. That is why most people decide to wait until spring and take the safer, longer route."

Anna not only wanted to get home, she *needed* to get home. It had been a long journey and she was tired. She couldn't imagine waiting until spring. Not now, not when the Crystal Palace loomed in front of her, beckoning her home. How could she not continue? They had been through so much, surely they could get through this as well.

"Will you tell us how to take the shorter route?"

Tedith couldn't believe his ears. "Anna, what are you saying? You heard what Zeebee said. It's not safe." Tedith didn't want to continue, he wanted to wait until spring. He saw no reason to take the risk when all they had to do was wait a few more months.

"Tedith, we didn't come this far to play it safe, and I am not waiting until spring," Anna said with a conviction that surprised even her.

"I don't know Anna," Tedith said, shaking his head. "Somehow I think this time it's different."

Anna knew what Tedith meant. This realm did feel different. Maybe it was because they were so close to getting home. Maybe it was because Donovan's presence was so strong.

"I know. But we have to at least try. Don't we?"

Tedith sighed. "Okay, if you want to give it a go, I am with you. I only I hope you know what you are doing."

Anna thought, "So do I, Tedith. So do I."

Anna turned to Zeebee. "Will you help us?"

"Are you sure this is what you want to do?"

Anna nodded, hoping she wouldn't live to regret her decision...or worse, *not* live to regret her decision.

"Okay, wait here." They watched as Zeebee slithered away and returned a few moments later with an old rolled-up map in her mouth.

Zeebee passed the map to Anna. "Spread it out."

"Okay, you are here." Zeebee used her tail as a pointer. "Travel straight down the mountain, until you reach Yali stream. It runs along the bottom of the mountain range. Find a place to cross the stream. The water is fairly low this time of year so that should be easy. Once on the other side, follow the stream going in the direction that the water flows. In two full days of walking, you will come upon a sheer rock wall. Right here," Zeebee said, pointing to the map.

"Find the opening in the rock wall. It will look like a cave but it's actually a tunnel. It's called the *Miniruk Tunnel*. It leads straight to the *Valley of Quilrum*. You shouldn't have any trouble in the tunnel; however the valley is a whole other story. There is no telling what you will encounter, it's different for everyone. Get through the valley as quick as you can. At the end of the valley is a grove of Bokada trees. "Here," Zeebee said again pointing with her tail.

"The grove is magnificent. The trees soar hundreds of feet in the air. Each tree is over a million years old. You will be safe in the grove. On the other side of the grove is the bottom of *Frofin Mountain*. Follow the mountain path until you reach the summit. Running along the top of *Frofin Mountain* is *Soopoil Ridge*. Carefully make your way across the ridge as swiftly as you can. I have no idea what you might encounter on the ridge. At the end of the ridge is a path that leads directly to the Crystal Palace. It's only a few miles from the bottom of the mountain. It's a dangerous journey. You will have to be vigilant and single-minded. If the weather holds and you don't encounter anything unexpected, you should make it to the Crystal Palace in four or five days. I have to ask you again. Are you sure you don't want to wait until spring, when you can take the longer but safer route?"

Anna took a deep breath, "Yes, I'm sure. We need to push on.

We'll take our chances."

"Okay. The woods will provide some measure of cover. But be on the lookout for Donovan. Once he gets word that you have made it to the Gold Realm he will do everything in his power to stop you. You can drink the water from the mountain stream and the forest is ripe with berries, nuts and seeds. But be careful what you eat. There are many poisonous berries. Eat only what the birds eat."

"Thanks Zeebee, for all your help," Anna said.

Zeebee nodded. "If you two are going you should leave now. That way you will be able to make it to the other side of the stream by nightfall."

Anna folded the map and put it in her back pocket.

"I wish you a light-filled journey. Remember, keep an eye out for Donovan and go as quickly as you can through the valley and along the ridge"

"Thanks Zeebee, we will," Anna promised. "Come on Tedith."

Tedith followed Anna, not at all sure they were making the right decision. Zeebee watched as the two travelers made their way down the mountain. When they were out of sight, Zeebee transformed back into Odin, smiled and walked up the mountain.

CHAPTER EIGHTEEN

YALI STREAM

Other than the occasional bird flying overhead, Anna and Tedith walked down the rest of the mountain alone. The landscape gradually changed from a mountain meadow to a lightly wooded forest.

They kept a constant lookout for Donovan but at least for the time being, there was no sign of him. Fatigue and hunger were their now constant companions and they were anxious to get to the stream before dark.

As the sun moved towards the horizon, turning everything a deep peach, they heard the sound of rushing water.

"Come on, Tedith, we are almost there."

With newfound energy, they ran the remaining distance to the stream.

They drank greedily. Water trickled down Anna's chin.

"Should we cross here?" Tedith asked, as he wiped his furry mouth with his equally furry paw.

Anna looked at the dying light.

"Yeah, let's cross and find a place to spend the night."

"Okay but what about food? We haven't eaten all afternoon." Tedith rubbed his ever-hungry tummy.

"Let's see what we find when we get to the other side. Come on."

Zeebee was right. *Yali Stream* was easy to cross. A few short hops from rock to rock and they were on the other side.

An enormous bird with turquoise wings, a hooked beak, and a long iridescent tail was eating small red berries from a nearby bush. Remembering what Zeebee said about eating only what the birds ate, Anna gingerly approached the bush. She expected the big bird to fly away, but instead, it squawked at Anna as it continued to devour the berries. When Anna was within arm's length of the bush, she reached out for one of the berries.

The bird pecked her hand. "Ouch!" Anna cried, quickly pulling back her hand.

"Go find your own bush. This one is mine," the bird screeched.

"I beg your pardon. I didn't mean to...it's only that we haven't eaten all day and Zeebee said to only eat from the bushes that the birds ate from."

"Well for heaven's sake, why didn't you say you were a friend of Zeebee? Any friend of Zeebee's is a friend of mine. I'm Floriane, which means flower. They call me that because my feathers look like a beautiful flower," the big bird said, stretching out her wings for Anna to admire.

Anna had to admit they were beautiful. "Nice to meet you, Floriane." Anna gently shook Floriane's outstretched wing.

"Here, help yourself. These are Talula berries and they are deee-licious!" Anna and Tedith popped several of sweet juicy berries into their mouths. "You ain't from these parts are ya?"

"No, we are trying to get to the Crystal Palace so we can get home."

"What? That's crazy," the bird squawked. "You won't make it before winter sets in. Everyone knows you can't travel the mountain passes during the winter. Zeebee must have told you that you won't make it in time. It's too far, unless of course, you take the short route...Hey, wait a minute. Don't tell me you are going to go through the *Valley of Quilrum* and over *Soopoil Ridge*."

Anna's mouth was so full of berries, she could only nod.

"Now I know you are crazy. Didn't Zeebee tell you how dangerous that is?"

Anna swallowed. "Yes, she told us, but we need to get home and I'm not willing to wait until spring."

"Well I never. I hope you know what you are doing."

"Yeah, me too. Do you know a good place for us to spend the night?"

Floriane thought for a moment. "There is a hollowed out oak tree not far from here. It wouldn't be a bad place to spend the night."

"That sounds perfect."

"Follow me," Floriane said as she flew downstream.

Tedith was reluctant to give up the juicy berries and grabbed a handful more before running after Floriane and Anna.

"Here it is." Floriane landed on an old tree with a hollowed out base. It was so large it was almost a cave.

Anna stepped inside. "This is great, thank you."

"You wouldn't know if there is anything else to eat around here would you?" Tedith asked.

"Why sure, there are all sorts of things to eat. The forest is overflowing with food this time of year. Look here." Floriane flew over to a tree. "The nuts from this tree are great. And over here," Floriane flew to a straggly shrub, "are some really yummy Sokaa seeds."

Floriane continued to fly from tree to tree and bush to bush, pointing out a dozen or more edible delights. Anna paid close attention while Tedith ran after Floriane, tasting each of the treasures. He popped a purple berry in his mouth and gagged.

"Yuck!" Tedith said, after he spat the berry out. "What was that?"

Floriane laughed. "What, you don't like Manura berries? I guess they are an acquired taste."

"They are the worst thing I have ever tasted." Tedith ran to the stream and rinsed his mouth out.

"Well it's getting dark," Floriane said, still smiling at Tedith's reaction to the berry. "I best be getting back to my nest while I can still see where I am flying. I bid you sweet dreams. I do hope you know what you are getting yourself into."

"Bye Floriane, thanks for the help." Anna waved as Floriane flew deeper into the woods.

"Come on Tedith. I'm tired. Let's settle in for the night."

"Uggg, I'm so full, I couldn't eat another bite." Tedith rubbed his protruding furry tummy.

They made a bed inside the hollow tree with leaves they gathered from the forest floor.

"There, that should do," Anna said surveying their work, "and not a moment too soon. I'm beat."

The leaves rustled and crackled as they settled in. Anna laid in the dark listening to the night until sleep finally overtook her.

Anna woke at first light to the early morning sounds of the

forest. She quietly made her way out of the tree, so she wouldn't wake up Tedith, who was no doubt dreaming of honey pots.

The morning air was cold. Anna could see her breath. She vigorously ran her hands along her goose-bump covered arms. It was a picture perfect morning, clear and crisp, without a cloud in the sky. Anna walked down to the stream. As she bent down to take a drink, she heard Tedith calling her. "Anna, Anna!"

"I'm over here Tedith, by the stream."

Tedith emerged from the forest. "Don't do that to me. You scared the pa-jeepers out of me. I didn't know where you were."

Anna rubbed his furry little head then took a long drink of the clear water. "Come on, let's get something to eat and get a move on. We have a long day ahead of us."

They ate from several of the bushes and trees Floriane had shown them. Tedith was careful to avoid the Manura berries. They headed back to the stream and began to follow the rushing water, as Zeebee had instructed them to do. The early morning sun glistened off the water, slowly warming Anna.

They walked for the better part of the morning, stopping occasionally to nibble on a forest delight or to drink from the stream.

"Let's rest here," Anna said, as she plopped herself down on a sun drenched patch of thick brown grass.

They both stretched out and let the rays of the sun soothe them. Anna was beginning to doze off when she heard voices coming from downstream, the direction they were heading. Anna nudged Tedith and put a finger to her lips. She motioned for him to follow her. They quietly left the banks of the stream and entered the cover of the woods.

They found a large bush that had yet to lose its leaves and crouched behind it. The voices grew louder.

"You really think they would be stupid enough to take the short route?" a man's gruff voice asked.

"I'm sure of it. Anna's desire to get home is strong and she is foolish enough to think that she can make it through the valley and over the ridge. Stupid girl."

Anna shuddered. There was no mistaking the voice or arrogance, they belonged to Donovan.

"We need only to follow the stream until we find them. I sense we are getting close."

Anna crouched down even further.

She waited until the footsteps and voices faded into the distance then motioned for Tedith to silently follow her. They continued to follow the stream, only this time instead of walking along water's edge, they walked in the protective cover of the forest. They could hear the stream but not see it. It was more difficult to travel through the woods, but safer. Donovan and his men were expecting them to walk along the banks of the stream.

After they walked for several minutes in silence, Tedith whispered, "Do you think it's okay to talk now?"

Anna looked around "Yeah, I think they are gone. Let's head back to the stream. We'll be able to make better time walking along the bank, but keep your ears open and be ready to head for the woods at the first sound of anyone approaching."

They followed the stream as it meandered through the mountain valley. Even though there was no sign of Donovan, Anna couldn't relax. She was so close to getting home, she could almost reach out and touch it. She just had to keep her wits about her and stay focused. With a little luck she would be home in a few days.

It was late afternoon when they reached a wide bend in the stream. The stream was much wider and deeper now and the water rushed past them. No longer could you easily hop from rock to rock to get across.

"Can we stop and rest for a bit?" Tedith asked.

"Okay but only for awhile. I'm worried that Donovan will realize that he passed us and head back."

As Tedith went in search of food Anna sat down on a nearby rock, took the map out of her pocket and unfolded it on the ground. She traced her finger along the stream until she reached a large bend.

"Look Tedith, I think we are here," Anna said, when he returned with a handful of nuts.

"There is another bend in the stream here," Anna said, pointing further downstream. "Let's try to make it there before nightfall."

"Okay. Well what are we waiting for? Let's go," Tedith said, feeling better now that he had eaten.

Anna folded the map and put it back in her pocket. She walked to the edge of the stream, bent down and took a drink. As she was wiping her mouth she noticed a large shell among the river rocks.

"How strange. I wonder how a shell got into the stream," Anna thought. She picked it up and washed off the sand. It reminded her of the conch shells she saw in the Natural History Museum. She put the shell up to her ear and listened.

"You are mine. You will not make it home!" the shell roared.

Anna dropped it as if it was on fire. The shell shattered on impact. "Come on Tedith, let's get out of here."

Anna wondered if she really would be able to make it to the Crystal Palace before Donovan found them. They still had several days to go and Donovan knew these parts like the back of his hand. She just had to get home; she had been gone such a long time. By now she was pretty sure they had given up looking for her. Maybe they had even held a funeral for her. It made Anna sad to think about how much pain she had caused her family and friends. This made her even more determined to get to the palace.

As they walked, Anna watched as the sun edged its way towards the horizon, turning everything deep amber. The days were definitely getting shorter as winter approached. Anna hoped the second bend in the stream wasn't too far away; there wouldn't be light for much longer. They continue walked into the fading sun.

Tedith tripped on a rock. "Maybe we should find a place to spend the night," Tedith said, "It's getting hard to see where we are going."

"Just a little further. We have got to be close to the second bend."

Within a few minutes the second bend in the river greeted them.

"Great. We made good progress today. Now let's find a place to sleep. I think we should go inland a little, in case Donovan and his men return along the stream looking for us. Stay close, there is barely enough light to see." They wandered inland a few hundred feet.

"Do you see a place...Look!"

"Do you think anyone lives here?" Tedith asked as they examined the old ramshackle cabin in front of them.

"By the looks of it, I don't think anyone has lived here for a long time. Let's take a closer look."

The door was falling off its hinges and the roof was full of holes. Anna crept quietly up to one of the broken glass windows and looked inside. There wasn't much light but there definitely wasn't anyone in there. She slowly pushed the door open and stepped into a net of cobwebs.

"Yuck!! Well, at least we know no one has used the door in quite a while," Anna said, wiping the webs from her face and arms.

It was a one-room cabin. There was a rickety wooden table with three legs, two wooden chairs, which couldn't be trusted to sit on, and a straw mattress covered with an old moth-eaten wool blanket.

"Wow, look at this place," Tedith said. "Do you think it is safe to sleep here?"

"Yeah, I guess so. I can't imagine Donavan will be looking for us at night."

"Come on. Let's get some shut-eye. We can explore this place in the daylight."

Anna gave the blanket a good shake. She coughed as dust flew everywhere. It was quite cold and Anna was grateful for the blanket, moth holes and all.

That night, Anna dreamt she was home in her apartment with Grandpa. She was sitting at the kitchen table doing her math homework. She was holding a feather quill instead of a pencil. She dunked the quill into an ink well and looked at the question on her homework. It was made up of advanced mathematical symbols that Anna wasn't familiar with. She stared and stared at the problem but couldn't make any sense of it. She asked Grandpa for help. He told her she had to do it herself. Anna protested, saying it was too hard. Grandpa smiled at her and said, "Remember Anna, you are never given more than you can handle." Anna woke up with a shiver. Pale pink light pushed through the dirty, tattered curtains of the cabin.

Anna crawled over Tedith. In daylight, the little cabin looked even worse. In addition to the table, chairs and bed, there was a stone fireplace with a wood box beside it. A few cupboards hung tentatively on the wall. A countertop made of a rotting wooden plank stood beneath the cupboards. Anna figured this part of the cabin had been the kitchen. She swept away cobwebs as she stepped over parts of the fallen roof.

She heard Tedith stir.

"Mornin'. How did you sleep?" Anna asked.

"Great. I had the most wonderful dream."

"Let me guess, you dreamt about honey?"

"No, actually I dreamt I was in your bedroom sleeping next to you. It felt so good to be home!"

Anna knew what Tedith meant. She only hoped they would make it.

Tedith jumped down from the bed. "This place is cool."

They explored the contents of the cabin. All the cupboards were bare, except for some mouse droppings.

Anna was anxious to continue their journey. "Come on Tedith there is nothing here."

"Wait! Look at this!" Tedith exclaimed.

Anna turned around to see that Tedith had lifted the lid of the wood box by the fireplace.

Anna peered inside. There was an old canvas backpack with a faded "D" embroidered on it. Anna didn't want to be paranoid, but she couldn't help but wonder if "D" stood for Donovan.

Then she noticed a faded old sign nailed to the inside of the lid. It was covered in dust. Anna took out her bandana and dusted the sign off. It was inscribed with strange characters that Anna couldn't make out.

She pulled out the backpack. A cloud of dust came with it. Anna unbuckled the leather strap and carefully removed the contents. There was a matchbox with two matches in it; a pair of glasses with only one lens; a dozen dingy white shoelaces; a bent spoon; a needle stuck into a spool of purple thread; a half-empty jar of honey and a green glass bottle with a cork.

"Look at this stuff," Anna said.

"Yeah, look at the honey," Tedith said, hopefully. "Are we going to take this stuff with us?"

"I don't know, Tedith. It doesn't belong to us."

Anna examined the broken glasses; then put them on. She covered the eye that didn't have the lens in front of it and looked through the one lens. Everything looked distorted. She looked at the sign on the lid.

"Hey, I can now read the sign," Anna said.

"What does it say?"

"*Finders Keepers. An Ancient & Honorable Tradition.*' Well, that answers that question. I guess we can take what we find."

"What about that honey?" Tedith inquired sheepishly.

Anna smiled and handed it to him. "Not too much. We may need it later."

Tedith opened the jar, bent the spoon straight, and dug into the sweet contents. "Yum!"

"I'm not sure we will need all this stuff but you never know." Anna repacked the backpack.

"Tedith, hand me the blanket from the bed." Anna stuffed it in. Then she buckled up the pack and swung it onto her back. "Come on, let's go. We have a long day ahead of us. I'd like to get to the tunnel before sunset."

It was even colder outside than the day before. A blanket of ground mist covered the forest floor. Clouds covered the morning sky. They stopped to eat breakfast from a few bushes as they headed towards the stream.

The morning went by quickly. Anna kept her eye out for Donovan and *The Loyal Forces of the Opposition* but had a sense they were nowhere around, at least for the time being.

They saw a few fish jump from the stream and the odd frog, but for the most part things were quiet. Anna kept hoping one of the frogs would turn into Odin but they were just regular frogs.

"Let's rest here," Anna said, stopping to sit on a large rock by the edge of the stream, which had continued to get wider and deeper and now looked more like a river than a mountain stream.

Anna pulled the map out of her pocket. "We must be somewhere along this part of the stream," Anna said, pointing to the map. "I'm not sure. There aren't any visible landmarks, but if I am correct, we should be at the rock wall in a few hours. We made really good time this morning." Anna looked up at the sky. "I'm not sure the weather is going to hold though."

During the morning the sky had turned thick with clouds. "Those are rain clouds. Let's go. I'd really like to get to the tunnel before it starts to rain."

The sky continued to grow darker and the clouds more threatening. The smell of the pending storm filled the air. The only question now was how soon it would be before it arrived.

The first drop of rain hit Anna on her head, then another and another. Anna knew they were in for it; this was not going to be any light sun shower. The clouds opened and Anna and Tedith were soon soaked clear through to their skin. Tedith looked like a half drowned orange rat.

The rain came down in sheets. The trees drooped as if weeping. They watched the stream rise higher and higher. The banks were all mud and as slippery as a newly-waxed floor.

Tedith lost his footing and began sliding down the bank towards the water. Anna ran after him. He slammed into an old tree stump before he reached the stream. Anna carried him back to the stream bank. His fur was matted with clumps of mud and was more brown than orange.

There was nothing to do but push on. The rain relentlessly pounded the weary travelers. Anna's whole body ached as if she had been beaten. It was much farther than it looked on the map, or maybe it was because they were so miserable that it just seemed longer.

Drenched, freezing, exhausted, and hungry they reached the massive stone wall.

CHAPTER NINETEEN

QUILRUM VALLEY

T he sheer rock wall shot straight up hundreds of feet into the air and seemed quite out of place beside a mountain stream.

"Look for the opening," Anna called out to Tedith over the punishing rain.

They scanned the wall. Tedith was the first to spot it. "Over there," he pointed.

They ran into the opening. Anna quickly took off the soaking wet backpack. She took out the blanket and began to dry off Tedith. He shook like a puppy right after a bath, spraying water everywhere.

"Gee, that was something," Anna said as she began to dry

herself off. "I've never been in rain that hard before. It actually hurt when it hit me."

Anna wrapped the blanket around them and surveyed the surroundings. Zeebee was right. At first glance, it looked more like a cave than a tunnel. It was difficult to see too far into it, as it became dark as soon as you moved away from what little light the entrance provided. The sound of the rain echoed through the tunnel, giving it an eerie feel. Anna was suddenly scared. The only thing that now stood between them and the *Valley of Quilrum* was *Miniruk Tunnel*. Lord only knew what was waiting for them there.

"Let's stay here tonight Tedith, and start out fresh in the morning."

"I'm freezing; maybe we can make a fire with the matches from the cabin." Tedith said, shivering.

"I don't think we would find anything dry enough to burn. Besides, we can't make a fire in the tunnel. It would smoke us out."

"What about food? I'm hungry."

"I am too Tedith, but I am not going out in the rain again. You can if you want."

He looked out at the driving rain and decided to go hungry. For once, his stomach would have to wait.

"Come on, let's get some shut eye, we have a full day tomorrow."

The ground was hard and cold. Anna pulled Tedith next to her under the blanket. They knew they needed rest for what lay ahead of them but neither of them fell asleep easily. They tossed, turned, and shivered until a restless sleep finally overtook them.

Anna got up at first light. She ached all over; her still wet clothes clung to her. She couldn't decide if she was more cold or hungry. Anna looked out of the tunnel. At least it had stopped raining but it had turned bitterly cold. It seemed winter would arrive early this year.

As Anna thought about what might lie ahead of them, she started to doubt her decision to take the 'short' route. The weather was certainly part of her hesitation. Based on how cold it had gotten, she wasn't sure they would make it before the snow set in. However, what really fueled her doubt was fear. Anna was more frightened now than at any other time since starting the journey. She was about to enter the *Valley of Quilrum*. She wouldn't even allow herself to imagine what was waiting for them there. She looked down at Tedith lightly snoring beside her and wondered what she had gotten her little friend into. She knew she wouldn't have gotten this far if it hadn't been for him. It wasn't only herself she was now putting 'in harm's way,' but Tedith as well. Perhaps this was a mistake. Perhaps she should turn around. It wasn't too late. They could go back to Zeebee and spend the winter with her. Then in spring, they could start again, taking the longer, 'safer' route. The more she thought about it, the more she was convinced that going back was the right decision. Anna stroked Tedith's furry little head. He slowly awoke.

He yawned, "How long have you been up?"

"Only a little while."

Tedith looked outside. "I'm glad it's not raining but, brrrrr, it sure is cold."

"Yeah, it's cold alright."

"Shall we get some breakfast?" Tedith climbed out from under the blanket.

"I guess so."

Tedith paused and looked at Anna. There was something odd in the tone of her voice.

"Anna, what is it? What's wrong?"

"I've been thinking," Anna took a deep breath. "I think it would be better to go back and spend the winter with Zeebee. We could begin the journey again in the spring after the snow has melted."

Tedith could barely believe his ears. This didn't sound like the Anna he knew.

Anna continued, "It's going to start snowing any day now. And, well, you heard Zeebee. She never heard of anyone making it through the Valley *and* over the Ridge. I don't know what I was thinking when I decided that we should take the 'short' route. It was foolish to think we could make it. We could be back with Zeebee in a couple of days. The winter will go by quickly. In spring we can set off again."

Tedith could scarcely contain his disbelief. "What has gotten into you, Anna? This doesn't sound like you."

Tears welled up in Anna's eyes. "'I'm frightened Tedith, really frightened."

Tedith took hold of her hand. He had never seen her so shaken.

"It's okay Anna. Whatever you decide is fine with me. You know I'm in this with you to the end. But are you really sure you want to go back? We have come so far. We are only two or three days from the Crystal Palace."

"Yeah, Tedith, but we have never faced what we are about to face."

"I know Anna, but we have been in some pretty tight situations before and have always made it through."

"This time it feels different. I really think it would be best to go back and start again in the spring. It's not as if I am giving up...I mean, not exactly. I'm just postponing the journey for a while."

Tedith was going to protest but he could see how scared she was and didn't want to push her. "Okay, if you are sure. We can start back right after breakfast." Tedith wiped the tears from Anna's cheek. "Come on."

Outside, the air was even colder. A thin layer of ice, which shattered as Anna walked on it, covered the ground. She had lost her appetite and her stomach was in knots with fear but she forced herself to eat. As Anna picked at some nuts, she thought about all they had been through together. It was certainly more than she had ever dreamed she was capable of. There were times she was sure they were doomed.

A bird called out as it flew above Anna. One of its tail feathers dropped and landed by her feet. Anna picked up the feather. It made her think about the dream she had the night they spent in the cabin. She remembered she was with her Grandpa and was writing with a feather quill. What was it that her Grandpa said to her? "You will never be given more than you can handle."

As she reviewed everything they had been through since beginning the journey, Anna realized there had been many times she thought they wouldn't make it. But somehow, someway, they found a way to overcome each obstacle they encountered. And if that was true about the past, then maybe, just maybe, it was also true about the future. Maybe Anna really did have everything she needed to beat the odds and make it through the valley *and* over the ridge.

Anna's thoughts then turned to her mom; her whole being ached to be with her, to be home—to have her life back again, the good and the bad, school, chores, homework, everything. She wanted it all.

Maybe it really was as simple as Odin said it was. Not easy but simple. Maybe she just needed to keep putting one foot in front of the other and believe she could make it. Maybe Anna just needed to trust herself and her path home—trust that if she continued to follow her heart, continued to keep going no matter what, she would get home.

"Tedith, Tedith!"

He came running. "What? What's wrong?"

"Nothing is wrong. Everything is very right. We are going to continue."

Tedith jumped into her arms. "Yea! I was hoping we would. I really didn't want to turn back. What made you change your mind?"

"Trust. My fear has been replaced with trust." Anna hugged him. "I'm going to trust that I have what I need to overcome whatever we encounter. What do you think of that?"

"I think that's great."

"Okay, let's get ready to go." Anna put Tedith on the ground and took the bandana out of her back pocket. "Here," Anna said, handing it to Tedith, "fill this with nuts and seeds. I'm going to fill the bottle with water. There may not be any food or water where we are going."

After they had stashed their provisions safely in the backpack Anna took the map out, spread it on the ground, and smoothed out the creases.

"The tunnel is quite long but pretty straight. There are only a few twists and turns but no forks to confuse us. I figure it will take us the better part of the day to get through it." Anna refolded the map and put it away. "It is going to be dark as soon as we leave the light coming from the entrance, so stay close. You ready?"

"Yep, let's go."

It wasn't long until they were walking in pitch-blackness. Anna, not able to see a thing, stumbled on a rock.

"Ouch," she cried, rubbing her foot.

Suddenly, high-pitched screeches echoed throughout the tunnel. Anna and Tedith covered their heads as a swarm of bats, having been awakened from their slumber, flew past them towards the entrance of the tunnel.

"Yuck, bats. Let's go."

Anna ran her right hand along the side of the tunnel to guide them. It was surprisingly smooth for a tunnel made of stone. Tedith followed close behind.

Thankfully, the tunnel was warmer than outside. The deeper they went, the warmer it became. It was also damp. Occasional drops of condensation fell from the ceiling, landing on their heads. The dark made it slow going. They travelled at a snail's pace.

"How you doing Tedith?"

"Great. Watch out for the rock!" But it was too late. Anna tripped on the rock and fell flat.

"Ouch!"

"Are you okay?" Tedith said, rushing to help her up.

"Yeah, I'm fine but how did you see that rock? I can't see a thing."

"You can't? That's funny. I can see at least four feet in front of me."

"Really? I know cats can see in the dark, but I didn't know bears could, or maybe it's only teddy bears. Why don't you take the lead? That way, at least one of us can see where we are going."

They walked for a while with Tedith in the lead but didn't make any better time. Anna kept falling behind and Tedith had to constantly stop and wait for her to catch up with him.

"I wish I could go as fast as you Tedith."

"Yeah, if we could hold hands I could guide you but the tunnel is too narrow for us to walk side by side."

"Hey, that gives me an idea."

Anna undid the backpack and rummaged around inside it until she found what she was looking for. She pulled out the shoelaces and tied the ends together, forming a shoelace rope. She then handed one end to Tedith.

"Here, you hold onto this end. I'll hold onto the other end."

It worked like a charm. Anna no longer fell behind. Their pace picked up considerably.

For the most part, they walked the rest of the morning in silence. When they did speak, their voices reverberated throughout the tunnel, giving it an eerie feel. Besides, Anna didn't want Donovan to hear them. He was sure to check the tunnel when he finally realized that they had slipped past him by the river.

Anna heard Tedith's stomach grumble. "Let's stop and have something to eat," Anna whispered.

Anna took off the backpack and laid the blanket out for them to sit on. She then fished around in the pack until she located the jar of honey, which, along with the spoon, she handed to Tedith. She then pulled out the bottle of water and the bandana containing the nuts and seeds.

"How much longer do you think?" Tedith asked through a mouthful of honey.

"I figure we are about halfway there. I was thinking we could sleep at the other end of the tunnel tonight, and at first light, make our way through the valley." Anna nibbled on a few seeds. Tedith scooped up another spoonful on honey and stuck it in his mouth.

"Let's not eat too much Tedith. We need to make this food and water last. We don't know what we will find in the valley.

Tedith frowned, but heeding Anna's words, licked the remaining honey off the spoon and screwed the lid back onto the jar.

"Water?" Anna uncorked the bottle and handed it to Tedith.

Tedith took a swig and returned it to Anna.

"Okay, let's go." Anna re-corked the bottle and put everything back in the pack.

Tedith took the lead again, with Anna right behind at the end of the shoestring rope.

"What do you think the *Valley of Quilrum* will be like?" Tedith asked quietly, after walking in silence for an hour.

"I don't have any idea, but if it's under Donovan's influence, it isn't going to be pretty. We need to be ready for anything. According to the map, the valley isn't very long. By the looks of it we should be able to make it to the other side in less than an hour. Of course it really depends on what the valley is like and what we encounter. We won't... ouch!" Anna cried, as she banged into Tedith who had stopped abruptly.

"Tedith why..."

"Shhhh, there's a light up ahead," Tedith whispered.

Anna strained to see down the dark tunnel. "I don't see any light."

"Trust me, it's there. It's faint, but there is definitely a light. You don't think we are at the end of the tunnel already, do you?"

"Not according to the map. We shouldn't reach the end for a few more hours. Let's keep going but be careful."

They slowly continued through the tunnel. It wasn't long until Anna could also see the light. It was coming from an opening, maybe they were at the end of the tunnel after all. Maybe the map was wrong. The light grew brighter the closer they got. The tunnel was also getting warmer.

As they approached the opening, Tedith handed the shoelace rope to Anna. She tucked it into the front pocket of her jeans. They got on their hands and knees and crawled the last few feet. They cautiously stuck their heads out.

Above, was a dome with a large hole in the center, through which you could see the sky. Directly beneath the dome, far below them, was a deep, round pit. In the center of the pit was a huge, roaring fire. Smoke billowed through the opening in the dome. Their tunnel connected with a walkway that encircled the massive fire pit. They were in a rotunda. The opening they emerged from was one of nine identical, evenly-spaced openings. The fire in the center of the rotunda was like a hub in the middle of a wheel.

'Wow, look at this place!" Tedith exclaimed.

"Yeah—look at this place," Anna replied, without Tedith's enthusiasm. "This explains why it kept getting warmer the further we went into the tunnel but I don't remember seeing anything like this on the map." Anna took the map out of her pocket and carefully examined it. "Nope it's not here. The tunnel was supposed to go straight through to the valley. How are we going to figure this out?" Anna looked worried.

"What do you mean? Figure what out?"

"Think about it, Tedith. If you don't count the opening we came from, there are eight possible entrances and only one of them leads to the *Valley of Quilrum*. The question is; which one?"

"I see your point."

Anna thought for a moment. "Let's work our way around the rotunda, one opening at a time. Maybe there will be something in one of the tunnels to let us know it leads to the valley."

Anna took off the backpack and removed the bandana. She then placed a large nut by the entrance of the tunnel. "This is so we don't forget which tunnel we came from."

They walked into the first opening to their right. It looked exactly like the tunnel they had just left.

"How far into each tunnel do you think we should walk?" Tedith asked. So far, nothing seemed remotely remarkable.

"Let's follow the tunnel until the light goes dim or until we notice something."

They carefully searched the walls and floor as they walked.

"I don't see anything, do you?"

"No, nothing." Anna strained to see as far down the tunnel as she could. "It looks exactly like the other tunnel."

"Okay, let's try the next one."

They examined the next tunnel but it too was unremarkable.

They inspected three more tunnels, finding nothing out of the ordinary. It was actually amazing how similar each of the tunnels looked.

Anna was getting frustrated; how were they ever going to find the tunnel that went to the valley? They had finished examining the fifth tunnel and were heading back when they heard voices coming from the rotunda.

Anna put a finger to her lips. Then quietly crept towards the opening until she could hear what was being said. The voices were coming from the entrance of the tunnel Anna and Tedith had just explored.

"They somehow eluded me by the stream but there is no way for them to escape from the tunnel." It was Donovan!

"Right now, Anna and Tedith are making their way through the tunnel that leads from the stream. A squadron is approaching from the rear. We will enter the tunnel from this end and trap them in the middle. It's so dark in the tunnel, they will be lucky to have gotten halfway through by now. Even if they could have made it this far, there is no way for them to know that *this* is the tunnel that leads to the *Valley of Quilrum*. They are close at hand; I can feel it. Come on, let's go."

Anna and Tedith took several steps back into the darkness of the tunnel. Donovan and his men walked right past them, as they headed for the tunnel that led to the stream. The one Anna and Tedith had been walking through all morning.

Before entering the tunnel Donovan stopped abruptly. "Wait, what is this?" He bent down and picked-up something. "It's a nut. What is a nut doing here?"

Anna held her breath.

Donovan looked around. "Something is not right about this, but I don't have time to deal with it now. Let's go."

Anna exhaled. As soon as she could no longer hear footsteps, she grabbed Tedith and ran into the tunnel next to them, the one Donovan said led to the valley.

They quietly and quickly made their way down the tunnel as the light from the rotunda faded. Convinced they were now out of harm's way Tedith said, "Geez that was a close one."

"I'll say. If you weren't able to see in the dark, which allowed us to move a lot faster, Donovan would have certainly caught us in the tunnel."

"Yeah and if we would have stepped into the rotunda thirty seconds sooner they would have caught us."

"...and if that wasn't enough, Donovan unwittingly told us which tunnel led to the valley. Talk about timing!" Anna exclaimed.

"I'm glad we got away but I am sure they won't stop looking for us. I'm hoping when they don't find us in the tunnel they will think that we turned around and went back to Zeebee."

Anna took the shoelace rope out of her pocket and gave one end to Tedith. "You lead. It's getting too dark for me to see."

They were eager to get to the other end of the tunnel and stopped only occasionally during the afternoon to rest.

"Look," Tedith said, stopping.

Anna had to strain to see it but there was definitely a faint light ahead of them.

"We must be nearing the end of the tunnel," Tedith said as he started to walk again but the shoelace rope didn't budge. Anna was frozen in her tracks.

"Come on Anna, we are almost there. Think about how close we are to the palace," Tedith urged, tugging on the shoelaces.

Anna took a deep breath and made herself walk. The closer they got, the more frightened she became. She remembered something her grandpa had once told her, "Courage isn't the absence of fear. It's moving ahead in spite of the fear." At the time she heard it she thought it was very clever but it was a lot harder to *do* than to *say*. Her mind was racing. What would the valley be like? What did Donovan have waiting for her? Would they make it to the other side?

As they reached the end of the tunnel Anna was completely unprepared for what lay before her in the valley. How could this be? She gazed out at the most exquisitely beautiful valley of pure white flowers. It was as if it were spring, rather than the beginning of winter. A warm breeze swept over the flowers. The smell was intoxicating, reminding Anna of her favorite flower, *Lily-of-the-Valley*. She breathed in deeply. The valley floor was far below them. A wood and rope suspension bridge led from the opening of the tunnel down to the valley floor. A path ran the length of the valley then disappeared into a grove of huge trees.

"Gosh, I wasn't expecting anything like this," Tedith said, gazing out at the magnificent scene.

"Me either," agreed Anna.

"I still think we should sleep in the tunnel tonight and start out at first light. The valley may look beautiful but I suspect there is more to it than meets the eye."

They watched as the setting sun painted the valley with its ever-changing light. First pale pink, then rose, then a dark crimson.

They ate a dinner of nuts and seeds covered with honey. It was actually quite tasty, reminding Anna of granola. Tedith pulled out the blanket and the two weary travelers made themselves as comfortable as possible on the stone ground. At least it wasn't as cold as last night. Together, they fell into a dreamless sleep.

Tedith was the first to awaken. The pure white flowers in the valley were a pale apricot color in the pre-dawn light. He gazed out at the light dew covering the valley. Everything glistened. It was hard to believe that this was the dreaded _Quilrum Valley_.

He watched Anna as she slept. She was squeezing the backpack, just like she used to squeeze him, when he was just a stuffed toy. Tedith had missed her so much after Old Jed had carried him away. He knew how much she missed her mom, and really hoped that what waited for them in the valley and along the ridge wouldn't stop them from reaching the Crystal Palace.

Anna gently stirred, then awoke with a start. "Where am I?"

"It's okay, Anna, you are with me," Tedith reassured her.

"Wow, was I ever sleeping soundly. My mom calls it 'the sleep of the dead.' I certainly hope that isn't a premonition of things to come." Anna chuckled, trying to hide her fear and hoping her statement wouldn't turn out to be true.

They ate breakfast in silence, lost in their thoughts as they contemplated what might be waiting for them. The valley looked even more beautiful and inviting in the morning light. Anna wondered how anything so beautiful could be so dangerous. Maybe Zeebee was wrong. Maybe the worst was behind them. After all, the map was wrong, it hadn't shown the rotunda. Anna could only hope.

They packed away what remained of the food and water. There wasn't much, only a small handful of nuts and a couple mouthfuls of water. Hopefully there would be food available when they reached the grove of Bokada trees. That is, if they made it to the grove.

Anna slung the pack onto her back.

"Okay, little buddy, you ready?"

"Ready as I'll ever be," Tedith said, trying to hide his nervousness.

Anna examined the suspension bridge. It certainly looked

sturdy enough but it was a long way down to the path on the valley floor.

Anna stepped onto the bridge. The world completely changed. Daylight became night. The light breeze turned into a howling, bitterly cold wind. The beautiful flowers wilted and became decayed and diseased. The lovely fragrance changed to the smell of decomposing flesh.

The valley floor was enveloped with grotesque, demonic figures. Rotting flesh hung from their skeleton forms. Their eyes hung from their boney eye sockets. They cried out as if being eaten alive as they strained and reached out for Anna and Tedith. They were more dead than alive.

Gasping for air, Anna stumbled back into the tunnel. The valley immediately returned to its former glory, peaceful and serene.

Anna's heart was racing. She was shaken to her core. She buried her head in her hands, as if protecting herself. Too shocked even to cry, it took several moments before she could speak.

"Oh my Lord, Tedith. I never thought it would be anything like this. It is far worse than I could have ever imagined. We will never get through the valley."

Tedith shook his head, he knew she was right. They would never make it though. "Maybe there is another way."

"There isn't Tedith. Our choices are to go back, where we are certain to encounter Donovan, or to go forward. Either way we are doomed. The Crystal Palace is just over the next mountain range but it might as well be a million miles away. We are never going to see it."

Tedith and Anna sat at the edge of the tunnel looking out at the tranquil valley.

Anna thought of all those she held dear—her mom, her grandma, all of her friends, classmates, and teachers. So close but so very far. The obstacles to reaching them were insurmountable. And yet, the thought of never seeing any of them again was unbearable. Filled with overwhelming sadness, Anna finally wept.

Warm salty tears burned down her cheeks. She wept for everything she had been through; she wept for everyone she would never see again; and she wept for home. She ached at the thought of losing it all. The loss was so immense.

Slowly Anna's sadness turned into a yearning, a deep profound yearning from the core of her being, the yearning that called her home. It begged her to continue. How could she abandon what she desired most? How could she give up? How could she be so close and not go on? She had to continue. She must continue. Every fiber of her being beckoned her home.

Anna wiped away her tears. "Come on, Tedith. We are going through the valley."

"What?" Tedith looked at Anna in disbelief. "Anna, do you know what you are saying? We are not going to make it through."

"I know it's a long shot Tedith, but I've got to try."

"Are you sure?"

"Yes, I am sure. Let's go home."

Before Anna could change her mind, she stepped onto the bridge. The scene instantly returned to her worst nightmare. The demons moaned and howled as they eagerly waited for them on the valley floor. The stench was so bad Anna had to keep herself from vomiting.

The raging wind whipped around them, violently swaying the bridge. "Stay close," Anna yelled over her shoulder. They held the rope railings for dear life as they made the slow descent to the waiting valley floor.

If they were hoping for relief when they reached the path, there was none. The demons lunged at them. Anna recoiled.

"You are ours. You will never make it to the other side," the demons mocked. But no matter how hard they tried the demons never touched Anna or Tedith. It was almost as if they *couldn't* touch them.

Then Anna noticed the path. It was glowing with a gentle white light. By Anna's feet was a tiny ladybug. It looked so calm, so certain that its world was safe and good.

In that instant, Anna knew that if they stayed on the path they would make it across the valley.

The demons continued to beg and scream for Anna to follow as they tried to lure her off the protection of her path. The fierce wind howled as decaying arms reached out for them. The darkness of these beings was relentless but Anna was determined not to let it consume her

Anna turned around to see Tedith a few paces behind her. He was struggling against the wind. "Oh no," Anna thought, "The wind is too strong for him." As she went back to help him, a gust of wind swept him off the path. The demons pounced on him. Tedith screamed. Anna grabbed his back leg and held on with all her strength but the demons were too strong; Tedith was slipping from her grasp. Anna knew she couldn't hold on for much longer. She also knew that there was no way she was going to let them take Tedith.

Just as she was about to lose her grasp, a profound calm engulfed her. She reached deep inside herself and with everything she was and everything she had, she pulled Tedith from the clutches of darkness and back onto the path. Anna cradled him. He was badly hurt and in shock.

The demons cried out in agony over their loss. Anna now knew she was stronger than the darkness and that nothing would prevent her from making it to the other side. The grove of trees at the end of the valley beckoned her.

Tedith was limp in her arms. She held him tightly. Anna was exhausted but she pushed against the wind and darkness until the

Bokada trees finally stood before her, like soldiers at attention. She stumbled into the magnificent grove and collapsed into its safety. The valley instantly transformed once again, to its tranquil state.

Tedith groaned.

"Tedith, Tedith are you alright? Please speak to me."

"Are we there yet?"

Anna smiled and hugged her little friend.

"Ouch, not so hard. I hurt all over."

"But you're okay?"

"Yeah, nothing that some honey wouldn't fix," he said with a weak smile.

Anna squeezed him again and took out the honey from the backpack.

CHAPTER TWENTY

SOOPOIL RIDGE

The Bokada trees soared into the air. They were as high as the Empire State Building and as wide as a cruise ship. Great big sheets of bark, which the trees shed as they grew, littered the ground. They were smooth and silky. As impressive as the size of the trees was, the leaves were even more amazing. Each leaf was as long as Anna was tall and their shape reminded her of a huge fan. The leaves were a glossy, dark green on one side, and a velvety soft, pure white on the other. The feel of them reminded Anna of the fuzzy bunny in her much loved childhood book, *The Velveteen Rabbit.*

The grove was a welcome respite from the nightmare of the

valley. An abundant array of bushes and shrubs lived under the protection of the grove's immense canopy. Anna recognized some of the plants from Floriane's instructions. Luckily, a few of them were still clinging to their precious seeds and berries.

Anna carefully watched Tedith lick the last drop of honey off the spoon.

"How are you little buddy?" Anna asked.

"Good, just a little sore," Tedith replied, getting up. "Ouch!" He called out and immediately fell back to the ground.

"What is it? What's wrong?"

"It's my foot. My left foot."

"Let's see." Anna gently lifted Tedith's foot to have a closer look. There was a gaping hole in his heel. White stuffing oozed out.

"Oh dear Tedith, you have a nasty gash," Anna said, looking and sounding worried. "You can't walk on it. You'd lose all of your stuffing."

Tedith lifted his foot up to examine it. It made him feel woozy just looking at it.

"Didn't we find a needle and thread in the cabin?"

"Yeah, but..." Anna said, not sure she liked where this was heading.

"Well then, you can sew me up."

"No...no way. I'm not sticking a needle in you."

"Come on. It'll be a cinch," Tedith said trying to sound more convincing than he actually felt.

"I don't know Tedith. I've never been very good with a needle and thread and it would hurt a lot. I don't think I could do it."

"Sure you can. It'll be fine. Besides, what other choice do we have?"

Anna didn't like this idea but Tedith was right; they didn't have a lot of options. He couldn't walk on it the way it was. "Are you sure about this?"

"Absolutely, I'll be fine. Really," Tedith said putting on his bravest face.

"Okay, I'll give it a go but if it's too painful I'm going to stop."

Anna wished she had paid more attention last year when Grandma wanted to show her how to mend a hole in one of Grandpa's socks. Anna reached into the backpack and pulled out the spool of purple thread and needle.

"I'm afraid the purple thread is going to look a little funny against your orange fur," Anna said, as her shaky hand threaded the needle.

"That's okay…it'll give me character." Tedith said, trying to hide his nervousness behind his smile.

"Okay, you ready?" Anna carefully lifted Tedith's foot and put it on her lap.

"As ready as I will ever be."

Anna tenderly pushed the white stuffing back into the hole. Tedith cringed.

Then, gently holding his fur together, she stuck the needle in.

"Ahhhhh!" Tedith cried out.

"I'm sorry. Maybe I should stop."

"No, you have to continue. I'll be fine."

Anna thought for a moment. "Wait here." She rushed into the forest and returned with a little stick. "Here, bite on this." Anna had seen this in old western movies.

Once the stick was firmly in his mouth, Anna continued sewing. Biting down on the stick seemed to help, but Tedith still winced in pain. Anna worked carefully and quickly.

"Last one." She pulled the needle through, tied a knot, and bit off the end of the thread.

"There, all done. How do you feel?"

"Okay. I'm glad it is over," Tedith said, getting to his feet.

"What are you doing? I think you should rest."

"I want to see if I can put some weight on it."

Tedith limped a few steps. "Not bad, much better than it was. As long as we don't go too fast, I should be fine. Do you think I could have some more honey? I think it will help with the pain."

Anna smiled and handed him the honey jar. Tedith was sure there must be something honey didn't make better but he really couldn't think of what that might be.

Anna took out the map and spread it on the ground. "It looks like we should be able to make our way through the grove by nightfall. We'll camp at the bottom of the *Frofin Mountain* and start up towards *Soopoil Ridge* first thing in the morning."

"Sounds like a plan."

"You rest here Tedith, while I replenish our food supply." Anna took the blanket out of the backpack and tucked it around Tedith. Then she removed the bandana and began filling it with seeds and nuts. She was hungry and ate as much as she stored. When the bandana and Anna were both full, she returned to Tedith and put everything back in the pack.

"Okay little fella, you ready?" Tedith nodded and off they went.

The going was slow. Tedith limped several steps behind Anna. She carried him periodically but he was too heavy for her to carry long distances.

Anna picked up a stick and handed it to Tedith. "Here, try using this as a walking stick."

It seemed to help and they were able to make better time.

Early in the afternoon, they came across a little creek where they stopped for lunch and refilled their water bottle before carrying on.

As dusk approached, they came to the end of the grove. *Frofin Mountain* loomed in front of them, blanketing them in its shadow. The path up was a series of hairpin turns that eventually ended at *Soopoil Ridge*. It would take them the better part of the next day to make it to the beginning of the Ridge. With any luck, they would make it to the other side of the ridge by nightfall. For now, however, they were content to set up camp. Tedith was exhausted. Anna collected some wood, and with one of the matches from the cabin, made a small fire. The weather had gotten increasingly colder. Anna gathered several of the large Bokada leaves and piled them together to make a soft bed. After they had eaten their usual dinner, they snuggled under the blanket next to the fire. Anna listened to the fire crackle as she drifted off into a deep sleep.

Anna woke at the first sign of light but did not get up. It was cold and the fire had long since gone out. Frost covered the ground. Dark clouds filled the sky. Tedith was curled up in a ball next to her. They had a long day in front of them and had better get started.

"Tedith, it's time to wake up." Tedith stirred but did not wake up. "Come on Tedith, we need to get a move on. I've got honey for you," Anna said, trying to lure him awake.

Tedith opened his eyes and right away Anna could see that something was wrong. She put her hand to his forehead.

"You're burning up." Anna examined his foot, it was red and swollen. "Your foot must have gotten infected."

"I'll be okay," Tedith said as he tried to stand but became light-headed and immediately sat back down.

"Oh dear Tedith, I don't think you are going to be able to travel like this." Anna tucked the blanket around him.

Tedith shivered as he looked up at the looming mountain. He hated to admit it but he knew Anna was right. In his condition he would never make it to the top of the mountain let alone along the ridge.

"You go Anna. Get to the Crystal Palace. I'll be fine here. You can bring back help." Tedith's teeth clattered together as the fever took hold of him.

"There is no way I am going to leave you. We are in this together," Anna said firmly.

"But we can't stay here. Winter is on its way and Donovan can't be far behind."

Anna knew he was right, but she also knew she wasn't going to leave him.

"How about some honey? I'm sure you will feel better after a bit of honey," Anna said, trying to lift his spirits.

"I don't want any, not right now. Maybe later."

Anna could barely believe her ears. Tedith not wanting honey! That was a first. She knew she had to do something. "Come on Tedith, we are going."

"I'm sorry Anna, but I'm really too sick to walk. I can barely stand."

"Who said anything about walking? I'm going to carry you...in the backpack." Anna began to remove the contents of the pack.

"What? I'm too heavy. There is no way you will be able to carry me up the mountain, let alone across the ridge."

Anna worried that he was right but she put on a brave face.

"I'll be fine." Anna opened up the bandana and ate the last handful of nuts then bandaged Tedith's foot with it. She then wrapped the blanket securely around Tedith and carefully placed him in the backpack. He fit perfectly. His furry little head stuck out from the top.

"There you go. How's that?"

"Not bad, not bad at all, but what about the rest of the items?"

"There is no room. We'll have to leave them behind. Okay, you ready?" Tedith nodded.

Anna picked up the pack and swung it onto her back. It was heavy and she almost lost her balance.

Once the pack was securely in place Anna said, "There, that's not so bad. You okay back there?"

"Yeah, I'm fine." Tedith shivered.

"Okay then, let's go."

Tedith wasn't the only one shivering. Anna's arms were covered in goose-bumps. She hoped walking would warm her up.

Dark, menacing looking clouds hung over Anna as she walked along the foothills towards *Frofin Mountain*. She walked all morning, stopping every half hour or so to rest and check on Tedith. His fever had intensified. Beads of sweat soaked the fur on his forehead.

By mid-afternoon the foothills had changed into rugged mountain terrain, which was steeper and much harder to maneuver. Slowly Anna made her through a series of hair-pins. Several times she stumbled on protruding rocks.

She tried not to think about what was waiting for her at the top. After the valley she didn't even want to imagine the horrors waited for her on *Soopoil Ridge*.

The temperature continued to drop and the thin, cold mountain air made it difficult to breathe. It reminded her of the time she used a skinny straw as a snorkel in the community pool. It didn't matter how hard she sucked in, she couldn't get enough air and finally had to surface to catch her breath.

Anna was exhausted and at the next hairpin turn took off the pack to rest. She was relieved to have the weight off her back. The leather straps had left her shoulders red and raw.

"How you doing little buddy?" Anna asked, stroking Tedith's furry little head.

Tedith smiled weakly. One moment he was shivering, the next, he was burning up. Anna could tell the infection was starting to spread through his body. She knew she had to get him to a doctor as soon as possible.

Anna studied the sky which had turned the color of charcoal; she knew a storm was brewing. Anna put the pack back on. She had to keep moving if she wanted to get to the ridge before the storm hit.

The temperature continued to drop the higher Anna climbed. It was now below freezing and her t-shirt and jeans did little to protect her against the cold. Anna rubbed her hands up and down on her exposed arms and blew on her fingers in an attempt to keep warm. The now icy ground, made walking even more treacherous.

Then delicate, white flakes started to fall. Anna took a moment to catch her breath and watch the falling snow. Even in the middle of all this, Anna admired the beauty of the world as it turned white. The mountaintops already covered in snow, looked like they were a postcard from the Swiss Alps.

Anna forced herself to continue. She just had to reach the summit before sunset. It wasn't long until the gentle snowfall turned into a raging snowstorm. Anna pushed on.

Finally, with the sun heading towards the horizon half frozen Anna reached the summit of *Frofin Mountain*. The storm whipped around her, as she looked out at the world. In the distance, beckoning her, stood the Crystal Palace.

Soopoil Ridge was now the only thing between her and going home. Anna took a deep breath and carefully walked to the edge of the ridge. The wind howled as Anna looked out in horror.

Soopoil Ridge ran along the top of *Frofin Mountain*. It was little more than three feet wide and was covered with ice and snow. A sheer drop on either side of the ridge guaranteed sudden death should she fall. How was Anna ever going to make it across?

She swung off her pack. Tedith was now in and out of consciousness. She wrapped the blanket more tightly around him and tucked him securely into the pack.

"Sorry, little buddy, but I need to put the flap over your head until we get to the other side of the ridge. You will be safer that way." Tedith groaned. Anna couldn't tell if he understood her or not.

Anna's lips were blue, her hair was matted with ice and her fingers were numb. She knew she had to move quickly; she couldn't stand this cold much longer. Anna didn't know how she could possibly get to the other side but she knew she must. There was now something even more important than getting home. She had to save Tedith.

"Here we go little fella." She swung the backpack on.

Anna braced herself as she took a step onto the ridge. The snowstorm lashed out at her. She steadied herself and slowly walked further onto the ridge. Anna looked down and became dizzy. She took a deep breath, then looking straight ahead, continued.

Anna inched her way along the ridge. The storm was relentless, but Anna was determined. "Thank goodness for all that practice on the balance beam in gymnastics," Anna thought.

She was just starting to believe she might actually make it across when a clap of thunder shook the skies. It startled Anna but she didn't lose her balance. Then, a flash of lightning struck *Soopoil Ridge* a few feet in front of her. It sent a tremor down the ridge.

Anna teetered but managed to hold on. She had never seen or heard of lightning in a snowstorm. Before she had a chance to fully recover, another lightning bolt struck the ridge, then another and another. Anna shielded her eyes and through the cover of her hands, watched in horror as the entire length of *Soopoil Ridge* was stuck by lightning bolts.

"That's it," she thought. "I will never make it across the ridge without being hit by lightning. There was no choice but to go back.

Anna turned around to head back just in time to see a bolt of lightning strike the ridge that lay between her and *Frofin Mountain*. The ridge shook violently causing a massive rockslide. Anna quickly knelt down and grabbed hold of the ridge for dear life. A huge portion of the ridge plummeted down the mountainside. A gaping hole now stood between Anna and safety on the other side. There would be no turning back. The only portion of the ridge that remained led to the other side and it was continuously being struck by lightning.

The wind wailed as if it was in pain. Anna could no longer feel her fingers or toes, the first sign of frostbite. She carefully took the pack off her back. Tedith was unconscious. She huddled on the ridge cradling the pack. She watched the lightning strike the ridge over and over again and realized her fate was sealed. She would never make it home. After everything she had been through, this was how it would end.

She stared at the lightning waiting for it to strike her. She knew it was only a matter of time. As she watched, she realized that there was a pattern to the lightning. There were six bolts of lightning, spaced about ten feet apart. They struck at different times, but each bolt of lightning struck in the exactly the same place and each strike was seven seconds from the last. She knew it would be risky, but if she timed it carefully, she might be able to dodge the lightning bolts.

With newfound strength, she cautiously got to her feet. She lifted Tedith up. As she swung the pack onto her back, a huge gust of wind knocked her off balance. Anna let go of the pack.

"Nooooooo!" Anna screamed. She watched in horror as the pack hurtled down the side of the mountain. Anna completely broke down. She huddled on the ground and sobbed uncontrollably. The thought of losing her best friend was unbearable.

All was lost. There was no point in going on. She was half-dead already. She had nothing left to give. It wouldn't be long until the storm seized her and she met the same fate as Tedith. Donovan had finally gotten his wish; Anna would not be going home. The storm continued to rage around her. The lightning and wind were relentless.

As she waited for the inevitable, a strange calm came over her. Within the calm Anna let go and accepted her now-sealed destiny. She let go of everything she had ever wanted and of everything she thought was important.

She let go of her family and friends. She let go of her hopes and dreams. Then, with a deep sigh, she let go of the one thing that had propelled her through this entire journey; her longing to go home.

Anna was no longer scared. Anna no longer yearned. She was ready. She was at peace. Then she heard him, as clearly as if he was sitting right next to her.

"It's time to go home, Anna. You haven't come this far to give up. *We* didn't come this far for you to give up. I will always be with you." It was Tedith. Anna knew this was impossible, but somehow Tedith was speaking to her.

"I can't, I won't, not without you."

"Yes you can. Finish your journey. Finish what you started."

As Anna listened to Tedith, a deep inner strength arose in her. "Okay Tedith. I'll do it. I'll do it for us. And if I don't make it, at least I will know I gave it everything I had."

Trembling, Anna slowly stood up. Carefully she walked up to where the first lightning bolt struck. She took a deep breath and waited. As soon as the lightning struck she quickly moved past it. Within seconds the lightning struck behind her.

Anna moved cautiously along the ridge and paused in front of the second bolt. As soon as the lightning struck, she swiftly walked past the charred ridge to the other side. Anna gained confidence as she moved past each lightning bolt.

She was doing it, she was actually doing it. She was going to make it to the other side. There was now only one more lightning bolt between her and the end of the ridge. She counted...she waited. Then an extraordinary bolt of lightning struck not the ridge but mountain just beyond the ridge. It was blinding. Anna shielded her eyes. When she removed her hands, Donovan was standing where the lightning had struck.

"You really thought you could get away from me?" He sneered. "I must say you have put up more of a fight than I expected but you have met your match. It's over, Anna."

"Why, why don't you want me to go home?" Anna cried out. "Why can't you leave me alone?"

"You need me, my dear, even if you don't realize it," Donovan snarled.

"I am not going with you," Anna declared defiantly. "I'd rather die than give in to *you*."

"You don't need to come to me. I'm only too happy to come get you." Donovan walked onto the ridge. The only thing separating them now was the continuously striking lightning bolts. Anna on one side, Donovan on the other.

Donovan's red eyes locked onto Anna's. As soon as the next lightning bolt struck, he reached across and grabbed Anna's arm and pulled her towards him.

"No!" Anna screamed as she struggled against his grip. She would not give into him. The lightning struck again, hitting them both.

CHAPTER TWENTY-ONE

THE CRYSTAL PALACE

Anna slowly opened her eyes. She was lying on a bed covered with a soft patchwork quilt. Next to the bed was a small knotty-pine nightstand with a lamp made from a small tree stump. The room looked strangely familiar but she couldn't place it. The last thing Anna remembered was being struck by lightning then everything went white. She was pretty sure she was dead but the afterworld didn't look anything like she had ever imagined.

She swung her legs over the edge of the bed. She seemed to be fine. She was wearing the same clothes, except they were like new. She pinched herself. "Ouch," she cried. She seemed to be real enough. She examined her hands and fingers. They seemed okay, no sign of frostbite.

She wondered where she had seen this room before. Was it in a dream? She cautiously walked towards the closed door.

She opened it a crack and gasped. She knew exactly where she was.

"Odin!" Anna called out, running into the room. "Odin!" There was no reply. A fire was burning in the fireplace. She sat down in the big green easy chair, the same one she sat in right before her journey began. What's happening? Anna wondered. Then she remembered Tedith and started to sob.

The front door swung open. Anna looked up and through her tears she saw her grandpa.

"Sweetpea!"

Anna was speechless. She ran to him and flung herself into his outstretched arms. He caught her in mid-air and held her. Anna sobbed even louder.

"There, there, little one. Shhhh, everything is fine."

"But, but, I don't understand. Why are you here? Does this mean I really am dead?" Anna tried to compose herself. "Oh Grandpa I am so happy to see you!" Anna hugged him even tighter.

"I know Sweetpea, I am happy to see you too." He placed her in the easy chair, took his bandana out from his back pocket and wiped the tears from her eyes. This made Anna feel better. He then settled into the rocking chair across from her.

"Am I, Grandpa…am I dead?" Anna asked, not sure she wanted to hear the answer.

Grandpa chuckled, "No, no, my dear you are not dead."

"But then, how can I be with you?" Anna asked, quite confused.

"*The Land Beyond the Clouds* is the place where your world and my world overlap."

"But why are you here? Why are you in Odin's house? Do you know him?" Anna asked, still trying to work everything out.

"You could say that Odin and I are very good friends, very good friends indeed."

A tea tray then floated into the room from the kitchen and landed on the small table between them.

"Hey, that is what happened when I was here with Odin," Anna said, watching the teapot as it poured them both a cup of warm tea.

"Yes, I know." Grandpa winked as he reached for the teacup floating in front of him. "You have had quite the journey, haven't you, Anna?"

"You know about my journey?" Anna asked as she took a sip of her tea.

"Yes, I know all about it."

Anna looked downhearted. "Then you know I was trying to get home and I failed. I never made it to the Crystal Palace. I did that whole journey for nothing...for nothing. I'm exactly where I was when I started, right back here, in Odin's cottage." Anna was almost in tears again.

"Hmmm, are you really back *exactly* where you started?" Grandpa asked, sipping his tea.

Puzzled, Anna looked at him then looked around the cottage. Yes, I am right back where I started. I know it was a long, long time ago, but this is *exactly* where I started. I sat in this very chair, drinking tea with Odin."

"And everything is *exactly* the same?"

Anna scanned the room. It had been put back together after Donovan's raid, but other than that it was the same.

"Everything seems to be the same," Anna said, not sure what

her grandpa was getting at.

"Well, I would say there is definitely one thing that is not the same."

"Really Grandpa, I don't see anything different. What is not the same?"

Grandpa looked Anna straight in the eye and said, "*You.*"

"*Me?*"

"Yes, *you*. In fact, I would say that you are very different. And, *you* being different makes all difference in the world. In fact, it is the *only* difference that really matters."

Anna frowned in confusion. She didn't feel any different.

"Let me ask you this. What did you learn along the way?"

Anna thought a moment. There were so many things. "Well, I learned that I am a lot stronger than I thought. Even when I didn't think I could go on any longer, I somehow found the strength to keep going."

Her grandfather nodded. "What else?"

I learned I only need to deal with what is in front of me. I don't need to have the whole thing figured out beforehand. I also learned that getting everything you *think you* want sometimes prevents you from getting what you *really* want."

Anna sat a moment in silence thinking about everything she had been through, it had certainly been a lot.

"But the most important thing I learned was to trust myself. I really do have everything I need right inside me."

"My, you have learned a lot." Grandpa smiled at her.

"But what difference does it make? I didn't make it to the Crystal Palace, which means I'm not going to make it home. I went through all of that for nothing."

Grandpa laughed. "This *is* the Crystal Palace, my dear. You *did* make it."

"What?" Anna looked around her. "This is the Crystal Palace? How can that be? It doesn't look anything like a palace, and it certainly isn't made of crystal. And what about the Crystal Palace I saw from the mountaintop?"

"I imagine that one of the things you learned on the journey is that things aren't always what they appear to be."

Anna nodded. If her journey had taught her anything, it was that there was often more going on than what she could see. Things are often quite different than how they first appear, like in Candy Land.

"But, if this is the Crystal Palace, why aren't I home?"

"That's just geography. You now have everything you need to go home. In fact, you should get going. I suspect there are a few people who would like to see you."

"But how am I going to explain this to everyone?"

Before Grandpa could answer, the door to the second bedroom flung open, and out walked Tedith. He stared in disbelief then threw himself onto Anna.

"Anna, Anna," he squealed in delight.

Anna hugged him with all her might. "Tedith, is it really you? But, I don't understand. You went over the mountain. How did you get here?"

"I don't know. One moment I was falling and the next moment I woke up in a bed. I heard voices in the next room...boy, am I glad to see you," Tedith said, giving Anna another teddy bear hug.

"...and are you okay?" Anna asked, lifting up the foot that she had mended. The purple thread was still there, but Tedith's foot had healed perfectly.

"Yeah, good as new. Like nothing happened. Hey, wait a second," Tedith said. "It's Grandpa!"

"It certainly is," Anna said, beaming.

"Nice you see you again, Tedith. You had us jumping through

hoops last summer looking for you," Grandpa said, rubbing Tedith under the chin.

"Yeah, but what are you doing here? Wait, does this mean we are dead?"

"No, far from it."

"But—" Tedith began.

"I know you have a lot of questions but Anna needs to go now. Home is waiting."

"Really, Anna is going home?" Tedith asked, barely believing his furry orange ears.

"That's right, let's go." Grandpa took Anna's hand and walked towards the door.

The flower beds of singing tulips serenaded them as they walked through the forest of giant yellow sunflowers and into the Technicolor meadow, exactly the same way Anna had come such a long, long time ago. Anna wanted to ask a squillon more questions but she knew her grandpa wanted to get her home.

They passed the stream where Anna had first met Odin. She sure had been through a lot since then. She wondered how long she had been gone. Two, maybe three, years? She couldn't be sure. She only knew it had been a long time, a very long time. It still hadn't begun to sink in that she would be home soon.

They came to the magnificent gates made of shimmering light. Grandpa pushed open the gate. They walked through and clouds immediately surrounded them.

"Wow, this is cool," Tedith called out as he skipped through the clouds. "It's like walking on marshmallows." Which was exactly what Anna had thought the first time she walked on the clouds.

"Does this mean that I am going to climb down Jacob's Ladder?" Anna asked.

"You'll see." Grandpa squeezed Anna's hand.

Soon, they came to an opening in the clouds.

"That's your way home, Anna."

"Wow!" Anna looked through the slit and saw a magnificent rainbow heading straight to earth. The colors were in perfect order; red, orange, yellow, green, blue, indigo, and violet, just like the rainbow in the pagoda.

"But how do I use a rainbow to get down?" Anna asked, gazing at the radiant colors.

"Why, by sliding down it, of course," her grandpa smiled.

"Boy, there is a lot more to a rainbow than its pretty colors."

"Yes there is Sweetpea. You ready?" Grandpa asked.

"...but what about you? You're coming with me aren't you?" Anna asked, not really wanted to hear the answer.

"No, we both know that I no longer belong to your world. But listen to me. *I will always be with you.* When you need me, you have only to close your eyes and think of me, and I will be there. I am as close as your next breath."

Anna nodded as her eyes welled up with tears.

"Hey, what about me? I can go, can't I?" Tedith asked, visibly concerned at the prospect of losing Anna again.

"Well, little fella, that's up to you. As you know, in *The Land Beyond the Clouds* you are alive but if you go back to earth...well, you will become a stuffed toy again. You can go if you like or you can stay here. It's your decision."

"Oh," Tedith said, unusually pensive.

"It's okay Tedith, I understand. You should stay here, where you are alive."

"No, Anna I belong with you, even if it means that I become a stuffed toy again."

Anna could barely believe her ears. "Really Tedith, are you sure?"

"I'm sure, but with two conditions. One, you keep Jed, that old hound dog away from me. And two, you keep a honey jar by me at all times. Preferable a large jar. Even if I can't eat it, at least I'll know it's nearby."

"You got it little buddy." Anna picked up Tedith and gave him a squeeze.

"Okay, you two, it's time to go." Grandpa gave them both a big hug then gently placed them on the rainbow. Anna's whole body tingled, just like it had when she had first touched Jacob's Ladder.

"Goodbye Grandpa, I'm going to miss you," Anna said.

"Remember Anna, I am always with you."

With Tedith securely on Anna's lap, Grandpa gave her a gentle push down the rainbow.

The brilliant colors engulfed them and the air swished by them as they glided towards earth.

Anna landed firmly on her feet with a soft thud. She immediately looked up at the hole in the clouds from where the rainbow had come. It was already starting to close. Anna thought she caught a glimpse of Odin before the opening shut and the rainbow disappeared.

Anna looked at Tedith. He was back to his old, stuffed self. She gave him a big hug.

"Thank you, little fella. I promise to take good care of you."

They landed in the same clearing in the woods where Anna had found the bottom of Jacob's Ladder so long ago.

Anna ran through the woods towards Grandma's house. She wondered if Grandma would be there or if she even lived there anymore.

She had no idea how she would explain where she had been.

She ran into the barnyard. Jed barked and ran up to her, wagging his tale.

"Boy, am I glad to see you," Anna said, catching her breath as she scratched him behind his ear.

Old Jed sniffed at Tedith.

"Oh no you don't." Anna protectively lifted Tedith out of Jed's reach. "You stay away from Tedith, you hear!"

Anna turned her attention to the farmhouse. It looked pretty much the same. She took a deep breath, walked up to the kitchen's screen door and cautiously peeked in. Her grandma was standing over the kitchen counter buttering bread.

The screen door creaked as Anna carefully opened it.

"Ahhhhh!" Grandma screamed as she saw Anna.

"Dear child, you scared me half to death."

Before Anna could say anything her grandma said, "How many times have I asked you not to sneak up on me? My hearing isn't as good as it use to be. I'm glad you are here. I wasn't sure you heard me calling you in for lunch. I didn't see you in the barnyard. Were you in the little forest?"

Anna just nodded. She was too confounded to speak. Her grandma didn't seem to be at all surprised to see her.

Grandma studied Anna. "Are you okay child? You look different." Grandma pushed a piece of stray hair back behind Anna's ear.

Anna nodded again, trying to figure out what was going on. It was as if she hadn't been gone at all.

"My, my, look what we have here." Grandma took Tedith from Anna's arms and held him up.

"Where in the world did you find him? In the woods?"

Anna remained silent.

Grandma frowned at Anna. "You sure you're okay?"

"Yes, I'm fine," Anna finally managed to say.

"Okay then, go wash up. Lunch is almost ready. Remember, we

are going into town this afternoon to do a bit of shopping."

Anna washed her hands in the bathroom then went into her bedroom. It looked exactly the same. She propped Tedith up on her bed.

"Tedith, how can this be? It's like I haven't been away at all." She wished Tedith could say something.

"Anna, lunch is on table," Grandma called out.

Anna returned to the kitchen, sat at the table and took a bite of the grilled cheese sandwich in front of her. Her grandma had made it exactly the way she liked it, with lots of cheese, so it oozed out the sides.

Her Grandma continued to study Anna. "You sure you're okay child?" Her grandma felt Anna's forehead.

"I'm fine Grandma, really," Anna said, trying to sound convincing.

"I don't know. You look different. There is something different about you."

"I'm just not very hungry. Can I have some honey?"

"Honey? I thought you said you weren't hungry."

"It's not for me. It's for Tedith."

Her grandmother looked at Anna, crinkled her brow and said, "Okay, it's in the cupboard by the refrigerator."

Anna got the honey and took it to her bedroom. She propped it up against Tedith.

"I'm going to be in the barnyard Grandma," Anna said when she returned to the kitchen.

"Okay. We'll be leaving for town in about a half an hour."

Anna nodded as she walked through the kitchen door. Everything looked the same—the same barn, the same fields, even the same chickens.

Then Anna noticed the little anthill that she had been watching right before it had started to rain. The ants were busy rebuilding their hill, which the rain had knocked down. She wondered where the little ant that was carrying that big piece of bread had gone. "That's funny," she thought, "the bread is gone."

Anna smiled. She knew exactly where the ant and bread were. Somehow, someway, that tiny ant had gotten the huge piece of bread into that little anthill. Anna was sure of it.

THE END

Valerie Bishop was born and raised in Toronto, Canada.
She moved to the USA in 1989 and now lives in Montecito,
California with Sadie, the dog; Nika, the cat
and her remarkable husband, Russell.

She would love to hear from you
mail@valeriebishop.com

www.valeriebishop.com

Printed in the United States
202665BV00003B/205-252/P